There was no qu— about — t—t that this version of him knew Siobhan was sweet and funny and sexy. Now he knew that her laughter immediately lifted his mood, even from a distance.

And he knew that magic was the reflection of fairy lights dancing in her hazel eyes.

"Just remember, when it comes to losing, a Kowalski can really hold a grudge," he said, injecting a lightness he didn't feel into his tone.

"Oh, I saw the look you gave me when I lost you the point," she said, her eyes sparkling. "It promised payback."

The way he remembered it, a *lot* of looks had passed between them during that volleyball game, and most of them hadn't been promising retribution. Every time their eyes met, he felt singed by the sparks arcing between them, and he didn't think he was imagining it.

Then Siobhan rested her hand on his forearm, and instantly it felt as if the blood in his veins had been replaced with lava.

Dear Reader,

When the Kowalski family gets together, chaos always ensues! In *A Kowalski Secret*, a family wedding brings together new characters, along with reader favorites, and there's more chaos than usual when a toddler with Kowalski blue eyes is added to the guest list.

When, during the writing process, I literally laugh out loud and even shed a few real tears, I'm always extra excited to share the story with readers, and this book really put me through the wringer. Whether you've laughed and cried with the Kowalski family in the past or you're meeting them for the first time, I hope you enjoy the sparks flying between Brian Kowalski and Siobhan Lowe—two people with a prickly past, brought together by *A Kowalski Secret*.

You can stop by my website at www.shannonstacey.com to find my latest book news, and while you're there, sign up for my newsletter so that book news comes straight to your inbox. And I love connecting with readers, so you'll also find links to where I can be found on social media.

Happy reading!

Shannon

A KOWALSKI SECRET

SHANNON STACEY

SPECIAL EDITION

Harlequin®
SPECIAL EDITION™

Recycling programs for this product may not exist in your area.

ISBN-13: 978-1-335-40226-4

A Kowalski Secret

Harlequin Enterprises ULC
22 Adelaide St. West, 41st Floor
Toronto, Ontario M5H 4E3, Canada
www.Harlequin.com

Printed in U.S.A.

A *New York Times* and *USA TODAY* bestselling author of over forty romances, **Shannon Stacey** grew up in a military family and lived in many places before landing in a small New Hampshire town, where she has resided with her husband and two sons for over twenty years. Her favorite activities are reading and writing with her dogs at her side. She also loves coffee, Boston sports and watching too much TV. You can learn more about her books at www.shannonstacey.com.

Books by Shannon Stacey

Harlequin Special Edition

Blackberry Bay

More than Neighbors
Their Christmas Baby Contract
The Home They Built

Sutton's Place

Her Hometown Man
An Unexpected Cowboy
Expecting Her Ex's Baby
Falling for His Fake Girlfriend
Her Younger Man

The Kowalski Series

Exclusively Yours
Undeniably Yours
Yours to Keep
All He Ever Needed
All He Ever Desired
All He Ever Dreamed
Love a Little Sideways
Taken with You
Falling for Max
What It Takes
A Kowalski to Count On
A Kowalski Secret

Visit the Author Profile page
at Harlequin.com for more titles.

For my husband and my brothers-in-law,
because men who love, support and hug their sons
are the backbone of this series, and my sons and
nephews are so blessed to have dads like you.

Chapter One

Siobhan Rowe had gotten through some hard times in her life, but she was afraid spending an entire week camping with the Kowalski family might be her undoing. She didn't like taking a week off of work. She didn't like camping. And she *definitely* didn't like the Kowalski family.

Except for Steph, of course. She and Stephanie Kowalski had been friends for years, which was how she'd ended up agreeing to be her last-minute replacement maid of honor at a campground wedding in the middle-of-nowhere northern New Hampshire.

"How many diapers are you taking?" Robin asked, looking at the pile on Siobhan's bed.

She sighed and looked at the woman who'd become a good friend since Siobhan moved into the apartment across the hall. Without Robin, she wasn't sure how she'd get through the exhaustion of being a working single mother of a boy two months shy of his second birthday.

"All of them?" she said. "I don't know."

"You're not taking him for a trek along the Oregon Trail. They have stores up there." Robin was obviously amused by Siobhan's packing pile, which wasn't a surprise.

As the oldest of five kids, Robin didn't sweat the small stuff when it came to little ones. As an added bonus, she was totally comfortable hanging out at Siobhan's in leggings and comfy T-shirts, eating pizza because going out on the town meant throwing off Oliver's sleep schedule.

When Oliver's sleep schedule went awry, Siobhan had a very bad day. A week of trying to get him to sleep in a campground was just going to add to the *fun*.

"Explain to me again why you're going camping for a week with people you don't like? It seems so sudden and you keep starting to tell me and then getting distracted."

Siobhan sighed. "I don't dislike *all* of them. Most of them, I don't know very well. And obviously, Steph and I are friends. But Brian Kowalski—one of the four brothers who bought the campground—was married to my sister, Kelly."

"Oh." Robin's eyes widened. "So you're spending a week with your former brother-in-law and his entire family?"

"Right. He's Steph's cousin. She and Kyle—the groom—met at that campground when they were teenagers and, since her cousins bought it in March, they decided it was the perfect place to get married. But Steph's maid of honor had to drop out at the last minute, and I was the next friend on deck."

"You could have said no," Robin pointed out.

"It's not that easy to say no to a friend in distress because her wedding's ruined," Siobhan replied wryly. "And I'd been having a miserable day when she called. I had left work early because Oliver had an appointment with his pediatrician, and traffic was backed up more than usual because they decided to pave that day. Also, the air conditioner in my car wasn't keeping up with August in Boston. The phone rang at the *one* possible moment when an all-expenses paid, week-long vacation in the woods in the middle of nowhere sounded good."

"With your ex–brother-in-law and his family."

"I didn't really think about that part until after. I was mostly focused on helping Steph and on the woods."

While they spoke, Robin was rummaging through the piles on the bed, winnowing out what she deemed unnecessary. "How do you and… Brian? I think that's what you said. How do you get along?"

"That's the fun part." Siobhan pulled the package of diaper wipes out of Robin's hand and put them back in the pile. She was taking all the wipes she had because they were going camping and, if nothing else, she knew there would be marshmallows in Oliver's future. "We didn't really like each other very much from day one and it went downhill from there."

"Why?"

"I didn't think Kelly was in the right headspace for a relationship, and for me it was about Kelly and where she was in her life, but Brian thought my reservations were about *him*. We just clashed a lot. And, of course, when she left him, he blamed me."

"Of course." Robin held up a small bag that was stuffed with tiny shoes. "Why are you bringing every pair of shoes Oliver owns?"

"One, I'm not. And two, he'll be running around a campground. His shoes will get wet or muddy or he might step in something sticky." She watched as her friend took two pairs of sneakers out of the bag and set them on the bed. Then she dumped the rest back into the bin Siobhan used for shoes. "We're staying in a camper, so we have plenty of room for shoes."

"I'm not worried about the camper. I'm afraid you won't actually have room for Oliver in your car by the time you're done packing his stuff." She cocked her head. "Whose camper are you using?"

"It belongs to somebody in the family, I guess. Steph borrowed it for her maid of honor, and now that's me."

"Way better than a tent."

Siobhan laughed. "There was a zero percent chance my answer to her asking me to be in her wedding would have been a yes if it involved me staying in a tent with a toddler. Honestly, I'm not staying in a tent at all, but especially with a kid who's figured out the basics of a zipper."

Robin put her hands on her hips and nodded, apparently satisfied with what remained on the bed. "What time are you leaving?"

"Shortly after Oliver wakes up from the nap I didn't want him to take." She sighed. "I'm sure he'll sleep in the car, too, since it's a three-and-a-half-hour drive. In a new place—especially in a camper—with bonus naps? My son's going to be line dancing at two in the morning."

"Let's get you repacked, then."

As if on cue, Siobhan heard the tinny electronic engine sound of Oliver's favorite truck and knew she was out of time. A minute later, her son padded into the room, his truck clutched in his arms. His blue eyes were still sleepy and his dark hair was sticking up in several different directions, and Siobhan smiled because it was one of her favorite looks.

"Auntie Robin," he said, lighting up when he saw her packing things into a duffel bag. "We go camping!"

And that's what it was all about, Siobhan reminded herself. She was going to stand next to Steph while she married the love of her life, and Oliver was going to have the fun adventure of camping for a week in the great outdoors.

For that, she was willing to ignore her former brother-in-law.

* * *

"I'm not sure how you plan to ignore the maid of honor for a week when we're hosting the wedding."

Brian looked at his brother Rob and shrugged. "It's not going to be that hard. She'll be fussing around Steph, since that's what the maid of honor does, and if she needs something campground related, she can ask you or Joey or Danny."

"And that's why you've been standing in front of that window with your arms crossed and a scowl on your face for the last half hour?"

He shrugged. "That's different from any other day how?"

"Fair," Rob admitted. "The being totally still for a half hour's different, though. People driving by probably think you're some kind of angry mannequin and are really confused about why we'd put you in our window."

Brian didn't really care what people thought. He had a lot on his mind and, regardless of what his facial expressions were doing, watching the birds circling over the river in the distance usually calmed his mind. Not so much today, though, because their family was descending upon them to kick off his cousin's wedding week.

And so was Siobhan Rowe.

She hadn't liked Brian before he married her sister. She hadn't liked him while he was married to her sister. And she *definitely* hadn't liked him since the divorce.

It didn't make sense to him. She'd made it clear from their first meeting that she didn't want him with Kelly, so her sister dumping him and walking out the door with no warning should have made Siobhan happy. But by the time the divorce was finalized, he'd become convinced that nothing short of him falling off the face of the earth would make her happy.

And they were going to spend an entire week together. Wasn't *that* fun?

"Dude, you're literally growling right now." Rob clapped his hand on his shoulder. "Either eat something or take a nap."

"I ate. And I don't have time for a nap. The family's going to start arriving any minute."

"Speaking of people arriving, Steph sent a group text asking us to babyproof Siobhan's site as much as possible. You never told me she had a baby."

Brian turned away from the window. That was news to him, probably because he'd been ignoring his phone for the last hour. "How old is the kid?"

"Almost two, she said."

"Since Kelly and I were already divorced when she would have had him and Siobhan didn't leave me on her Christmas newsletter list, how would I have known?"

The bell over the door rang, and Brian sighed. The combination campground office and store was also something of a social hangout thanks to the chairs and the abundant amount of snacks for sale, and every time that bell rang, he wanted to rip it down and run it over with his truck.

Seeing Hannah Shelby walk through the door cheered him up, though. Rob's fiancée had come into their lives as a seasonal camper in the spring, intending to leave at the end of last month, but now she'd be a permanent fixture in their lives. Brian liked her and she not only made Rob happy, but she fit right in with the family.

She held the door so Stella could follow her in. Brian's yellow Lab was the best dog he'd ever had in his life, and she loved everybody she met. Of course, she loved him best, but she'd spent the morning roaming around the campground with Hannah, doing last-minute cleanup before the family arrived.

"Your mom sent me a text," she informed them. "They're about five minutes out."

Brian sighed again. "Let the chaos commence."

"I sent them the campground map yesterday," Hannah said. "I marked which sites everybody's in, but we'll see how that goes."

Rob chuckled. "What are the chances they pull into the campground in the order they need to arrive so they won't jam each other up?"

Chaos was the right word for the next two hours. As the family arrived—most of them pulling campers and definitely not in any kind of order—Brian and Rob helped get everybody parked at their sites. As soon as Joey arrived with his wife and daughter, he jumped in to help.

Even though he owned a quarter of the campground and should have been around to help, their brother Danny wasn't arriving until Saturday afternoon. Just because she was getting married in a campground didn't mean Steph was skimping on the details, so he'd be picking up the white chairs, tables and the arch from the rental place on Saturday and driving them up. He'd miss out on some of the festivities, but nobody wanted to do four hours round-trip of driving the day before the wedding.

When a small red car he didn't recognize pulled into the campground, Brian assumed Siobhan had arrived. The way Steph squealed and ran toward the car confirmed it.

Since he was stuck helping level his grandparents' very large motor coach–style RV, the dirt road that led to the camper Siobhan would be staying in was directly in his sight line. She drove slowly because Steph was walking beside the car, talking the entire time.

When Siobhan parked and got out, the first thing she did was stretch. Brian tried not to look, but—again—she was in his line of sight. And she was wearing a red tee that hugged her curves, so that didn't help. Her hair was a darker blond than Kelly's, but the sun showed off lighter highlights running through the strands. He knew from the many times she'd tried to set him on fire with them that her eyes were the same hazel as her sister's.

"That's not how *ignoring* works," Rob said as he walked by, keeping his voice low so it wouldn't carry. "And stop growling like that. I swear, you've been turning more and more feral since we bought this place."

Brian turned his back on Siobhan as she opened the rear door of her car. "Are we done here?"

"Yeah. I'm going to do the hookups for them, but you can resume the angry mannequin position in the store again if you want. You know, if you stop shaving and put on a flannel shirt before posing, you'll look like Paul Bunyan and we can become a tourist attraction."

He almost rose to his brother's baiting, but then Brian took a deep breath. His family was gathered to celebrate a happy occasion and even though they were a pain in his ass, there was no bottom to the depths of his love for his family. He was *not* going to spend the week growling and scowling at people.

Siobhan Rowe was a nonfactor, and he wasn't going to be a gloomy dark cloud casting a shadow over Steph's wedding because of her presence. They didn't like each other. That was fine. They were adults, and they could be in each other's orbit for a week with no drama.

Then they'd go their separate ways and, if he was lucky, they'd never see each other again.

Chapter Two

The camper they'd be staying in for the week was small, but it was clean and had plenty of room for her and Oliver. And sometimes on weekends or when they were feeling under the weather, he'd sleep in Siobhan's bed, so sharing this one wouldn't be a big deal.

"The guys opened it up this week, so the AC's on and the fridge is cold," Steph said. "I think it has everything you need, but if not, just ask. Between the store and all the family, somebody will have whatever it is."

Siobhan sighed. "According to Robin, I have more than what I need."

Steph and Robin had met a few times at Siobhan's, and Steph laughed. "How's she doing? I haven't seen her in a while."

"Good. She sends her congrats, of course. And she managed to hide being jealous that Oliver and I get to be away from the city for a week."

"You have no idea how much it means to me that you're here." Steph's eyes welled up with tears. "Really. I'm sorry I—I'm just glad you're here."

Siobhan knew some women would resent being a bride's second choice maid of honor, but she wasn't one of them. She and Steph had been college roommates, and they were close friends, but it wasn't the same relation-ship as a lifelong best friend from childhood.

"I'm thrilled I could be here for you. I'm also thrilled there wasn't an official maid of honor gown because a dress made for Vanessa would have covered half of me."

Steph laughed, and the last of any awkwardness dissipated with the sound. "The dress you sent me a picture of is perfection."

Oliver ran across the camper, a board book in his hand. He was heading for Siobhan, but at the last minute, he veered in Steph's direction. Leaning against her knee, he offered the book and grinned up at her.

Something flitted across Steph's face—the amusement fading to something else. Siobhan couldn't tell exactly what it was, but there was some confusion in there.

Then Steph smiled at Oliver. "You've gotten so big since the last time I saw you."

"They grow so fast, and it's been a few months," Siobhan said. "Plus, he kind of changed from baby to little boy while I wasn't looking."

"Beep beep," Oliver said.

"The book has a truck and there's a lot of *beep beep* going on," Siobhan explained. "Oliver, Steph doesn't have time to read to you right now."

"I think if you're my maid of honor, I get to be Auntie Steph. At least for the weekend."

"Well, Auntie Steph, if you take that book from him thinking you'll read it one time really quickly because that adorable little grin is so hard to resist, you'll be wrong. Once you start, he's more of a constant loop until your voice gives out kind of guy."

"Good to know." She ruffled Oliver's dark hair and that same expression clouded her face again. "I should run, though. I heard somebody pull in and we're waiting for Kyle's family to show up. I want to make sure to greet them when they get here."

"Don't worry about us. I'm just going to put some stuff away and then, since this guy was in the car for a long time, we might go for a walk."

It didn't take Siobhan long to find places to stow their stuff and put away the groceries they brought, and Oliver tried to wait patiently. He was a high-energy little boy, and he quickly got bored with exploring his new environment.

Once she tied his sneakers on, slathered him in sunscreen and plopped his sun hat on his head, she helped him down the camper steps. After a moment's hesitation, she decided to take him for a walk around the back part of the campground. Not only was there more shade, but most of the Kowalski family was milling around the front part.

She'd met most of them at least once—at Brian and Kelly's wedding. She'd been her sister's maid of honor because Kelly didn't have anybody else, but she hadn't been happy about it. Her sister simply wasn't ready for marriage and it had taken all of her strength to fake it through that day. And Steph had assured her the family would be thrilled to see her again, but she had her doubts, so into the woods they went.

Oliver was fascinated. They spent a lot of time at parks, but the woods lining the dirt road weren't isolated trees planted in cultivated lawns. There were sticks and rocks and piles of leaves to explore. Siobhan hovered, ready to intervene if she spotted poison ivy or insects of the biting variety, or in the unlikely event a car went by, but mostly she let him wander freely.

By the time they'd walked the back loop of the campground, Oliver's energy was flagging, so she held his hand to keep him from tripping over his own feet. Slowing the pace, they made their way back toward the open part of the campground and their camper.

About halfway down the hill that led to the break in the tree line, movement caught her eye and she saw Brian leaving a small cabin. He was looking down at his phone as he walked, and they were on an intercept course.

She almost turned around, but retracing their steps up the hill and around the loop would be a lot for Oliver. Scooping him up and running would just be ridiculous. Instead, she slowed their pace even more, hoping he'd stay engrossed in whatever he was looking at and walk down the hill without ever knowing she'd been behind him.

It wasn't meant to be. As he reached the end of the cabin's driveway, he slid his phone into his pocket and looked up—directly at Siobhan.

It had been over half a year since she'd seen Brian Kowalski at a holiday open house Steph and Kyle had hosted. She hadn't expected to see her former brother-in-law there, and when he'd given her a tersely polite hello, she'd been so taken off guard that she turned her back and walked away.

Not one of her finer moments.

Determined not to bring any negativity into Steph's special week, she forced her lips to curve into a stiff smile. "Hello, Brian."

"Welcome to Birch Brook Campground." The words were flat, and the smile he gave her didn't reach his blue eyes. His gaze shifted to Oliver and his face softened. "Who's this?"

"My son," she said in a wooden voice. "Oliver."

"I heard you had a kid. Congrats." There was no warmth in his words, but then Brian gave her son a grin that knocked the breath out of Siobhan's lungs. "Hey, Oliver."

"Beep beep." Oliver returned the grin, and that same strange look slid into Brian's expression.

Oh, no. No. Absolutely not. "We're on our way to… over there, but it was good to see you again."

She swung her son onto her hip and started walking before Brian could say anything else.

Oliver was happily babbling about something, but Siobhan couldn't hear him over the buzzing in her ears. Her skin was hot, and her breath felt quick and shallow—she couldn't fill her lungs—and she forced herself to slow down.

The blue eyes. The dark hair. That damn adorable grin. Kelly had lied to her.

Brian watched Siobhan walk away as though somebody was chasing her and shook his head. *He* certainly wasn't going to be the one chasing her, that was for damn sure. The hope he could get through the entire week without interacting with her had been futile, of course, but that didn't mean he'd go out of his way to talk to her.

Cute kid, though. When he'd smiled, there'd been a second when Brian thought he looked a lot like his cousin Josh's boy when he was that age. It was weird how much little kids could look like each other sometimes.

When he reached the large canopy they'd erected for shade near the playground, he found most of the family gathered. His grandparents and the original Birch Brook Campground campers, Leo and Mary, were holding court from two camp chairs by the fire ring. There wasn't a fire burning in it because it was hot and too early for campfire stories, but fire rings were usually the central point of any campground gathering. The actual flames were optional.

He spoke to his parents, Mike, and Lisa, and then talked

to everybody for a few minutes. His brother Joey's wife, Ellie, was uncovering snack trays with the help of her six-year-old daughter, Nora. Rob and Hannah were adding ice to the coolers of drinks. His aunt Terry—mother of the bride—and her husband Ethan, then his uncle Joe and aunt Keri. Uncle Kevin and Aunt Beth. And there were cousins everywhere. His dad's cousin, Sean, who was one of the Maine branch of Kowalskis but had chosen to live in New Hampshire, was there with his wife, Emma, and their kids.

The rest of the Maine family would be making a day trip over for the wedding on Monday. They owned the Northern Star Lodge & Campground and it was their busy season, so weekends were tough. It would be a long day with a lot of driving, but they wouldn't miss it.

"This is amazing," Kyle said, appearing at his side.

Brian looked at the plate of finger foods the groom was holding. "You think that's good? Wait until the desserts come out."

He looked confused for a second and then gave him a sheepish smile. "Sorry, I meant this whole thing is amazing—that you guys are doing this for us."

"It's going to be fun," Brian said, and he was impressed when it came out sounding like he actually believed it. "We're going to do everything we can to make your wedding the best day ever."

That part was true, at least. And he was sure there would be some fun times. There always were when the family was gathered in one spot. But being one of the hosts and owners was a lot of pressure.

"And the cabin we're staying in is perfect. It's so comfortable. And roomy."

"I'm glad you like it."

The logistics of lodging for everybody had been a nightmare. He, Rob, Hannah and Joey had lost an entire day to making the drive to Maine and back with campers borrowed from the family. On Monday evening, after the wedding, most of the Maine family would head home, but a few of them would crash in the house.

That wouldn't be fun. The campground had two buildings on it—the store that also served as the office, and a small house that needed a lot of TLC. Brian and his brothers stayed in the house during the camping season, though only Rob didn't keep a primary residence in the southern part of the state. They hadn't had TLC to spare for the house yet, though, and throwing a couple more guys in there would be tough. They might have to break out tents. Then the Maine family would drive the campers back on Tuesday when everybody left and the newlyweds took off for their official honeymoon in Bar Harbor.

They'd decided to give the big cabin on the hill to the bride and groom because, even though they'd have to use the bathhouse, it was the most private. And Kyle's brother and best man, Wes, along with his sister-in-law, Amber, and Ron, Wes and Kyle's grandfather, would be staying in one of the campers. Kyle and Wes had lost their parents to a car accident when they were in college, so it was just the four of them.

Everybody had a place to sleep, but Brian and his brothers had burned through a lot of sticky notes figuring it out. It was like a seating chart, but for beds, and he hoped they'd never have to do it again.

"We definitely appreciate it," Kyle said again. "I

haven't spoken with your grandparents yet, so I'll catch you later."

"Make sure you bring a chair because once they get going, you'll be there awhile."

Sometime later, while Brian and Stella were sharing some food in a shady spot under a tree, Steph wandered over and sat on the ground next to him.

"Have you seen Siobhan yet?" she asked, not being one to beat around the bush.

His shoulders tensed. "Briefly. We said hi."

"Is it going to be okay?"

He wasn't sure what she meant by *okay*, but he turned and looked at her. There was an anxiety in his cousin's eyes that he didn't like seeing there, so he dug deep and gave her a genuine smile. "It's going to be okay, Steph."

She blew out a relieved breath. "I'm glad. I know it was a big ask, so thank you for being okay with it."

"Her kid's cute."

She gave him a thoughtful look that didn't make sense to him. It was a pretty standard comment to make about a person's child. "He is. Quite the blue eyes."

He snorted and nodded his head toward the gathering of people. "No shortage of those around here. I guess he'll fit right in."

Steph stared at him for a few seconds and then pushed herself to her feet. "I guess if it's going to be okay between you, I should go find her and tell her to come join us. I need her to meet Kyle's family, and plus, our family's been asking about her."

He nodded, but she still hesitated a moment before turning and walking away. She was acting a little weird, but she was probably just really afraid any awkwardness between him and Siobhan would put a damper on the festivities.

"Not going to happen," he told Stella, who looked ecstatic about it. Or maybe it was the cube of cheddar cheese Brian slipped to her. "We're just going to sit over here and mind our business, girl."

Chapter Three

Siobhan sat in her camper, staring at her cell phone, while Oliver played with puzzles on the floor. Of course Kelly's number had been disconnected. She didn't even know where her sister was living right now, but if there was one thing she did know, it was that she didn't pay her bills and went through pay-as-you-go cell phones like candy.

She didn't want to call their mother. Siobhan had worked hard to maintain a separation between them, and reaching out would be an invitation for a flurry of renewed contact before Janelle Rowe got distracted and forgot about her again.

Instead, she stared at her reflection in the darkened cell phone screen and remembered the day Kelly had shown up at her door with her car stuffed with her belongings. She had to leave Brian, she'd said. He was awful and she'd fallen in love with somebody else. She was pregnant and afraid of how Brian would react to her cheating and carrying somebody else's baby.

Siobhan had questioned her so thoroughly, trying not to judge her for the adultery. Kelly was definitely a lot like their mother. How could she be so sure it wasn't Brian's baby? Because they fought all the time and hadn't had sex in months. Why had she run? She was afraid. Brian had a temper and she was afraid he wouldn't let her go.

Seeing her younger sister so distressed, her body heaving from the sobs, had been her undoing. She'd helped Kelly move in with her new love, and she'd been the one to show up on Brian's door to demand the rest of her sister's things. Whenever possible, she'd been Kelly's liaison in the divorce, which thankfully had gone quickly, and Kelly was still able to hide her pregnancy the last time she was forced to see Brian.

The man had been like ice, with anger simmering below the surface, and Siobhan had been weak with relief when the legal connection between him and her sister was finally severed.

Oliver was three months old when Kelly and her boyfriend showed up at her door and asked her to adopt him. They hated being parents because they had big dreams and they were going to travel. If she didn't take him, they were going to surrender him to the state and let somebody else adopt him.

Siobhan had taken Oliver and made him her son, even though she knew it would mean seeing less of Kelly. Their mother had always been selfish, often leaving the girls to fend for themselves. Since Kelly knew how it felt to have a mother like that, Siobhan had hoped becoming a mom herself would change her sister. It hadn't, and Siobhan knew it was for the best that Kelly had bailed while Oliver was still an infant.

But she also knew that, like Janelle, Kelly avoided anything that made her feel guilt and shame—or anything resembling a complicated emotion, really—so she knew their relationship would shift to a distant one.

Why, then, was the realization Kelly had lied to her knocking her sideways?

Her sister must have been pregnant with Brian's baby when she left him. She'd cheated on her husband and wanted to leave him for her new boyfriend. But she knew Brian wouldn't let his baby go, and that Siobhan wouldn't help her take Oliver away from him if she knew the truth. Even for Kelly, it was a new low.

Oliver was her son now. It didn't matter that she hadn't given birth to him. She'd loved him from the second he drew his first breath while she held his biological mother's hand, and the day the adoption became final was the happiest day of her life.

She'd moved to a new position that offered more money and benefits, even though she hated the job. Then she moved to a two-bedroom apartment in a fairly decent suburb inconveniently far enough outside of Boston to make it just barely affordable. The only person actively in her life who knew her son was adopted was Robin.

But now, what was she supposed to do about Brian?

Not telling him wasn't an option. Of course, she didn't know *anything* for a fact. But if there was the slightest possibility Oliver was his son—and there definitely was—she had to have that conversation with him.

Fear rippled down her spine when she thought of Brian taking her son away from her. If he forced a test and it confirmed his paternity, proving Kelly had lied on the legal documents, was that enough to overturn the adoption?

She was so tense, a knock on the door almost made her scream, and Siobhan covered her heart with her hand as she stood.

"Auntie Robin," Oliver said, making her aware of just

how seldom they had company who wasn't their neighbor. But her life had been pretty busy since he came into her life and she was honestly content with just the three of them.

"Not Auntie Robin," she said, picking him up so he couldn't tumble out of the camper when she opened the door. "Let's see who it is."

It was Steph. *Auntie* Steph, she thought, and she had to force back the hysterical giggle that threatened to erupt.

"Everybody's here," Steph said. "We're all gathering near the playground for a casual meet and greet. And there are some snack trays and water and lemonade."

Siobhan in no way felt solid enough to leave the shelter of the camper, taking Oliver out to meet all the people who might actually be his biological family. But with Steph grinning up at her from the bottom of the steps, she couldn't say no. She was the maid of honor.

"Sounds great," she lied. "We'll be right over."

She took her time getting Oliver ready, and then she washed her face with frigid water. Staring at her reflection in the mirror, she told herself she could be wrong. So they both had dark hair and intense blue eyes. So what? A lot of people did. She'd get through this week, and then she'd reach out to people and see if she could find Kelly.

They'd almost reached the large grassy area at the center of the campground where the family was gathered when she stopped because the anxiety was making her body shake. She could take Oliver home. She could claim he didn't feel well or that he wasn't doing great in the camper. It would take some juggling, but Robin could probably stay with him while she returned for a shortened stay to fulfill her maid of honor duties.

Anything to keep Oliver and Brian apart until she could

wrap her mind around what might or might not be happening.

"Siobhan!" It was Lisa, her sister's former mother-in-law, who saw her first and waved her over. Her voice sounded a lot more welcoming than Siobhan had anticipated. "It's so good to see you again! And we can't wait to meet that adorable boy of yours!"

Despite telling Stella they'd mind their own business, it wasn't long before Brian got sucked back into the family gathering. There were too many stories being shared that he didn't want to miss out on, and Joey always downplayed his role in shenanigans. Brian wanted to be around to make sure his brother got the full blame for his childhood crimes.

Also, some desserts had been brought out, and he was a sucker for baked goods. But as he milled around, joining and leaving conversations at random, he picked up on a strange vibe. There were a lot of whispers happening. A lot of glances bouncing back and forth between him and Siobhan. He wasn't sure why, since absolutely nothing had happened to make the family fear they might start yelling and throwing things at each other any second.

There had been a lot of discussion before Steph asked Siobhan to be her maid of honor. Being the sister of the woman who'd broken Brian's heart—and the woman who'd put herself between him and Kelly multiple times during the divorce—meant the Kowalski family as a whole didn't love her. But they'd all agreed to leave that in the past and embrace her as one of Steph's best friends.

Since there wasn't a fire in the ring yet, Siobhan's little boy—Oliver, he reminded himself—was free to roam. Siobhan had tried to keep hold of his hand so he'd stay at her side, but she'd been assured everybody always kept an eye out when there was a little one around. And Nora was having a blast playing with him, despite the years between them.

"Show Gran," he heard Nora say, and he saw the mangled dandelion in Oliver's hand.

He even found himself smiling as he watched the boy toddle over to his grandmother and show her the flower. Mary bent low to see it, and then she brushed Oliver's sweaty hair back from his forehead. He looked up at her, grinning at his prize while she did so, and Brian saw his grandmother flinch. Her brows drew together and she studied the boy intently for a long moment before her smile returned.

Then his grandmother and his mother exchanged a long, pointed look before his grandmother nodded. Brian's stomach coiled into knots when his mom then turned and looked at him.

"Brian, can you let me in the store for a minute? I forgot to pack a few things I need."

His mother didn't forget *anything* when it came to camping. Brian wasn't even sure that was possible, since it seemed as if she brought everything she owned with her. "I think Rob's over there. He can let you in."

"Brian."

Because they were in front of everybody, she didn't actually middle-name him, but it was heavily implied and he pushed himself out of his chair. "Fine."

He knew he was in trouble when he caught his mom gesturing to his dad with a slight jerk of her head in his peripheral vision. A lecture was coming, and he gave Stella the stay signal so she wouldn't crawl out from her comfy spot in the shade just to hear her human get spoken to in the opposite of a *what a good boy* tone of voice.

They didn't speak until he'd unlocked the store, stood back so they could go in first, and then locked the door behind him. His dad went and sat in one of the chairs, and Brian assumed his mother would take the other, but she was pacing in a tight circle.

That was a *really* bad sign.

"Explain yourself," his mother commanded suddenly as she stopped pacing and crossed her arms.

"Can you be more specific?"

Her eyes narrowed. "You want specific? Okay. Why do I have a grandchild I don't know about?"

Her question slammed into him so hard, Brian actually took a step back. "What? Mom, no. Are you talking about Oliver? You do know other people in the world have dark hair and blue eyes, right?"

"It's not just the blue eyes," his mother insisted. "Although they *are* a pretty distinctive shade of blue. His expressions are so familiar to me, it's like seeing the past—when you boys were little—laid over the present. I know Gran saw it. I've caught Steph looking at him like she sees it. That boy is a Kowalski. I just know. I can *feel* it."

"Then go talk to my brothers because I'm not that child's father."

"Brian," his father said in a stern voice, a signal that Brian's tone was close to that *don't talk to your mother like that* line. "We love you and whatever's said in this room stays in this room because we have your back always. But I have to ask."

Bracing himself, Brian focused on breathing and staying calm because he wasn't going to like whatever his dad was about to ask him, but he had to contain his response.

"Did Kelly leave you because you had an affair with her sister?"

The tremor started deep in his muscles, spreading until Brian realized he was literally shaking. "No. *No.*"

"We need to know what's going on here," his mom said in a worryingly soft voice.

"You think I cheated on Kelly?" He dropped into a chair because he was afraid his legs might stop holding him upright. "With her sister?"

"I'm sorry, honey, but I'm trying to figure this out. You've always said you don't know why Kelly up and left you, but maybe you didn't want to tell us the truth?"

"You really think I did that? That it's something I'm even capable of?"

His mom looked at him for a long time, her gaze locked with his. "No. I really don't."

"I don't, either." His dad sighed. "It had to be asked, but it would be so out of character for you, it would make even less sense than what's already going on."

"I swear on my dog, Dad—on Stella." He didn't know how to make it any more plain. "I have never touched Siobhan. Not even once."

"I don't understand how this is happening," Lisa said, shaking her head.

"I don't, either," Brian said in a grim voice. "But I'm going to get some answers."

Chapter Four

Siobhan kept her eyes on her son, but through her peripheral vision, she saw Brian storming out the back door of the store—it was the only word for it, really. He definitely stormed. Lisa trotted after him and eventually caught him by the arm. Their exchange of words looked intense, and then they looked toward the gathered family.

Brian looked at Oliver, and Lisa looked directly at her.

The last thing Siobhan wanted right now was a big scene in front of Oliver—or the rest of them, for that matter—so she stood and started toward her son.

"Oliver, Mommy forgot something. Let's go up to the store while they're still up there."

"Nora and I can keep an eye on him," Ellie said. "So you can…"

When her words died away and several people shifted in their chairs, Siobhan realized most of them knew something was going on. She didn't want people whispering all week, so the best thing to do was meet it head-on.

"Thanks." She smiled at her son and then headed across the grass toward the store.

When they saw her coming, Lisa let go of Brian's arm and said something Siobhan couldn't hear. Then Brian turned back toward the store while his parents gave her tight smiles and headed back to the others. Because she knew everybody present was probably watching her, she didn't hesitate before stepping through the door Brian had left open.

He didn't wait to see if she followed, but walked straight to one of the leather chairs and dropped into it. When she closed the door, maybe giving it a little more oomph than she intended so it was almost a slam, he looked up at her. There wasn't a hint of softness or warmth in that look, and she shivered.

She could deny everything. So what if Oliver had blue eyes. Millions of people did. She could look Brian in the eye and tell him Oliver was her son. Technically, at least, that was the truth. A denial probably wouldn't be enough, though. If the entire family wasn't in one place, the facial expressions and mannerisms wouldn't make the resemblance so obvious. Surrounded by them, though, it was hard to deny he was one of them.

Leaving wasn't an option. Steph might feel as if a second maid of honor bailing was some kind of a sign she shouldn't get married, even though there were plenty of women in her family who could step in.

And even if Brian suspected Siobhan was running from a mess of Kelly's making, he might not care. Based on how quickly he turned on his wife, he wasn't exactly a devoted family man. He'd been awful to Kelly, and she'd referenced his temper more than once. Maybe he didn't *want* a son.

But Kelly had lied.

Siobhan pressed her lips together, dismissing the thought with one sharp shake of her head. She couldn't deny her sister had lied about who Oliver's father was, but she couldn't really blame her sister for not wanting to be tied to Brian Kowalski for the rest of her life. Not if he'd ever looked at her the way he was looking at Siobhan right now.

She sat in the other chair so she was facing him, but she had no idea what to say. This wasn't the kind of conversation she'd ever imagined herself having, and the words to get it started wouldn't come to her.

Brian didn't seem to know what to say, either. He'd inhale slightly, as though about to speak, but then his jaw would clench and nothing.

The silence grew so oppressive it was almost a physical weight crushing her. "The answer to the question you haven't asked is I don't know."

His face didn't soften, but his broad shoulders dropped and he sighed. After an endless moment, he shook his head before flopping back in the chair and staring at the ceiling.

Siobhan was silent, waiting. And when he leaned forward again, she got a glimpse of his raw emotions before he got control of his face again. Confusion. Anger. Overwhelmed.

"I don't even know the right questions to ask. You don't know what?"

"I don't actually know who Oliver's biological father is."

He considered her words for a moment, and then his eyes narrowed. "Who actually gave birth to him?"

"Kelly." Just one word—her sister's name—and Siobhan knew it was going to change everything. But she wasn't going to lie. Not about this.

Brian dropped his face into his hands, elbows rested on his knees. Judging by the rise and fall of his shoulders, he was taking long and slow deep breaths, and Siobhan wasn't sure if he was trying to control his emotions or his temper.

I'm scared of him, Siobhan.

"How old is he?" Brian asked as he lifted his head. He

didn't look happy, of course, but he didn't look angry or dangerous.

"Twenty-two months. He'll be two in October."

She let him do the math himself, and when the color drained from his face, she knew he'd done it. "We were still married when Oliver was conceived."

"Barely, but technically yes."

The anger came now, tinting his face and neck red. "You helped her take my son away from me."

"No. She told me you two fought all the time and you hadn't slept together for months. She was already hooking up with Steve and I—I believed her." She paused, taking a breath. "And for the record, I *still* don't know for a *fact* who Oliver's father is."

"We will as soon as I can manage it," he vowed. "Why do *you* have him?"

"When Oliver was three months old, they decided they didn't want to be parents anymore and told me that either I adopted him or they were surrendering him."

"Surrendering him." The flush faded and he swiped his hand over his mouth. "So you legally adopted him. But that guy signed the papers. He lied. They both lied."

"I don't know if he thought he was Oliver's biological father or not. She probably lied to him, too, especially if she planned to stay with him. But I thought he was." It was important to Siobhan that he knew that.

His phone chimed and she'd usually be annoyed by him responding to it while they were talking, but she was thankful for the interruption. A glass of water would be nice, but at least she got a respite from being pinned by Brian's intense blue gaze. Whatever was on his screen made him close his eyes for a solid five count, and then he held the phone out toward her.

She frowned, but he gave her a go-ahead gesture with his head, so she took it. On the screen was a text from his mom.

This is always in the favorites album in my phone.

And there was an old photo of four young boys. It had the grainy look of an older print photo that Lisa had taken a picture of with her phone, but Siobhan got the message. Not only were the Kowalski genes so strong that they were basically a stamp on Brian and his brothers, but if Oliver was digitally added, he'd look like he belonged. The resemblance really was uncanny.

Despite the heat in the room, Siobhan was shivering, and after handing his phone back to him, she crossed her arms and tucked her hands under her arms. Part of her wanted to walk out, but she wasn't sure her legs would support her.

"I didn't see it until you smiled at him up on the hill," she said quietly. "He just had a growth spurt and part of it was his face changing and losing some of the baby fat so he looks like a little boy now and I haven't seen you in a long time and I've certainly never seen you smile at me like that, so I just didn't see it." She realized she was babbling and forced herself back on track. "I know this is hard for you, but you also need to know that I'm his mother and I'm not conceding a damn thing without a paternity test."

"Five bucks says my mother's already got the instructions for how to do that loaded on her phone."

Siobhan closed her eyes briefly, and then sighed. "Zero chance we keep this between us, I guess."

"Since half my family knew before I did, no, there's no chance."

"Great."

"My parents accused me of causing the divorce by having an affair with you," he told her, and the underlying tremor in his voice made it hard for her to swallow.

"I'm sorry this is happening, Brian. Maybe I should go. I know Steph will be devastated, but I'm sure one of her cousins can stand in for me. I think it's important that there be boundaries until we know for sure, one way or the other."

He looked at her for a long time, his expression unreadable, before he spoke in a low voice. "No. I don't want you to go."

Brian had no idea what the right thing to do was in this situation, but he was sure of one thing—he didn't want Oliver to leave the campground. And keeping the boy around meant he had to convince Siobhan to stay.

He'd known this week was going to be tough, but he didn't think it was going to turn his entire life upside down.

Maybe. There was a chance this was all a strange coincidence and the test results would come back proving his ex-wife had a baby with some guy she'd cheated on him with and then his former sister-in-law had adopted him. He couldn't let himself get attached, just to have his emotional rug yanked out from under him *again*.

It was already too late, though. He knew Oliver was his son as surely as he knew Mike and Lisa were his parents.

"I know we're all blown away right now," he said, "but Steph's getting married and she's so excited about this wedding. She'd be crushed if you left."

"I'm sorry it'll be hard for Steph, but I don't want to be here."

Even though he'd spent the last several years nurturing a serious dislike for this woman, Brian tried to put himself in her place. He imagined what it would feel like if he had a child and when he showed up at a campground, an entire family tried to claim that child as their own.

He and his kid would be out of there so fast he'd probably leave a cartoon puff of air behind him and half his tire tread out on Route 3 from peeling out of the campground.

"I understand," he said. "But look, it's a long drive. You and Oliver just spent hours in the car. By the time you could pack everything up again and eat, it'll be late and it feels like an even longer drive when you're exhausted. At least spend the night and see how you feel tomorrow. I'll keep my family in line."

"You have to tell them," she said quietly. "You can't let them believe that you and I...you know."

"I was pretty emphatic about that not being a possibility, but yes. I'll tell them what we know to be true. You adopted Oliver from Kelly, who was still married to me when he was conceived, and it seems likely—though not certain yet—that she lied to both of us."

"I don't want...the family names, you know? Until we know for sure if those are his aunts and uncles and grandparents out there, I don't think it's healthy for anybody to go there yet."

Daddy.

Brian scrubbed his hands over his face, willing his voice to be steady even though his entire body was trembling. "That's fair. Just as a heads-up, though, my family loves kids in general so they're going to be all over him, but that would be the case no matter whose kid he is. Some random camper could show up with a toddler and by the time the parents unhooked the camper, the kid would be sucked into the Kowalski vortex."

"Okay. But as a heads-up right back at you, if I get uncomfortable, I'm going to take him into the camper and we'll stay inside until we leave tomorrow."

"Fair enough. I can send them a text now, so we don't have to talk about it when we go out there."

When she nodded, he pulled up the family group chat on his phone. It took him a minute to compose the text message, especially since his hands were trembling slightly and he kept messing up so badly even autocorrect wasn't sure what he wanted to say.

Kelly is Oliver's bio mom and the math says he could be mine. Siobhan adopted him, but K lied to her about our situation and she didn't know. S might stay if we don't make it awkward. Will do paternity test after wedding. Until we get the results, be chill and focus on the wedding, please. And don't blow up my phone with replies or I'll block all of you.

"Do you want me to read it to you before I hit Send?" he asked.

"If you don't mind." After he'd read it aloud, she shrugged. "That's all there is to say right now, I guess."

"We should probably give them a few minutes to read it and get the initial burst of talking about it out of their systems."

"I know he's not even two, but I hope they'll remember Oliver is listening."

"They will." He hit Send.

After the whooshing airplane sound told them his family was now in the loop, a tense silence settled between him and Siobhan again.

Quiet wasn't good. Since the moment he realized he might have a son, his head had been like a snow globe. Every time somebody spoke, the snow globe was shaken and his thoughts were the flurry of flakes. But in the silence, the snowflakes got a chance to settle and Brian could make sense of his thoughts. One in particular was picking up steam, like a snowball rolling downhill.

Maybe Kelly had lied to her sister, but if Siobhan hadn't hated Brian since day one and had supported their marriage, maybe Kelly wouldn't have left him for some other guy. Maybe they would still be married, raising their son together.

He didn't say it out loud. Right now, his only objective was getting to know the child he knew in his gut was his son. To do that, he needed to keep Siobhan at the campground, and that would be challenging enough without rehashing the years of animosity between them.

"I didn't know," she whispered, and since she was looking at her hands, Brian wasn't sure if she was talking to him or to herself.

"If you'd known, you probably wouldn't have shown up at a gathering of my entire family with him."

She couldn't have known how strong the resemblance really was, of course, because she had no way of knowing what Brian and his brothers had looked like at that age. But if Siobhan believed there was even a hint of a possibility Brian was Oliver's father, he didn't think she would have even come herself, never mind brought the boy with her.

"You're right about it not being fair to put Oliver back in his car seat for hours," she said. "But I'm probably going to leave tomorrow. There's no way this isn't awkward."

"Give my family a chance," he said. "For Steph's sake, at least."

Siobhan looked him in the eye, her gaze unflinching. "I adore Steph. We've been friends for years. But there is literally nobody on this planet more important to me than Oliver. If I think it's a bad idea for us to be here, using Steph's wedding to emotionally blackmail me into staying won't work. As soon as one of my boundaries is crossed, we're gone."

"I'm sorry. I love Steph, so that was a genuine ask, but I can see how it looks like I'm using her to manipulate you. And maybe I am on some level, I guess. I'll try not to anymore."

"Thank you."

There didn't seem to be anything else to say, so Brian stood. "I'll go out and make sure they're settled down."

"I'm going to use the restroom first—maybe splash some water on my face—and then I'll be out."

As he walked across the grass, he knew the moment he was spotted because everybody snapped into *act natural* mode. They weren't very good at it, and he chuckled before his gaze landed on the little boy who looked like a replica of his own baby pictures and the sound died in his throat.

His son.

Brian wasn't sure how he was supposed to keep his family's expectations in check when he couldn't even control his own, but he wanted Siobhan and Oliver to stay. He had to try.

Chapter Five

Walking back across the grass to where her son was being watched by the Kowalski family was one of the hardest things Siobhan had ever done.

Regardless of what she'd said to Brian, the urge to take Oliver and run was strong. Sure, he'd be upset about being back in his car seat for another three or four hours, depending on the flow of traffic, but he'd get over it. What he might not get over was his mother falling asleep at the wheel, and she was tired. When the emotions currently coursing through her body like an electrical current faded, she'd probably be utterly exhausted.

Then there was the fact that, even though he hadn't understood exactly what they'd be doing, Oliver had been so excited to go on this trip.

At that moment, she heard his laughter and spotted him on the playground. Stella was running after a tennis ball, which she brought back to Nora. The little girl threw it again, and again Oliver laughed.

Siobhan stopped walking, taking in her son's joy in the game and letting it refill her emotional well. While she was shaken to her core, he was too young to know anything was going on. The only way his happiness could be disrupted would be him sensing his mommy wasn't okay and feeding off of her chaotic energy.

There were so many of them, all sitting around the unlit campfire. As Steph's aunts, uncles and cousins had finished setting up their campsites for the week, they'd wandered over with chairs. Joining them would be daunting even if she *hadn't* shown up with a surprise child, but all she could do was maintain a pleasantly neutral expression—which wouldn't be easy—and sit quietly. There were enough family members talking to and around each other, trying to catch up since the last time they'd been together, that it should be easy to blend into the background.

She had to admit they did their best not to stare at Oliver. He ran around with Nora—who was great with him— and Stella, and every so often somebody would have them sit in the shade and drink some water. When he brought her a rock he found in the grass, she admired the smooth gray stone, and then she laughed with the others when he went from person to person, showing off the rock.

Brian was the end of the line, having dropped his chair near his uncles, and it seemed Oliver grew bored with the game just about the time he reached him. After handing Brian the rock, who assured him it was the best rock he'd ever seen, Oliver left it with him and went back to where Nora was using blocks of wood to make a tower.

As Siobhan watched, Brian turned the rock over in his fingers a few times. Then he brushed his thumb over the surface and tucked it into the pocket of his jeans.

Over the next couple of hours, thanks to easy conversation, old stories and a lot of laughter, the overall tension in the group seemed to melt away, and by the time talking of firing up the barbecue grills started, Siobhan was feeling maybe not relaxed, but definitely less stressed.

Emma, who was married to Mike's cousin Sean and seemed really warm and friendly, was wandering through the groupings of family with a small notebook. Siobhan wasn't sure what that was about until Emma reached her.

"I'm doing the burgers and dogs count," the woman explained. "Hamburger? Cheeseburger? Hot dog? One of each? And Oliver put himself down for a hot dog and I just thought I'd confirm he'd actually like a hot dog and didn't just ask for what Nora was having."

"Oh." She'd had some vague idea she and Oliver would duck back into the camper when mealtime came around, but she had a hunch trying to separate her son from his plan to eat hot dogs with his new best friend wouldn't go over well. "He loves hot dogs, and I'd like a cheeseburger, please. Is there something I can do to help?"

Emma looked around, and then laughed. "Honestly, I think there are already too many people helping. Just relax and enjoy the down time before the little ones are refueled."

"Oliver's going to sleep well tonight, for sure."

"I think we all will." Emma looked around and then leaned in close. "Listen, there are going to be two potato salads. If you *like* potato salad, make sure you take a little of each and no matter what, you love them equally."

Siobhan's hand went to her mouth, stifling a giggle. "Whose are they?"

"Terry's and Beth's. About nine years ago, there was some confusion about the summer cookout sign-up list thanks to a spill-proof tumbler lid that wasn't at all spill-proof, and they both brought potato salad. Nobody would admit to liking one more than the other, and they just keep bringing them, waiting for some unsuspecting person to like one more than the other."

"So in Kowalski-speak, this would be a Potato Salad Grudge Match of Doom?"

Emma's laughter turned heads. "Yes! Who told you about the doom?"

"Steph's mentioned it a few times over the years, how the family uses it to mean epic or whatever. Just a childhood thing that nobody outgrew."

She put her hand on Siobhan's arm. "Exactly."

"And Steph also told me she tried not to let this be a Wedding of Doom, but she stopped fighting it once the family group chat latched onto it."

"Resistance is futile, as they say."

"Emma, I need that food count," Leo shouted.

The family patriarch had a booming voice and Emma rolled her eyes. "And there's the family's official PA system."

Twenty minutes later, while most of the family was occupied setting up the tables under a canopy and loading them with condiments and everything else they needed, Steph joined Siobhan in sitting on the grass to watch Nora explaining to a rapt Oliver how caterpillars became butterflies.

"There you are," Siobhan said, giving her friend's pink cheeks and mussed hair a sideways glance. "I was looking for you earlier."

"Sorry." Steph grinned. "Kyle and I needed a little nap."

"And that's why you're in a cabin with solid log walls and not a camper."

She laughed. "One hundred percent. But how are *you* doing?"

"I'm good," she replied, realizing it was mostly true.

"You know, if you want to leave, I'll understand. I know everybody wants you to stay—especially me. And Brian, of course. But nobody expected this and I get that it's a lot. I don't want you to stay just for me if it's too hard. Brianna can be my maid of honor." She paused and took a shaky breath before giving Siobhan a falsely bright smile. "Third time's the charm, right?"

The way Steph was putting up a brave front for her benefit brought tears to Siobhan's eyes. She *really* didn't want to let her friend down. And the damage was already done. This family was sure Oliver was one of them and leaving wouldn't change that. As long as Brian took her boundaries seriously, it might be okay.

"I don't *want* to leave. I want to be your maid of honor." She blew out a breath. "I told Brian I would wait and see how I feel tomorrow, but mostly it's up to your family. Oliver is having a good time and I promised him he could go in the pool, so as long as everybody is chill, as Brian put it, I'll probably stay."

Steph winced. "I can promise you we're all devoted to *trying* to be chill, but this situation knocked *everybody* a little sideways."

"So far everybody's been great. Let's just focus on you and your wedding and see how it goes."

"Burgers and dogs are ready," Leo announced.

Steph leaned close. "Has anybody told you about the potato salads?"

Brian finished banging the last peg into the *tots' tent*, as his family called it. It was a small, modified tent his family had been using for years as a combination of play fort and napping spot. It hadn't left his grandparents' garage in a few years, but after they'd eaten, he and Joey had given it a once-over and it was still in good shape.

Because it was new to Nora, she was excited to get inside and Brian wasn't surprised when Oliver went right in after her. The boy had definitely latched onto

Nora—his cousin, Brian thought—and he was grateful she didn't seem annoyed to have a toddler shadowing her every move.

"Is it okay if he goes in there?" Siobhan asked, startling him because he hadn't noticed she was standing next to him. "If she needs a break from him, I can distract him."

"I think she's happy to have somebody to play with, even if he's younger. And my money says, they'll both be asleep before an hour's up."

"That explains the mats you put in there," she said, and he nodded. "It reminds me of the domes made out of screens that you put over paper plates to keep the flies off."

"Similar idea. My uncle made it when my younger cousins were little. Basically it's just a little pop-up tent, but he replaced two of the panels with screen that has magnetic strips."

"It's held up well."

He chuckled. "It's seen a few repairs over the years, but it's also seen a lot of use. It keeps the little ones with us, but away from the fire and bugs. Since they always fall asleep, those screen panels just lift up so it's easier to pick the kids up and carry them to bed."

"Your family seems very good at camping."

"We've always enjoyed it, especially the annual trips here when everybody came."

"Steph told me about the camping trips, and she said the whole family was happy when the four of you bought this campground."

He nodded, aware of how strange it felt to be having a conversation with Siobhan Rowe. In the days leading up to her arrival, he'd been so focused on how they were going to ignore each other. Since she'd never liked him any more than he liked her, he'd assumed they'd both do the necessary social dance steps to ensure they were never in the same space at the same time without other people to interact with.

Then Oliver had happened. And, honestly, she seemed like such a different woman. She wasn't exactly warm with him—understandably—but he'd seen her talking and laughing with his family all afternoon and she fit in so well.

She also smelled good, which was something he'd rather not be aware of. It was probably just the bug spray, he told himself. His family tended to use the stuff that worked really well, but didn't smell that great. Being new to camping, Siobhan might be using one of the ones that smelled good and claimed to be skin friendly, if you didn't mind the bug bites.

"Hey, Brian," Terry called, breaking the spell Siobhan's scent had cast over him. "Did I get a package delivery here today?"

After smiling at Siobhan, he turned back to the campfire, which was roaring now. "Today? You've gotten packages delivered here every day for the last week."

"It made more sense than having them delivered to my house, only to load them into our camper and drive them up here."

He was aware of Siobhan peeking through the screen to see that Oliver and Nora were playing with the stuffed animals she'd brought with her, and then she moved back to her seat next to Steph.

To put distance between them, he took an empty chair on the other side of the fire, between his grandfather and Kyle's grandfather. It was a mistake, not only because he ended up sandwiched between two men with big voices, but because sitting across from Siobhan meant she was in his line of sight.

It was hard not to notice the way the flames reflected in her eyes and the way it shimmered over the lighter blond strands in her hair. And every time he managed to focus his attention elsewhere, she'd laugh or move her head in a way that made her ponytail swing or she'd bounce the sandal dangling from her foot.

Her toenails were painted a soft shade of pink.

Finally, for his own piece of mind, he took a walk up to the store for a quick bathroom break and then, when he returned, he joined a different conversation and sat in a chair that didn't face Siobhan's direction.

Sometime later, when the fire was burning low and the exhaustion of arrival and setup day was setting in, he noticed Siobhan by the tots' tent. She peeked in and then turned to say something to Ellie, who laughed.

Then she peeked inside again before putting her hands on her hips. He could tell from her body language that she was considering how exactly she was going to manage to get the boy out of the tent and up to her camper.

Indecision kept him in his chair. If he offered to carry Oliver to bed, would she take that as him trying to push his way in? It was a very dad thing to do. But even if she was able to carry him to the camper, how would she get the door open? Waking him up and having him walk was always an option, but not usually a parent's first choice.

Siobhan turned and caught him watching her. Her gaze held his for a few seconds, and then she dipped her head toward the tent. Taking that as an invitation to join her, Brian pushed himself to his feet and made his way around the chairs.

"He's a heavy sleeper," she said in a low voice. "He

sleeps through almost anything, and he's a monster if I wake him up, but carrying him from the couch to his bed isn't bad. He's getting heavy, though, and I wouldn't bet on me carrying him across the grass and up the hill and getting the door of the camper open without dropping him. Would you mind carrying him for me?"

Would he *mind*? "Of course not."

Once Siobhan had lifted the screen panels, Brian crouched and slid his hands under the boy. It had been a while since he held a child, but he supported him the best he could as he lifted him into his arms and stood. Oliver stirred slightly, but then found a comfortable spot against Brian's chest and quieted again.

He looked down at the boy's relaxed face and smiled. Oliver had the tiniest eyelashes. Thick and dark, but so tiny. His nose was adorable, and there was the tiniest hint of an upward curve in his mouth as he slept.

Everything seemed to fade away, until Siobhan sighed and he heard the tremor in her breath. He cleared his throat and turned to follow her in the direction of her camper. When they reached it, she opened the door and stood out of the way.

He had to turn sideways to ensure he didn't hit Oliver's head on the doorjamb, which made the stairs tricky, but he managed. Once he was inside, he moved back so Siobhan had room to enter, and she pulled the door closed behind her.

"Where do you want him?" he asked in a low voice.

"You can just lay him on the bed and I'll take it from there."

He did as she asked, bending low to set Oliver on the bed. When he slid his hands out from under the boy, he sighed in his sleep and rolled onto his side.

"Don't you have to wake him up to change him or anything?" he asked as he backed away.

She chuckled softly, and he tried not to stare at how soft the lines of her face were when she was looking at Oliver. "He'll sleep through it, believe it or not. I'll change him and use a warm wipe to give him a quick wash, and then I'll put his pajamas on him."

"And he won't wake up?"

"Usually not, though he might here because it's a strange place. Babies are so funny. Oliver is a terrible napper, but sleeps like a rock at night. A friend of mine has an eight-month-old who's a dream when it comes to napping, but wakes at the slightest disturbance when it's dark."

"I guess it's probably nice to have a break while they nap, but I'd choose a good night's sleep every time."

"Me too, so I got lucky."

They lapsed into silence, and Brian knew it was time for him to go. Reluctantly, he turned away from Oliver and managed a tight smile for Siobhan.

"I'll go so you can get him to bed."

"Thank you for carrying him."

Thank you for letting me. He didn't say the words out loud, though, since he couldn't be sure how she'd take them. "Anytime."

Once he'd quietly closed the camper door behind him, Brian closed his eyes and inhaled the comforting scent of woods, lingering barbecue and campfire smoke.

Soft voices and laughter his family was trying but failing to muffle drifted to Brian from the campfire. Usually he'd jump at the chance to enjoy their company, but right now he needed a few minutes by himself.

He should have known he wouldn't get it. Stella spotted

him first, of course, and she left her place by the fire to join him. Then his dad stood. Brian heard the low rumble of his voice, but he couldn't make out what was said. He could guess, though, because when his dad started toward him, nobody else moved.

The last thing Brian wanted right now was a paternal talking-to, but the man's purpose was clear and the only way out of it was turning his back and deliberately snubbing him. No way would Brian ever do that, no matter how much he wanted to be alone.

With Stella on his left and his dad falling into step on his right, Brian walked up the hill into the dark, wooded part of the campground.

Much to his surprise, his dad didn't say anything. They walked in silence, which suited him just fine. And it was enough. His presence offered much-needed comfort, and with every step he felt a little steadier.

They were at the top of the hill, following the road that would go down past the cabins and come out on the other end of the playground when Brian felt ready to talk.

He had to clear his throat a couple of times first, though. "Holding him was…something else."

"I'm proud of the way you've handled this. Both of you, actually, because this can't be easy for Siobhan, either."

"I really can't speak for her, but I know I'm only getting through it because you're all being so great about it."

"Whatever you need, son." His father's hand rested briefly on his shoulder before rubbing his back a few times. "Always."

Sometimes, over the years, Brian would think about the day he'd have a child of his own and hope he could be as good a father as his was.

He hadn't expected that day to come so soon.

Chapter Six

Siobhan waited until she heard Brian's footsteps crunching on the gravel road before she sank onto the dinette bench and dropped her face into her hands. The look on that man's face when he held Oliver for the first time was seared into her memory—probably forever.

There were so many emotions running through her, she couldn't even begin to process any of them. It was obvious Brian wasn't the kind of man who would walk away from his child. She'd never had to share Oliver with anybody, but she was going to have to now, and she didn't know how. She didn't want to.

And she was so angry with Kelly. Not only because she'd put Siobhan and Oliver in this position, but because she'd robbed Brian of the opportunity to be a father. Even though everything would be different if Kelly hadn't lied—Siobhan probably wouldn't be Oliver's mother— she couldn't help being upset on Brian's behalf. Maybe he hadn't been the greatest of husbands—according to Kelly, anyway—but he didn't deserve to be erased from his child's life.

She was sad. She was scared. Confused. Unsure of what to do next. Part of her still wanted to put her son in the car, drive home and lock themselves in their apartment.

But it wouldn't stop the inevitable. And while Steph could find yet another stand-in maid of honor, if the family was saddened to have met Oliver only to have him whisked away so abruptly, that could put a damper on the entire wedding week.

Siobhan pushed herself to her feet and poured herself a cup of water, which she downed half of in one shot. What she needed to do was sleep on it. First, though, she needed to get her son into bed.

It was probably being away from home that did it, but Oliver didn't sleep through getting cleaned up and changed as she'd hoped. He was cranky and kept trying to push her away, but she was finally able to get him into his pajamas and tucked into bed. She only made it halfway through his book before he fell back to sleep.

Once Oliver was softly snoring, Siobhan slid out of the bed and went to the other end of the camper to sit at the dinette with her phone. She pulled up Robin's name in her contacts and hit the button to call her, desperate to talk to possibly the only person in her life who would one hundred percent take her side.

"Please tell me you're having fun," Robin said in lieu of hello.

"That's not exactly the word I'd use." Siobhan kept her voice low. Even though there weren't any campers super close to hers, people could be walking around and she wasn't sure how soundproof campers were. Probably not very. "You might want to get comfortable."

"I'm wearing a tank top and men's boxers, I have cupcake frosting on my phone, and my TV's paused with a very attractive duke about to slide his hand up under his lady love's dress, so I'm not sure it's possible to be *more* comfortable."

"So you're sitting down, then?"

"What's going on, Siobhan? You just got there today. How bad can it be already?"

She choked down the hysterical giggle that bubbled up in her throat. "Well, there's a good chance Brian Kowalski is actually Oliver's biological father."

"What the— Dammit. Hold on a sec." There were rustling sounds, punctuated by Robin muttering curses, and then she was back. Siobhan could tell by the sound quality her friend had put her earbuds in. "Sorry. You made me drop my cupcake and it has blue frosting and I know better because the blue food coloring stains everything. But *what*? How is that even possible? Brian being his father, I mean. Who cares about cupcakes? And why do you even think that?"

When her friend finally stopped and took a breath, Siobhan filled her in on everything that had happened since her arrival at Birch Brook Campground. Robin listened intently, her gasps the only interruption, until she got it all out.

"You can't really be sure, though," Robin said when she was caught up. "I mean, Kowalskis aren't the only people with dark hair and blue eyes."

"Trust me, I tried that defense. But Robin…you'd have to see it. I swear, he's like a little Brian clone. The test is just going to confirm what's already obvious to everybody here, even though I'm not going to admit that to *them*."

"You could refuse to allow the paternity test, you know. You're his mother and people can't just go around sticking swabs in your kid's mouth whenever they want. They need your permission."

"I thought of that, but I feel like he has a strong enough case to get a court order." Siobhan sighed. "And then, if

I make it adversarial, what happens when he can prove he's Oliver's father and Kelly lied on the adoption papers? Robin, if I fight him, I might lose."

"You're legally his mother. They can't just take him away."

Siobhan wasn't so sure of that, and she definitely wasn't sure enough to risk a court battle. "I'm hoping it doesn't come to that."

"Do you want me to come up there? I can tell my job I'm sick or something and be there…um, sometime in the middle of the night, I guess."

Siobhan laughed, even though she knew Robin was serious. "No, you don't need to come up. I appreciate the offer, but I'll get through this."

"If you get a bad vibe, just come home. We'll pack up what we need and go on the run with Oliver and we'll find a small town to hide in somewhere out west. We can pretend we're sisters and open a bakery or something and nobody will ever find us."

Siobhan laughed, and then smothered it with her hand so she wouldn't wake her son. "Nobody who knows us will *ever* think to look for us in the back of a bakery, that's for sure. Our only cupcake skills are eating them and smearing the frosting all over the place."

"I swear, I'm as bad as Oliver sometimes." There was a long pause. "But I was only half joking. You know I've got you, right?"

"I know."

"You don't think *he* would try to go on the run, do you?"

There was one sharp jolt of terror, but she was able to laugh it off. "No, he wouldn't do that. This is a big, close family and he might be a jerk, but they're nice people. I'm very confident if he even hinted at something like that, they'd set him straight. I mean, they're going to take Brian's side, of course, but they wouldn't support him doing something like that."

"I should probably stop dumping my tendency toward high drama all over you."

Siobhan sighed. "I feel like I'm the one living in high drama right now."

"If it gets to be too much, just come home. We'll hire a lawyer and let her handle it."

"I will. I promise."

"Okay. Try to get some sleep and call me tomorrow."

Getting some sleep was much easier said than done. She couldn't really toss and turn without disturbing her son, but spent a lot of time staring at the ceiling. Finally, she slept, but it was fitful and her mind was filled with flashes of blue eyes.

Siobhan wasn't surprised Oliver woke up earlier than usual. They were in a strange bed and the sun was hitting the side of the camper like a spotlight. Even though she'd struggled to fall asleep, the brightness of the camper and emotional restlessness had woken her just a few minutes before her son stirred.

She was already looking forward to an afternoon nap, whether it was here or at home. Several hours of thinking about it in the dark hadn't made up her mind one way or the other.

Oliver blinked at her and then his mouth curved into a sleepy smile. "Swim in the pool today, Mommy?"

"Yes, honey. Later we'll swim in the pool."

It didn't mean she'd decided. They could have breakfast and then play outside. Toward the middle of the day, Oliver could spend some time in the pool. They could have lunch, and then hit the road.

"And the playground?" he asked, so excited he was bouncing on his butt on the mattress.

"And the playground, too."

As she grabbed the diaper bag, Siobhan knew she wasn't going anywhere. At least not today. She didn't want to rush her child through his adventure and then go back to their apartment, where she'd probably spend the rest of her time off pacing the floor, worrying about what was to come.

If she stayed, she could enjoy a week off with her son. And for better or worse, most of the people in the campground were going to be a part of Oliver's life, one way or another. Staying and getting to know them would be in everybody's best interest.

Her phone chimed, and she picked it up to see a text from Steph.

We're doing a buffet-style breakfast and you're welcome to join us, of course.

Since she'd come to terms with the fact that she was going to see the week out, she should probably embrace her maid of honor duties. But she and Oliver enjoyed their breakfast. Maybe it was only oatmeal or scrambled eggs and cut-up fruit, but her boy was definitely a morning person. Siobhan always protected their mornings together before she had to drop him at daycare and head to work.

We're about to eat, actually, but we'll be out soon to visit for a bit before Oliver goes in the pool. It's all he'll talk about.

She hoped that was enough to signal she was staying without having an entire conversation about it.

"What flavor do you want today?" she asked Oliver once they'd gone through their morning routine.

"Apple!"

It was his favorite. Apple cinnamon instant oatmeal with sliced apples on the side. "At least *you're* predictable, little man."

And Oliver laughed and clapped, even though he had no idea what she was talking about.

Brian's first thought when he opened his eyes was *Oliver*. His second was pushing Stella's face out of his because her morning breath was not a great way to start his day.

Excited her favorite human was finally awake, Stella bounded off the bed and waited impatiently for Brian to get up and open the door. After scrubbing his hands over his face, he followed his dog through the house, but then veered off toward the window that looked out over the part of the campground where Siobhan's borrowed camper sat.

Her car was still there.

"She hasn't left yet," his mother said, and Brian spun, barely managing to swallow the curse that rose in his throat.

His mom was sitting at the kitchen table with a mug of coffee in front of her, and he probably should have seen that coming. At least he would have been wearing more than a pair of boxer briefs.

"Be right back," he muttered, and then he retraced his steps to his bedroom.

Brian had been so focused on whether Siobhan had left, he'd forgotten he wasn't alone in the house. When he and Stella were at their actual home, almost two hours south, they lived alone. He and his brothers all settled within twenty minutes or so of their parents, who were outside of Concord, though Rob had given up his apartment to be at the campground year-round. Family visits were usually planned—or at least announced—in advance, though, after Joey came very close to catching their mom and dad having fun on the couch.

During the spring, when they were working nonstop to get the campground ready to open, he and his brothers had all stayed in the house together. They didn't care that it was small and in desperate need of renovation—they just wanted a place to sleep at night. Then Joey and Danny had gone home, and Rob had moved into the camper with Hannah. When Brian went home for the winter, they'd stay in the house. That was the plan, anyway.

Rob and Hannah were actually staying in the house now, with Joey and his wife and daughter staying in the camper. It was a merry-go-round of lodging, and with his entire family present, Brian should have been prepared for literally anybody to be in the house. And he might have been if he wasn't looking for Siobhan's car.

After getting dressed and making a pit stop in the bathroom, he opened the door to let Stella out and poured himself a cup of coffee. He had no idea where Rob and Hannah were. They'd either gone out early or been exiled by their mother, who obviously wanted to talk to him.

"Today should be fun," she said as soon as he sat down. "I didn't sleep well, and I know you and Siobhan didn't, either. Your father, of course, copes by sleeping, so he's well rested. But it's already hot today and most of us could use a nap."

"Have you talked to her?"

"As far as I know, she hasn't come out of the camper yet." She shrugged. "But that doesn't mean anything.

Maybe she's packing, or maybe she's the mother of an active toddler and knows that as soon as she lets him outside, she doesn't get to rest until he drops from exhaustion. All we can do is wait and see what she decides."

"I hope they stay."

"Me too, honey." She sipped her coffee, and then after a few seconds of silence, shook her head. "I don't know how it fell through the cracks. Even though she lied about who the father was, the date of the divorce decree and the birth certificate should have flagged the authorities during the adoption process. Sure, most couples probably aren't intimate in the period leading up to filing for divorce, but doing a paternity test to eliminate the man she was married to at the time of conception is standard procedure, isn't it?"

"I don't know, Mom." He leaned back in his chair, hands wrapped around the warm mug. "I'm sure she didn't tell anybody she was pregnant until after it was finalized and yes, the dates should have been flagged because there's a window around a divorce in which the husband is the presumed father. So maybe it's two different systems or something got entered incorrectly, or maybe it just got overlooked. Somebody dropped the ball, but this is where we are now."

"It has to be quite a shock for Siobhan. She *really* didn't like you very much."

He snorted. "That's an understatement. And you used the past tense there, but she's not going to magically like me now. If anything, she might even like me less."

"I think the feeling was mutual. Certainly none of us have been her biggest fans. But that was in the past and we're going to let bygones be bygones because there's

Oliver to consider. We are *not* going to pull that child in different directions."

"Mom, you can't..." Brian couldn't figure out what to say next, so he paused and scrubbed his hands over his face to buy himself a few seconds to think. "It's complicated."

"It certainly is."

"Until we get a paternity test done, I don't think it's a good idea for you to get too emotionally invested—for any of us to get too attached. Sure, she's been handling it okay, but she's also up here in the middle of nowhere, surrounded by us. For all we know, she's as good an actor as her sister, and she'll be on the phone with a lawyer before she's five miles down the road. I might have to fight just to get a court order for a paternity test, and who knows how long *that* would take."

"You'll both need lawyers no matter what because, as you said, it's complicated. That doesn't mean it's a fight, though. It just means there's a legal knot that needs untangling. Don't go borrowing trouble." She sipped her coffee and then smiled at him over the rim. "But if she chooses to make it a fight, we'll win. No matter how long it takes."

"Custody Battle of Doom," he muttered, and his mother snorted. "Where is everybody, anyway?"

"Setting up for breakfast." She drained the last of her coffee and stood. "Speaking of, I should probably get out there. I just wanted a quiet minute with you before the day starts."

Brian stood and after his mom put her mug in the sink, he stepped forward and opened his arms. She wrapped her arms around his waist and held him close. As he had since the day he was tall enough to do it, he rested his cheek on the top of her head and just breathed.

She didn't fuss. She just quietly held him while his

breathing and his heart rate gently slowed. His parents really did give the best hugs. Over the years, he'd figured out his dad's hugs often gave him strength and his mom's gave him comfort, but they both made him feel like everything would be okay.

Once his body was relaxed and his mind somewhat calm, he kissed the top of her head and she let him go.

Then she cupped his face in her hands. "Come have something to eat."

"You know I don't like eating when I first wake up. I'm going to get some stuff done and then I'll grab a bowl of cereal. That'll hold me until lunch. But do me a favor and keep an eye on Stella? She'll convince every single person out there that nobody has given her bacon and she doesn't know when to quit."

"I seem to recall saying the same thing about you once, when you were very little."

The grin she gave him over his shoulder before walking out the door made him laugh, and he was still smiling when he poured a second cup of coffee to take with him to the campground office in the store.

He spent an hour there, chipping away at some of the smaller tasks on the to-do list that tended to get overlooked. None of them were particularly urgent, but he didn't want to be outside if Siobhan and Oliver left. One, he didn't want her to feel like he was pressuring her in any way. She'd had her world turned upside down, too—finding out her son's dad was a man she couldn't stand probably sucked—and he was going to give her space even if it killed him.

And secondly, he wasn't sure how it would feel to watch that car drive out of the campground with Oliver in the back seat, but he knew it wouldn't feel great. He'd rather not watch it happen.

Once he was pretty sure that if Siobhan woke up determined to leave as soon as possible she would have left already, he put the sign with the *closed but here* message and Rob's cell phone number in the window and locked up. They'd blocked off the wedding week back at the beginning of the season, so they had no transient campers, but a few of the seasonal campers were up. They probably wouldn't need anything, but he and his brothers tried to be available.

Outside, it was already warm and heading toward hot, and he wasn't surprised to see people sitting quietly under their camper awnings. Some were in small groups, chatting. Emma was reading while Sean was either really interested in the underside of the awning or taking a nap that his neck muscles would regret later. There was a group of people gathered under the awning next to the playground, though, and he could hear both of his parents' voices coming from that direction.

He found Stella sprawled on the grass in the shade of the big red maple tree at the edge of the grass, not far from the canopy. It was one of her favorite spots because the shade was dense and kept the ground cool, and she could see much of the campground without moving, so it was usually the first place he looked. But he didn't expect to find Oliver lying on his back with Stella as a pillow, pretending to read a board book to the dog.

He'd always assumed he'd have kids one day. Eventually he'd fall in love again and start a family. It wasn't something he actively thought about, really, especially since they decided to buy the campground. He kept busy and tried not to think about his failed marriage and his lack of dating.

But looking at Oliver and Stella, his heart aching and his throat tight with emotion, he knew he'd never wanted anything more. He savored a moment of what would be his perfect life, and then he cleared his throat and turned away.

It was just his luck, of course, that the first person he made eye contact with was Siobhan.

She held his gaze for a few seconds, her lips pinched together, and then turned to watch Oliver.

And then he looked at his mother, who gave him a raised eyebrow that very clearly communicated how ironic it was that he'd lectured *her* about getting too attached to Oliver before they got confirmation of his paternity.

"Good morning," was all he came up with.

"Good morning."

He wanted to ask her if she was just letting Oliver have a little more time outside before they left or if she was going to stay, but he didn't. If she hadn't made up her mind yet, he ran the risk of making her feel put on the spot.

"I promised Oliver he could go swimming in the pool. And I told him we'd play on the playground and watch his auntie Steph get married."

"Actually she'd be his…" He let the sentence fade away. "Oh, auntie in the friend-of-mom sense, not…you know."

Kevin laughed. "And you told *us* not to make it awkward."

Brian ignored his uncle, hoping he hadn't blown it so soon after she told him they were staying. He was relieved to see amusement in Siobhan's eyes, though. And while he didn't get quite as much warmth as she'd given others, her mouth curved into a smile.

And somehow, despite the history between them and the stressful shock of the last twenty hours or so, he didn't have to force the return smile.

"Rob was looking for you earlier," his mother said. "Something about lights, but then Hannah asked him about something else and Danny called and then your uncle Joe started talking about a book idea that centered around an old photo, so they started talking about camera stuff, and I think he forgot he was looking for you."

"I'll go find him," he said, casting another look over his shoulder at Oliver, who was still leaning on Stella. The dog lifted her head, but then dropped it again, clearly content to stay. "If he comes this way, keep him here or we might just chase each other in circles around the campground all day. Ask me how I know."

Chapter Seven

Before Siobhan could even see the pool, she could hear the utter chaos coming from that end of the campground.

She kept walking, with Oliver bouncing along beside her, tugging at her hand. What was going on might be a mystery, but knowing Oliver would throw the tantrum of his life if he couldn't go in wasn't.

When the pool came into view, she realized the chaos involved a lot of Kowalskis, a great deal of shouting and a huge inflatable ball.

Some of the women were watching from the safe side of the fence, including Ellie, who was holding Nora's hand. The little girl was dressed for swimming, too, so it was clear the little ones would be getting a turn soon.

Ellie turned and saw them approaching. "They're playing Water Ball of Doom, but one of them just yelled last point, so I think they're almost done."

Siobhan watched the chaos in the water, trying to figure out the objective of the game. "How do they score a point?"

"I'm not really sure, to be honest. I think it's mostly a vibe—if you do something that makes the other team mad, that's a point."

"So basically Water Ball of Doom is just an excuse to horse around in the water."

"More or less. But by having points involved, you can keep claiming you need a few more minutes." Hannah chuckled. "There is some structure, though. I think to *them*, it's an actual game with points and winners and losers. It's just a little short on rules."

Siobhan looked at Ellie, and then down at Nora. "You don't worry about...you know?"

"Not at all." Ellie rested her hand on her daughter's head. "They're great with kids in the pool. The whole family loves the water, so the last thing they want is a little one being afraid of it or feeling unsafe around them."

Siobhan nodded, unable to bring herself to confess she wasn't really worried they wouldn't be safe around Oliver. She herself had a fear of pools, though, and she avoided them whenever possible. And the behavior she'd been watching for the last few minutes was actually a big reason she was afraid of them.

She saw the ball get slapped hard and then it deflected off of somebody, though she couldn't see who. A roar went up—half of them cheering and gloating, while the other half shouted and tried to drown them.

"And there's the point," Hannah said.

Somebody let out an ear-piercing whistle, and Siobhan watched the entire vibe change. Everybody was laughing and chatting now. Some of them got out of the water and grabbed towels. Others floated around, talking to each other.

She breathed a sigh of relief when Brian hauled himself out of the water. The muscles in his back and arms flexed when he shoved himself up and twisted so he was sitting on the cement lip, and she could have done without noticing that. But it gave her hope he was going to leave the pool area and go find something else to do before it was time to strip off her cover-up and take Oliver into the water.

"Nora," Mike yelled. "What are you waiting for?"

Nora was waiting for Ellie to open the gate, and as soon as she did, the little girl speed-walked into the enclosure and to the edge of the pool—getting as close as she could to running in the pool area without actually breaking the rule.

Within seconds, she'd kicked off her flip-flops, thrown her towel in the general direction of a chair, and then she was jumping into the water—one hand pinching her nose closed and the other reaching for the grandfather she trusted to scoop her up.

With a tight hold on Oliver's hand, Siobhan watched Nora surface with Mike's hands on her waist. The little girl laughed and wiped the water out of her eyes before throwing her arms around Mike's neck.

Siobhan took her time getting Oliver ready to go in the water. She'd already slathered them both with sunscreen in the camper, but she added another dollop to his nose, cheeks and the tops of his ears. Then she put on his little flotation vest. As she adjusted the straps and fastened the one that passed between his legs she was pleased that none of the pool-loving Kowalskis made a comment about him not needing one. One of the things adopting her son had taught her was that people loved to give advice.

By the time Oliver was ready, most of the adults were gone. A few remained, lounging in the warm sun. Unfortunately, Brian was one of the adults who'd chosen to stay. He was at the far end of the enclosure, pulling toys out of what looked like a plastic garden shed.

"More noodles, Uncle Brian," Nora called. "I want the pink one."

Brian threw the pink noodle like a javelin, and it landed in front of Nora and Mike with a splash that made her giggle. Then he tossed in a couple of small balls and a float that looked like a frosted doughnut. The frosting was pink, of course.

Siobhan tried to ignore him while she pulled off the gauzy cover-up she'd thrown over her plain black tank suit and swim shorts. Oliver was struggling against her in his excitement to join his new best friend in the pool, so she kicked off her sandals and hoisted her son onto her hip.

There was no dipping her toes in because it didn't matter how cold the water was, and there was no time for acclimating, anyway. Oliver wanted in and he was on the verge of wriggling right out of her grasp like a fish.

As soon as her feet touched the bottom of the pool, she let him go and he paddled toward Nora as fast as he could. There was more splashing and giggling than forward motion, but that looked like part of the fun for both kids, so she let him be.

Nora invited him to play her favorite game, which involved Mike lobbing a small squishy ball toward her. When she hit it with the noodle, Mike would dive to catch it. She and Oliver took turns and though he missed a lot more than Nora did, Oliver didn't care.

Siobhan relaxed after a few minutes of watching, when it became obvious everybody was being careful around her son. Pools made her too anxious to actually leave the water while he was in it, but she pressed her back to the pool wall, lowering herself so the water line was at her chin. It was refreshing, and the motion of the water was calming.

The view of Brian sitting on the edge of the pool, talking to one of his uncles, was less relaxing.

His dark hair dripped water that ran over his bare sun-kissed skin in sparkling rivulets, capturing her attention and holding her gaze until they met the elastic band of his swim shorts.

Her face heated and she wished she had the ability to dunk her head underwater without panicking and breaking the surface with an attention-grabbing combination of coughing and flailing so she could cool her cheeks. She would move to the other side of the pool so Brian wasn't in her sight line, but then she'd be too far from Oliver for her own comfort.

It was a relief to finally see Steph and Kyle walking toward the pool, hand in hand. Even though they'd planned to meet up here, Siobhan had started to think they weren't going to make it.

She smiled when Kyle opened the gate and held it for Steph. Then, after making sure it latched securely behind him, Kyle crossed the cement apron in two long strides and executed a cannonball into the deep end that doused Brian and his uncle Joe.

Steph chose to take the stairs in, wincing as each step caused the cold water to inch up her body.

"It's nice once you're in," Siobhan said. "I'm never going to get Oliver out of here."

Her son was happily paddling around in his vest, waving the noodle whenever Mike threw the ball in his direction. Oliver's batting average was actually improving, and his laughter made Siobhan smile.

"No, it's definitely freezing," Steph insisted, and then she sucked in a breath when she dropped off the final step.

She looked at the trace of whisker burn on her friend's jawline and chuckled. "It probably doesn't feel as cold if your body's not so overheated when you get in."

"I think all the fresh air is really making Kyle frisky." Steph grinned. "And the cell signal in the back of the campground sucks, so there's not much else to do."

Siobhan laughed, but the instinctual urge to turn her head and look at Brian took her by surprise. Very deliberately keeping her eyes on Oliver, she reminded herself that it didn't matter if Brian was physically attractive. And didn't matter if he actually seemed to be a good guy and not the jerk her sister had painted him out to be.

He was her sister's ex-husband. He was probably Oliver's biological father. Under no circumstances could the mention of sex triggering thoughts of Brian Kowalski in response be allowed to become a thing.

Of course the man had to choose just that moment to laugh at something Kyle said, so putting him out of her mind wasn't that easy. She loved his deep laugh, and when he relaxed around people whose company he enjoyed, he laughed a *lot*.

"How long have you been in?" Steph asked.

Talking to her friend gave Siobhan an excuse to turn her body farther away from Brian while still keeping Oliver in her peripheral vision. "Not long. We got to watch the end of a Water Ball of Doom game."

"I can't believe I missed it. Maybe tomorrow." Steph's face lit up. "You know Gram and the others would love to keep an eye on Oliver if you want to play."

Siobhan laughed at the thought. "I absolutely do *not* want to play. I'll cheer you on, even though I might cheer at the wrong time because I have no idea what's going on."

"That's okay. Nobody does."

When two heads popped out of the water not far to her right, Siobhan yelped and instinctively headed toward Oliver. It was Kyle and Brian, who had apparently decided to swim the length of the pool underwater, and she caught herself before actually snatching up her son and racing out of the pool.

"Speedboat," Steph said, taking Oliver's hands and pulling him through the water.

Siobhan started to reach out, intending to stop her, but she withdrew it when he laughed his big joyful laugh. Kyle took Nora's hands and did the same, only faster, and both kids squealed.

She retreated to the steps, sitting on the top one so she was still in the water. Brian floating over and sitting on the other end of the same step surprised her, but she kept her eyes on Oliver.

"I'm sorry we startled you," he said quietly, looking at her in that way that said he saw more of her than she was comfortable having be seen.

"No, you're fine. I don't love pools, so I overreact sometimes. They make me nervous and I try not to put that on Oliver, so here we are, but it's hard sometimes."

"Does he take swim lessons?"

She chuckled. "We're trying again soon, I hope. We went once, but I couldn't do some of the things I need to show him in a group class. I can't afford private lessons, so my friend Robin's going to take him this winter if we can work out a schedule that fits."

"It's awesome that you still want him to be comfortable in the water and don't just avoid the pool. Some people would."

The compliment pleased her more than it should, getting a small smile out of her. "My mom used to take us to a town pool when we were kids and there were always bullies who'd splash and dunk you, or grab your legs and pull you under."

His scowl was deep and immediate. "They should have been banned. That won't happen here. I mean, you might see us do it to each other—and you saw Water Ball of Doom, of course—but none of us would do it to anybody else. Especially somebody who doesn't look comfortable in the pool."

Her cheeks heated again. "Does it show that much?"

He gave her that crooked grin that, no matter how much she hated the feeling, sent warmth curling through her body. "We can be a little rowdy in the water, obviously, so we were taught very young to be aware of who was in the pool with us at all times."

"Your parents really had their hands full with four of you."

"Yeah. They definitely did. When we were kids and acted up, we'd get a time-out and have to do multiplication tables."

She laughed. "Seriously?"

"Yup. Sometimes we weren't too bad and it was just low numbers, like one through three, but other times we'd work our way up to twelve."

Imagining Brian and his brothers sitting in a row, reciting math problems, made her laugh again. How did she laugh so much around in this man? "I'll make a note of that one."

As she watched, Kyle lifted the buoy line across the middle of the pool, towing Nora—who had a noodle under her arms—under it and into the deep end. Steph and Oliver followed and, for a moment, Siobhan tensed up. But despite the fact that he was wearing a little life jacket, Steph never took her hands off of the child. Oliver was clearly having the time of his life, and with Mike also nearby as Kyle pulled Nora around, she had nothing to fear.

Instead, she made herself enjoy the sun warming her muscles while the cool water kept her from overheating.

It would have been a lot *more* relaxing if Brian wasn't sitting so close to her, the breeze carrying the beachy scent of his sunscreen to her. He was utterly distracting on every level, and it made no sense.

Nothing did anymore.

Brian prided himself on his self-control, as a rule, but keeping his eyes off of the way the simple black swimsuit cupped and lifted his former sister-in-law's breasts was *not* easy. "This is so strange."

"What's so strange?"

He winced, not having intended to say that out loud. But he was in it now and they were as close as alone as they could get. "You and me sitting here, hanging out."

"Well, I'm sitting here watching my son in the pool. You're the one hanging out."

"True. I sat down to apologize, but it's comfortable and it's just strange how easy it is to talk to you."

She chuckled. "I'd pretend to be offended, but I know what you mean and yes, it *is* strange. You're kind of a nice guy now, I guess."

"I always have been, for the most part. We all have our moments. But you never gave me a chance."

"A chance to what?"

He watched Kyle spotting Nora as she swam the width of the pool, while Steph and Oliver played with the pink noodle. "To be a good husband, I guess. From day one, you were against me marrying your sister."

"I'm sorry you thought that."

"What was I supposed to think? When I was in eighth grade, I replaced all my algebra teacher's dry erase markers with permanent markers—even the boxed ones in her storage cubby—and there was more approval in the look *she* gave me when she found out it was me than in any look you ever gave me."

"How did she find out it was you?"

He noticed she didn't deny it. "My pain in the ass younger brother always had a digital camera with him— usually still does, actually—and he took some pictures to use as blackmail at home. But he was showing his friend in study hall and didn't realize the principal was looking over his shoulder."

"Oops."

"Yeah, but circling back to the point, even Mrs. Rundell didn't look at me with as much disapproval as you did."

"It wasn't really about you."

"I was the only man she was marrying." He snorted. "That I know of. Looking back, who knows."

"Don't. I know this is hard, but Kelly's my sister and no matter how furious I am with her right now, I'll feel compelled to defend her."

"You think she deserves that?"

"Maybe not, but…she's my sister. I don't know. But I can't help it and I don't want to argue with you right now."

"Okay." He stretched his legs out, aware he wasn't going to sit on the cement step much longer. "But if it wasn't really about me, what was it about?"

"Kelly wasn't ready to marry *anybody*. Whether it was you or some other guy, it was going to end in disaster."

"So you decided the best way to work the problem was to hate me and hope she caught on?"

"I didn't *hate* you." When he gave her a skeptical look, she shrugged. "I didn't know you well enough to hate you. But I guess I—I don't know. It's hard to explain. I think

I distrusted the fact that *you* couldn't see it. If you truly knew her well enough to marry her, you should have been able to see she wasn't ready for that kind of commitment."

He thought about what she'd said for a few minutes, and then he nodded slowly. "I guess that's fair. Obviously I didn't know her as well as I thought I did."

"It's hard to know Kelly," she said in a quiet voice. "The real Kelly, I mean, because she doesn't always share the most authentic parts of herself."

Brian thought about her words, letting what she *wasn't* saying out loud sink in. Having brothers himself, he knew how hard even that little bit had been for Siobhan to admit, so he let it be.

The silence stretched on until she sighed. "It's time to bring everybody's peace and quiet to a screeching halt— literally—by dragging Oliver out of the pool. He's had enough sun for today, but he's having some of the most fun he's ever had. I should probably apologize in advance."

He chuckled and then called out to the other end of the pool. "Hey, Dad!"

When his dad turned, Brian pointed to Oliver and then jerked his thumb toward the gate. Mike nodded.

"You tuckered me out, kiddos. I'm going to dry off and go see if there are any frogs by the pond."

"Frogs?" Oliver and Nora yelled at the same time.

When Nora started swimming toward the side of the pool with Kyle at her side, Oliver began flailing, trying to turn himself toward Siobhan.

"Mommy, there are frogs," he yelled before spluttering because he'd splashed himself in the face.

Siobhan stood, but Steph was already lifting the back of the life vest slightly, so Oliver could paddle the length of the pool.

"Can I see the frogs?"

Siobhan turned to grin at Brian, who was in the process of standing because her leaping to her feet in case Oliver needed her had put her butt in his line of vision and he didn't think it would be good to get caught admiring it.

"Oh, you guys are good at this," she said.

"It's been a while since a toddler needed wrangling, but remember my dad had four of us and we weren't always old enough to recite multiplication tables. Deflect, distract and, if necessary, bribe. Somebody can always come up with a fun activity to throw in the mix."

"They say it takes a village, and you definitely have quite a village."

There was something in her voice that made Brian want to dig deeper. Did she have a village? He wasn't sure if Kelly was still around, and he'd picked up during the time he was involved with the family that Siobhan and her mother weren't very close. She'd mentioned a friend named Robin, but were there others? Parenting was no joke and he wondered who she turned to for support when she needed it.

But as she reached out and pulled Oliver through the water and into her arms, both of them laughing, he realized it wasn't really his business. Even if and when the paternity test confirmed what they all already believed to be true, Siobhan wouldn't be his business. Oliver was obviously healthy and happy, and that's where his involvement would end.

"I want to find frogs, Mommy." Oliver squirmed in his mother's arms, and Brian felt an urge to reach out and take him—to carry him out of the pool and wrap a towel around him while explaining they'd get changed and then head over to the pond.

Instead, he turned and stepped out of the water. After grabbing his towel and slinging it over his neck, he walked to the gate.

"Uncle Brian, I have to pee," Nora said, speed-walking toward him with her mom on her heels. Ellie had their towels and her bag in her arms, and she gave him a grateful look when he opened the gate so they could get through. As soon as they cleared the cement, Nora took off running toward the bathroom.

Before leaving, Brian turned back. "Last one out needs to double-check that this gate latches behind you."

"Kyle and I are going to stay in for a bit and relax," Steph told him. "I'll make sure it's closed when we leave."

Brian nodded, but then arched an eyebrow at his cousin. "Just so you know, the camera on the store covers the pool area, so don't even think about getting frisky in that water."

After ensuring the little ones were out of the pool, Steph pushed backward and used her foot to fling water at him. "As if we'd get frisky in the middle of the day with my family literally everywhere."

"It runs all night, too. Just so you know."

"According to Ellie, it's Joey you forgot to tell."

Brian laughed. "Joey knew about it. He got carried away and forgot about it, but luckily he woke up in the middle of the night, panicked and wiped the entire drive."

"She said if he hadn't remembered and one of you guys saw it, he might have ended up on one of Hannah's true crime podcasts."

"So I guess when I turned off the sound alerts to my phone because a raccoon kept setting it off, I saved his life."

She rolled her eyes. "You're supposed to check the

alerts in case somebody is breaking in. Otherwise, what's the point?"

"Hey, Stella's not just a pretty face, you know. And mostly we wanted the wireless doorbell and then somebody decided it would be a good idea to have video to be able to check if something happened and suddenly my phone was chiming every time a chipmunk sneezed."

Then he left before Steph could say anything else because Siobhan was almost finished gathering their things and he didn't want to get pulled into a frog-spotting adventure to the pond with them. It sounded fun and he'd love to see the little boy's face when he spotted one, but it was too hard to stay hands-off. Even though he'd warned his mother against it, the attachment tugged at him, and it would be too easy to get sucked into an illusion that might break his heart.

But he heard the low rumble of his father's voice and then Siobhan and Oliver laughing as he walked away, and he was still smiling when he went in the house to change.

Chapter Eight

Siobhan never wanted to move again. She was in a very comfortable chair in the shade, with a tumbler of ice-cold water in the cupholder. On one side of her, Oliver and Stella were sound asleep on the blanket she'd spread on the grass, and on the other side sat two empty chairs.

After helping prepare lunch while Mike and Sean took the kids exploring around the pond, and then the intense Kowalski family time that seemed to be *every* meal, and then trying to keep Oliver from making himself sick from running around the playground right after they ate, she was *done*. After half the family had departed through the back of the campground on ATVs and in side-by-sides, she'd parked herself and Oliver in the shade, thankful only Stella followed. She'd even considered folding up the two extra chairs and hiding them, but that felt like a step too far.

Instead, she leaned her head back against the chair and closed her eyes, welcoming the light breeze. She couldn't let herself fall asleep because there was no doubt that the second she nodded off, Oliver would wake up and wander off in search of Nora. Since she was having quiet time in her parents' camper, who knew where her son would end up.

It shouldn't have come as a surprise when she heard

the creaking of somebody sitting in the chair nearest her. Camping with this family was a fully immersive experience. Opening her eyes, she swiveled her head to see Lisa considering her thoughtfully.

"I didn't think you were sleeping," she said in a quiet voice.

"Not without duct taping Oliver to a tree first."

Amusement softened Lisa's face, but Siobhan could see the serious intent in the woman's eyes. "I try not to hold it against you, you know."

"Oliver?" She thought they'd already covered the fact this was as much a surprise to her as it was to them.

"Your sister." Lisa sighed. "When we talked about you being Steph's maid of honor, I was *not* on board. Kelly did a job on my son, and you were a part of that. You were so cold to him during the whole thing, and I'm his mother. Oliver's still little, but I think you're starting to get an idea of how you'll feel about a person who hurts him."

Siobhan stared off into the distance where some of the family was milling around. As much as she'd wanted to be alone before, she wouldn't mind somebody interrupting now. "She's my sister, and I think if any family knows what that means, it's yours. And I only knew what she told me, and what she told me was that their marriage had been over for a while, but she was afraid of him."

"That was a lie."

"One of many," she admitted. "If I had even suspected there was a chance he was Oliver's father, I wouldn't have let her do it. I mean, I would have supported her in the divorce still, but I wouldn't have let her go through with it without a paternity test."

"I believe you." Lisa chuckled softly. "The second that boy smiled at me, I thought it was so obvious and how could you not see it, but I've raised four of them. I've seen every mood and expression, across every age."

"The last time Steph saw him in person, he was still in the baby phase. But when we got here and she saw him again, I think it clicked for her. I saw something on her face, even though I didn't know at the time what it was."

"They have this way of sweetly grinning that's so cheeky, but also melts your heart."

Siobhan knew that look well. She'd just never seen it on Brian's face.

"Do you plan to tell Oliver he's adopted?" Lisa asked.

"I've always planned to, probably when he starts show-ing curiosity about where babies come from. It seems most natural when talking about babies coming from their mommies' tummies to explain how some come from a different mommy, you know? I've talked to his pediatri-cian about it a bit." She sighed. "But even if I didn't want to, I'd probably have to. I don't trust Kelly not to waltz back into our lives and drop that bomb—accidentally or not—just for the attention."

"It sounds like you don't like her very much."

"I love her. She's my sister." After a few seconds of staring down at her hands, Siobhan shrugged one shoul-der. "My mom and my sister are the only family I have, and I love them. But, no, I don't like them very much and don't talk to them often."

"I'm sorry. That must be hard."

"It can be." She tried for a bright smile, but suspected it came off a little sad. "Especially when I'm around a family like yours."

"I'm definitely blessed," Lisa said. "We have our stuff, of course. Every family does. Believe it or not, there have been days I've considered just walking away and finding myself a little one bedroom cottage with a garden and not giving a single one of them my forwarding address."

Siobhan put her hand over her mouth, stifling a surprised giggle. "Okay, I was going to hide the empty chairs when I came over here and I felt bad about it."

Lisa made a scoffing noise. "Trust me, I've done it. But there aren't many opportunities to talk alone, and I wanted to ask you about you and Brian."

Siobhan hoped her cheeks didn't look as hot as they felt, but she didn't dare try to hide her face. "What about us?"

"You seem to be getting along pretty well."

"Surprisingly, yes. I think with Kelly at the center of our past interactions, we maybe had some misconceptions about each other. He seems like a good guy."

Lisa couldn't hide her pleased smile. "I like him."

"And I see how he's gone out of his way to respect my boundaries with Oliver. All of you, really. I appreciate it, and I'm very glad I stayed."

"We're *all* glad you stayed, honey. And I'm glad you and Brian are getting along and that you fit in so well with everybody because—assuming paternity, of course—you'll be part of the family, and not just Oliver. You're his mother, so you'll be welcome anytime, and if you need anything at all, we'll all be here for you."

Siobhan knew she should say something, but with her eyes welling up and her throat clogged with emotion, all she could do was nod.

It wasn't about her, she reminded herself. She knew that. They would embrace her because of Oliver, but the contrast with her own family couldn't be ignored. She wasn't sure her mother or sister would put themselves out on Oliver's behalf, and that was sad.

"That's all I wanted to say," Lisa continued, pushing herself out of the chair. "I'll let you have a few more minutes of peace before the others get back from riding. There's not much chance of Oliver sleeping through that."

Siobhan wasn't so sure about that. The kid was out like a light, and he hadn't even stirred when a logging truck roared past the campground.

But sure enough, fifteen minutes later, when the first machines made their way down the hill to the center of the campground, Oliver sat up like it was Christmas and he'd just heard a reindeer bell.

Stella took off across the grass, going straight to the third ATV in the line that parked around the edge of the playground. As Siobhan watched, Brian pulled his helmet off and leaned over to tousle his dog's fur. As he moved, puffs of dirt released from his shirt, and she couldn't imagine what they'd done to cover themselves and their machines with so much dirt and mud. Judging by the laughter, whatever it was had been fun.

Then he looked up, glancing around the campground until he spotted her in the shade. He smiled and waved, and she did the same without even thinking about it, a thrill shooting through her at the thought he'd sought her out.

Thankful nobody could see her blush from where they'd gathered, she took Oliver's hand before he could run toward the big muddy machines. Brian hadn't been looking for her, of course. He'd been looking for Oliver and she needed to stop having these ridiculous reactions to the man immediately. Lazy summer vacations and fresh air might give rise to all sorts of imaginings— especially since she hadn't been on a date since the day Kelly knocked on her door with Oliver—but she absolutely wasn't going to allow herself to become infatuated with Brian.

No matter how seeing him straddling the four-wheeler with his head thrown back as he laughed stirred things that hadn't been stirred in years.

She just had to put a lid on it. And then put a brick on top of the lid.

They were fixing dinner plates when Siobhan stepped back to avoid getting doused with ketchup by a six-year-old who forgot the cardinal rule of making sure the lid was closed before shaking the bottle, and Brian put his hand on Siobhan's back to steady her and keep her from falling.

There was nothing wrong with that. The problem was that he didn't want to let her go.

His palm rested against the small of her back and his fingers spread, feeling the warmth of her skin under her thin cotton T-shirt. For the space of one breath and then another, he savored the weight of her against his hand as he inhaled the scent of shampoo and sunscreen. Her hair was in a ponytail, so he saw the tips of her ears and her neck blush a light shade of pink.

Then she shifted, muttering an apology, and he curled his empty fingers into a loose fist for a moment before turning his attention back to his plate. The line moved and he grabbed a small spoonful of coleslaw in order to leave room for the ever-present dual helpings of potato salad.

When it was time to sit, he deliberately chose a camp chair instead of one of the picnic tables. After turning the chair so he could put his feet up on the fire ring—which conveniently kept his back to Siobhan and Oliver—he sat and rested his plate on his legs. Stella sat beside him for a few seconds before remembering she had a better chance of food being dropped by the kids.

He wasn't surprised when his grandfather and dad joined him, as well as his uncles Kevin and Joe. Eating with your plate on your lap wasn't ideal, but the older you got, the less appealing picnic table benches became.

They made small talk while they ate, mostly about the ATV trails and a trip some of them had planned for the upcoming snowmobile season. It gave Brian's mind the freedom to keep returning to that moment when Siobhan had almost, though not quite, been in his arms.

He couldn't make sense of his attraction to her, though he'd reached a place where there was no point in denying it to himself. She was beautiful, of course. That didn't hurt. But it wasn't as if he'd felt a need to touch every beautiful woman he'd ever crossed paths with. There was something about Siobhan that made him toss and turn at night— much to Stella's annoyance—and think about her all day.

Avoiding making eye contact with her wasn't that hard when he put conscious effort into it, although making sure he went about it in a natural way so his family's radar didn't get pinged was harder. They were a perceptive bunch, and it wouldn't take much to attract their attention.

After they ate, Brian would have preferred to keep himself busy, but he and his brothers had worked hard leading up to this week to ensure they'd be able to relax and spend time with the family, so there wasn't a lot for him to do. Taking the tractor up to bring down another load of split firewood from the pit took him a few minutes.

Then he volunteered to grab the box of marshmallows, chocolate, crackers, sticks and wet wipes from the store when his mother said the words he'd loved as a kid, but didn't like quite as much now.

"Time for s'mores."

Being one of the adults responsible for campfire safety and making sure sweets weren't left all over to attract furry woodland creatures took some of the fun out of it.

"Who's having s'mores?" he asked as he dumped the supplies on the picnic table closest to the campfire.

"S'mores!" Oliver yelled, clapping his hands. "Mommy, s'mores!"

"Somebody sure loves his s'mores," Mike said with an affectionate chuckle.

"He's actually never had one," Siobhan said, and then she laughed when half the family actually gasped. "They really frown on open campfires in my neighborhood."

"Smart people," Brian muttered.

"Ignore him," Hannah said, grabbing the marshmallow sticks and handing them out. She handed Nora one after glancing at Ellie for approval, but Siobhan took Oliver's. "Campers and campfires have become his personal monster under the bed over the last couple of months."

"Okay, how do you *not* know what happens if you throw gas—"

"Stop." Hannah held up her hand, cutting him off. "It's s'mores time. Ooey-gooey marshmallow and chocolate, Brian."

His younger brother had been smart to talk this woman into moving all the way across the country to marry him, Brian thought. "I do like ooey-gooey marshmallow and chocolate."

"You sound so funny saying that," she said, and then she laughed. Others joined in, but he didn't mind because Siobhan was one of them, and he liked the sound of her laugh so much, he'd chant the words if they kept it going.

And that thought reminded him he needed to keep

himself busy so he didn't pay too much attention to Siobhan and Oliver. Which he did by keeping the mess on the picnic table in check, though he did manage to make a s'more of his own.

And he made sure he was looking when Oliver took his first bite. Siobhan was helping him hold it, and when he got his first mouthful of ooey-gooey marshmallow and chocolate, his blue eyes widened. Then he grinned, his little mouth coated in melted sugar and graham cracker crumbs.

Then Siobhan started turning her head and he looked away before their gazes could lock and they could silently share the moment. He didn't feel strong enough right then to feel that connection with her—celebrating an adorable moment for the child they might be sharing for the rest of their lives. And the connection between them that had nothing to do with Oliver. He wasn't sure which knocked him for a bigger loop.

Most of them only had one or two s'mores, but the younger crowd went hard and they burned through a lot of marshmallows and chocolate before Kevin's son, Gage, and Sean's son, Johnny—the last two standing at what Brian thought might be five each—called it quits. After assigning the teenagers to clean up the debris, and laughing when they groaned and held their stomachs, he went around the circle, offering wet wipes.

When he got to Siobhan and Oliver, it was clear she'd need some help with the child squirming on her lap. Despite his resolve not to get involved, he pulled out a wipe and knelt in front of her. "This won't help much, but maybe you can get him back to the camper without him sticking to you or the grass or anything he comes in contact with."

She chuckled. "I'm not sure how much he even got into his mouth."

"But he enjoyed it, and that's the point." He swiped at the boy's sticky cheeks, but it was a lost cause.

"You need to be a little more assertive with that wipe or you're just going to smear the top layer of marshmallow around all night."

"Maybe we should switch places," he said, pushing himself to his feet.

He took Oliver so she could stand, not minding the sticky hands gripping his T-shirt. Once Siobhan moved, he sat down and settled the boy on his lap.

Siobhan knelt in front of them, resting her hand on Brian's knee as she lowered herself to the grass.

That single touch broke through what remained of his resolve and he allowed himself to enjoy the warmth and pressure of her touch for the regrettably short time he could.

Why did it have to be her? Even though his divorce had left him bitter and disillusioned, he'd known he'd meet a woman someday who'd snap him out of it. He was surrounded by too much love and too many happy marriages not to believe that, despite a pretty staggering setback, he'd have that, too.

But of all the women to stir that desire in him again, why did it have to be Siobhan?

After a few minutes, she heaved a defeated sigh. "Isn't one of the benefits of having a dog supposed to be the fact that they lick a kid's face clean?"

He chuckled. "Absolutely, but not when chocolate is involved."

"Right. Well, that's the worst of it," she said, once again using Brian's knee to push herself to her feet. He tried to ignore the renewed awareness as he set Oliver on his feet. "The rest is going to need hot soapy water."

"Beep beep," Oliver murmured, and Siobhan ran her hand over his hair.

"It's his favorite book," she explained. "He's ready to curl up and read, which is his way of admitting he's actually tired. I think we'll head inside early tonight."

"I think a lot of people will," Emma said, glancing sideways at Sean, whose chin kept dropping until he'd jerk himself awake.

"Just wait until after the volleyball game tomorrow," Steph said, looking a lot more chipper than the rest of them.

Leo gruffly cleared his throat. "Excuse me, after the *what* now?"

She sighed and rolled her eyes. "After The Annual Kowalski Volleyball Death Match Tournament of Doom."

Siobhan's eyes widened. "Okay, that sounds even less fun than Water Ball of Doom."

"If we wait until Saturday, Danny can play," Brian pointed out.

Steph shook her head. "Tomorrow's going to be cooler and overcast and Saturday is going to be wicked hot and humid. If we wait for Danny, the whole *death* match part might be literal and not just some ridiculous name you guys picked when you were too young to be allowed to name things."

"We'll cheer you on from well outside the sidelines," Siobhan said, shaking her head.

"My first year playing, a bunch of us ended up on each other's shoulders, like playing chicken in the pool, trying to be taller," Keri said, her mouth curved in a nostalgic smile. "And Leo grabbed my butt."

"It was an accident," her father-in-law said. "And I was

trying to keep your butt from hitting the ground. You were falling, so you should have thanked me."

"For grabbing my butt?"

"Beep beep," Oliver said again, and they all laughed.

"On that note," Siobhan said, straightening and taking Oliver's hand in hers. "Say good-night, Oliver."

They all said good-night, and then Brian watched them walking hand in hand toward their camper. The little guy was so tired he stumbled on some rocks in the dirt road and Brian was going to get up and offer to carry him, but Siobhan easily swung him onto her hip and kept going.

He relaxed back into his chair, though he didn't look away until she'd opened the camper door and set Oliver inside. Then he turned his focus to adjusting the straw in his tumbler lid so he wouldn't have to look around and see if his family was watching him as he watched Siobhan and Oliver.

If this is what it felt like for reality television stars to have camera crews in their faces twenty-four-seven, they weren't getting paid enough.

"Oh, no," Steph said, and the urgency in her voice caught Brian's attention. He and his brothers had worked with their aunt Terry to make sure every single possible wedding emergency had been thought of and taken care of *before* the family arrived. "Tell me somebody brought the volleyball. I don't even know who keeps it. Where does the volleyball live?"

Mary laughed. "I have the ball. It lives in the closet in my RV, which means if you all decide to forget to invite your old grandparents one year, no volleyball."

Brian chuckled as everybody rushed to assure her that would never happen. She knew that, of course, but she probably liked hearing it. And he was also glad she kept the volleyball because locating it had never occurred to him. It wasn't an actual volleyball, but a slightly larger and softer ball because they played volleyball with the same intensity they did everything else and the real version really hurt when you took it to the face.

Kind of like an unexpected and unwelcome attraction to your ex-wife's sister and the adoptive mother of the son you didn't know you had, he thought with a self-derisive snort.

"Do you disagree, Brian?" Keri asked, jerking his attention back to the conversation going on around him and the fact he'd missed a chunk of it. He had no idea what he was or was not agreeing with.

"I was thinking about something else," he said, but then he realized he didn't want them wondering what else might be on his mind. "I was supposed to place an order this morning, and I forgot and I was just giving myself hell."

Keri nodded and everybody moved on with the conversation, except for Rob, who'd watched him place the order. He shot his younger brother a look that basically meant he better keep his mouth shut or else, which earned him a challenging raised eyebrow and a questioning head tilt.

After another few seconds of glaring that risked attracting the attention of their parents, Brian picked up the long metal stick they used for poking at the fire. He moved the burning logs around, settling them in a way that would help them burn down more quickly.

It had been quite a day and all he wanted now was for everybody to go back to their campers and cabins so he could go to bed and stare at the ceiling half the night, wondering what the hell was happening to his life.

Chapter Nine

The sun was still coming up when Siobhan slowly slid out of the bed without disturbing Oliver. He was sprawled on his back, covers thrown off and his arms over his head, as usual.

She wasn't surprised to be up so early. They were early risers anyway, thanks to the daycare and work commute. And after a rough first night and then a day spent outside in the fresh air, she'd slept early and deeply.

As quietly as possible, she hit the brew button on the Keurig, wincing at how loud the final blast of liquid sounded in the stillness. Oliver didn't stir, though, so she made her way to the dinette without turning on any lights.

It probably would have been smarter to stay in bed and try to force herself back to sleep. Keeping up with the Kowalski family took a lot of energy. But the opportunity for some quiet time alone with a leisurely cup of coffee was too good to pass up. Thinking maybe she could spot some small campground critters before everybody started moving around and they skittered back into the woods, she hooked the end of a curtain panel and pulled it back.

The only campground critter in sight was Stella, who was trotting around, sniffing the ground as if to scope out whether any four-legged visitors had wandered around her property while she was sleeping. When Brian came into view, strolling behind the dog, Siobhan dropped her hand and let the curtain fall back into place.

She almost laughed at herself, hand over her chest as her heart raced. Then, unable to resist, she hooked the very edge of the curtain with a single fingertip and pulled just enough to see Brian again.

He had on a gray zip hoodie and jeans, and she could tell it was unzipped because he had his hands in the pockets. Even though he was facing away from her, his shoulders looked relaxed, and she wondered if he was doing the same as she was—sacrificing sleep in exchange for starting the day off like this.

Then he bent to pick up a stick and nothing short of her son waking up and screaming for her could have made her look away from the sight of denim stretching over his backside and thighs.

What was wrong with her? Was it all the fresh air going to her head? The pollen? Had she inhaled too much bug spray? There had to be a reason she was peeking out her window at the crack of dawn, ogling her sister's ex-husband's butt.

Still, a disappointed sigh actually escaped her when he straightened. Sure, it was wrong to indulge in admiring the way he filled out his jeans, but the occasional guilty pleasure was good for a single mom.

Then he turned to look at her camper and she gasped, yanking her finger back. The curtain closed and she prayed it hadn't moved enough to catch his eye.

When a hysterical giggle rose in her throat, she clamped her hand over her mouth to stifle it. She'd learned over the last couple of days that the soundproofing in campers wasn't great, and being caught *laughing* while spying on Brian would just up the awkwardness factor to an untenable degree.

Once her amusement at her herself was under control, though, she couldn't summon the willpower to *not* take another little peek. Not touching the curtain this time, Siobhan leaned forward until she glimpsed him through the gap where the two curtain panels almost met. He'd put his hands back in his pockets, and he was standing very still, looking at her camper. Not at the window or the gap in the curtains, thankfully, but at the camper as a whole.

His expression was quiet and contemplative, even as Stella trotted in a circle around him with the stick in her mouth. Siobhan knew he was thinking about Oliver in that moment, and it chased away her inexplicable attraction to the man outside her window, grounding her back in reality. More than likely, the little boy who was sleeping behind her and was her entire world also belonged to him.

Slightly shifting her body away from the window, Siobhan sipped her coffee and waited for Oliver to stir. Once he woke up, he was going to go nonstop all day, so she cringed at every sound and every voice as the campers around them started their day.

By the time they joined the family for breakfast, which had sounded like a good idea last night when she said they'd be there, Oliver was fully in high gear and Siobhan was already pre-exhausted. It was going to be a very long day.

It helped that Cat, who at twelve was a bit of an island age-wise, decided to hang with Nora and Oliver rather than fighting to be included by her older brother and cousins. Once her son was sitting at the kid-sized picnic table with them, Siobhan served herself and sat in the empty chair Hannah nodded her head toward.

Brian's future sister-in-law had set the chairs a little apart from the group, and Siobhan figured she either needed a little distance from the breakfast chaos, or she wanted to have a private chat.

"I can see why they basically shut the rest of the campground down for this," Siobhan said as she settled her plate in her lap. "This is not a quiet family."

"I'm pretty sure we could take these chairs across the street, past the fields and down to the river, and *still* hear Leo and Ron," Hannah agreed. "They're all good people, though."

"They are. It just takes a little getting used to."

"I'm still new to the whole Kowalski family thing." Hannah chuckled. "Technically, I'm not even part of it yet, but I will be. Rob and I haven't set a date yet, but there's already been talk about next year's Family Camping Trip of Doom."

"Are you okay with that?"

"I think so. My family's in California, but they enjoy camping, so it might be the most fun way to do it. But we're also considering eloping because—" She stopped talking and just swept her hand over their view of all the Kowalskis milling around.

"Has he run that by Lisa yet?"

"Oh, hell no." They laughed together, drawing the attention of the people they were talking about.

And, of course, Mike and Lisa hadn't sat down yet, so they dragged their chairs over and joined them—probably because they looked like they were having fun. Siobhan would have liked to continue talking with Hannah, but she made sure none of that showed on her face.

After having a discussion with Stella about a child-sized picnic table not also being dog-sized, Brian was one of the last to fill a plate. He glanced in their direction, but thankfully opted to sit with Joey and Ellie. Siobhan wasn't sure if it was because of her or because he wanted to stick close to Stella and her insatiable appetite for whatever the humans were eating, but she was thankful for it.

"Are you still living in Boston, Siobhan?" Lisa asked. "I didn't think to ask Steph when we were planning other than she told me about what time you'd be arriving."

"I'm a little north of the city now. A questionable over-sized closet in a questionable neighborhood with a some-what strange roommate is fine when you don't have a child. A miserable commute is the tradeoff for being able to afford a decent apartment in a nice neighborhood."

"And what do you do for work?" Mike asked. "Something in banking, right?"

"I'm a loan officer with one of the big national banks." She wrinkled her nose. "I really, *really* hate my job, actually, and I was thinking about quitting before Oliver came into my life. Once I had him, I stayed for the stability and then ended up accepting a promotion with better benefits. You can put up with a lot for financial security once you're not the only one to take care of."

A lot of the parents nodded, but she didn't miss the fact that Lisa opened her mouth to say something until Mike gently kicked her in the ankle. The conversation moved on, veering in a different direction, but Siobhan couldn't help wondering what Brian's mother had been about to say.

Some kind of assurance that Siobhan wasn't alone anymore? A promise that she'd have their support going forward? Or maybe she was going to accuse Siobhan of knowing all along, but deciding to come forward to get the child support payments.

No, she told herself. She'd gotten to know his family and if any of them—especially his mother—thought she was trying to work an angle of any kind, they wouldn't be shy about saying so. It had probably been nothing more than telling her she wasn't alone anymore and her husband reminding her that nothing was official yet.

It was something Siobhan herself was having trouble remembering whenever she was caught up with the family activities. Even after they'd moved on from breakfast, though, she had a hard time shaking off the feeling that she should be holding more of herself—and Oliver—back.

There was the breakfast cleanup and then she and Steph took a walk around the campground with Oliver and Nora. They had the kids with them, so they couldn't really talk about anything personal, which worked for Siobhan. Oliver might be oblivious to the drama going on around him, but there was a good chance Nora would repeat every word she heard. Probably at the worst possible moment, too.

Right now they were all living in a strange limbo, focusing on the vacation and the wedding, while avoiding the gigantic conversational elephant in the room.

Over the course of the morning, there was the usual milling around, with people dropping in and out of conversations. Siobhan tried to get Oliver to sit in the shade of their awning to play quietly for a while, but he was having none of it. Some of the other kids had already mentioned the pool, and he was afraid he was going to miss it.

By the time Oliver had worn himself out in the water, he was cranky and overstimulated. It was a mood Siobhan shared as she showered the pool water off of him in the tiny camper bathroom.

"I want chicken nuggets."

"We don't have any, but we can make sandwiches and watch a show on my tablet if you want," she said, willing to let him sit in front of a cartoon if it slowed him down a little.

"No. Chicken nuggets," he insisted, and then his bottom lip jutted out as warning a battle of wills was about to commence.

It was a battle she didn't have it in her to wage. Oliver needed a break. She needed a break. And his whining for chicken nuggets triggered a craving for French fries Siobhan couldn't shake. Hot, salty, fried potatoes always helped.

She'd been a good sport, joining in most of the family's activities, so there was no reason to feel guilty about wanting one meal that wasn't absolute chaos. The food was always plentiful and delicious, of course, but the noise level and trying to wrangle a toddler with a paper plate kept her on her toes.

"Auntie Steph said there's a restaurant not too far up the road," she said. "We can go see if they have chicken nuggets, but if they don't, I bet they can make you a grilled cheese."

She'd never been to a restaurant that couldn't serve a child a grilled cheese sandwich, so if they couldn't get his favorite food, they could get his second favorite. When he instantly cheered up, but quietly, without getting overexcited, she knew it was the right call. It would do them both good to get away, and after getting herself ready, she grabbed her bag and keys.

She'd just finished strapping Oliver into his car seat when Brian walked up, slightly out of breath as though he'd been hurrying but not quite running.

"Hey," he said, trying and failing to look casual. "What's up?"

"We're not leaving." She chuckled when he looked at Oliver in his car seat and then back to her. "Okay, we *are* leaving, but we're coming back. We're going off in search of chicken nuggets and French fries."

"Ah. I'm pretty sure we have chicken nuggets in the freezer, but I think my family's used all the potatoes in the county making potato salads, so I don't know about rustling up French fries."

"I think we could use a break," she said, belatedly realizing he might take offense at her wanting to get away from them.

He smiled, his eyes warm with amused affection. "We can be a lot, for sure."

"Your family's wonderful, but we're not used to so much…everything."

"Kenzie has great popcorn chicken," he said. "She and her dad own Corinne's Kitchen, which isn't far up the road. Not quite nuggets, but they're delicious and their fries are unmatched."

"Ooh." She grinned. "That's a big claim. You should know I judge people on their food recommendations."

"Trust me. I don't praise fries lightly. I'm bummed I'll be here eating more potato salad instead of being there to gloat when you try one."

"You're welcome to join us," Siobhan said, and then her skin prickled when she realized what she'd done.

She hadn't been thinking at all. Instead of remembering Brian was a man best kept at arm's length for a number of reasons, she'd gotten lost in his blue eyes and that smile. It had been almost like flirting, and she'd gone too far.

"I could go for some popcorn chicken and fries," he

said, his gaze returning to Oliver, who was starting to squirm with impatience in his car seat. "If you're sure you don't mind."

It occurred to Siobhan then that Brian could probably use a break, too. He was as central to the current drama as she was, but his family probably didn't need to tiptoe around the topic with him. As intense as the last several days had been for her, they'd probably been even more so for him.

"Sure." She looked around the campground and saw that people were starting to notice her and Brian, and the open car door. "Maybe we don't invite everybody, though?"

He looked over his shoulder and chuckled. Then he gave a hand signal to Stella, who made a woofing sound and galloped back to the group of family that included Rob and Hannah. "Okay, let's make a run for it."

Brian was in the passenger seat with the door closed before Siobhan even had time to ask if he was going to ride with her or take his own truck. After double-checking Oliver's harness, she closed his door and climbed into the driver's seat. The windows were already down because her air-conditioning wasn't as good as it used to be, and she returned the waves of the others as she drove slowly out of the campground and took a right onto the main road.

Once she was at speed, she became very aware of the man sitting next to her. Other than Robin occasionally, the seat was usually empty, and he seemed large in her small car. If she shifted her right arm at all, there was a good chance their upper arms would brush.

She was careful not to shift her arm.

"I apologize for pushing myself on you two," Brian

said. "I heard somebody say you were leaving and I—I don't know. Even if you were, it wasn't my business, so I'm sorry about that."

"I appreciate that. I did send a text message to Steph, but she might not have told anybody yet. And as for pushing yourself on us, if you weren't welcome, I wouldn't have invited you." Not that she'd invited him after careful consideration, but he didn't need to know that.

"Thanks."

They rode in silence broken only by Oliver occasionally describing things they passed. He was especially excited when they went by a small farm and he started yelling about the cows.

"I promise he's seen cows before," she said, and Brian laughed.

Then he pointed toward a small building coming up. "That's it there, on the right. Corinne's Kitchen."

"And is it actually? Corinne's kitchen, I mean."

"It was. Corinne cooked and waited tables and her husband cooked. She passed away, so he still cooks, but their daughter Kenzie took over the front of the restaurant. They're good people, and the food's excellent."

Once they were parked, he opened Oliver's door, but made her laugh when he admitted he had no clue how to free the child and stepped back. After getting Oliver out, she set him on his feet and took him by the hand. She saw Brian start to reach out, as though to take him, but he shoved his hands in his pockets instead.

There were a few customers having lunch, but Siobhan found an empty table away from the other diners. Oliver usually behaved well when they were out in public, but there was always the accidentally flung ketchup-covered French fry to consider. And not too long ago, her son had learned some fun new vocabulary words from a group of businessmen at a table next to them.

It was clear from the way Kenzie greeted Brian that he was a frequent visitor, as were his brothers, and then she turned to Siobhan.

"What can I get you today?"

"I'd love a coffee, please, and he'll take a small milk with a lid and straw. And we're separate checks, please. The little guy is with me."

In her peripheral vision, she saw Brian look up, clearly about to speak, but then he just smiled wanly and went back to looking over the menu.

"Sure thing," Kenzie said. "Do you know what you want to eat?"

Siobhan ordered popcorn chicken and fries for both of them. She probably could have gotten away with sharing the adult portion, but his came with the drink and a small dish of soft-serve ice cream, so it was worth the splurge.

Then she laughed when Brian said he'd have the same. "That was a lot of menu reading for somebody who knew what he was having before he walked through the door."

"True, but you never know when something else jumps out at you. The only thing I knew for sure was that I was *not* ordering a hot dog. Or potato salad."

After Kenzie walked away, she gave him a thoughtful look. "Thank you for not trying to overrule the check situation. It didn't look easy for you."

"I told you I'd do my best to respect your boundaries." He took a sip of his soda and then leaned back in his chair. "This was a good idea. Although it's so quiet and cool that once I have a meal in me, the hum of the air-conditioning might put me to sleep."

"If you and Oliver nod off here at the table, I'll just sit

here and read a book on my phone. I'd probably enjoy it, to be honest."

"If you think the campground's a lot right now, wait until the Maine crew shows up." When her eyes widened, he chuckled. "Sean stayed in New Hampshire after he met Emma, but my dad still has four other cousins in Maine, and they're all married and they had kids around the same time, so there's an entire pack of teenagers coming."

"If the *entire* family plays Water Ball of Doom, you're going to need a bigger pool."

His laugh was deep and warm, and Siobhan definitely didn't like the way it made her want to lean closer to him. "The doom is limited to this bunch, for the most part. And the family in Maine also runs a lodge and campground on ATV trails, so needless to say, it's their busy time, too. By getting married on a Monday, Steph made it so they can come, but most of them will only be coming for the day. There shouldn't be time for swimming, especially since we'd have to do it in shifts to fit everybody."

"You have *so* much family. I only have…" Her words trailed off as she remembered who she was talking to. "Well, my mom and my sister, as you know. And Oliver, of course."

She felt the energy shift when she brought up her family, as if she'd summoned a rain cloud to hover over their meal. And she thought about a rapid change of subject— just saying anything that had nothing to do with Kelly— but Kenzie walked up to their table with their drinks, and the tension just hung there between them.

Brian wished he could go back in time and steer the conversation into any direction that didn't lead to his ex-wife. They had to talk about her eventually, though, and maybe it was best done quietly, away from his large and very curious family.

Siobhan managed to fend off conversation for a while by focusing on Oliver. She drew shapes on the back of his placemat and they went through color names as he used crayons Kenzie provided to color them in. He watched them in silence, wishing he could find the right words to restore their easy way with each other, but nothing occurred to him and eventually their food arrived.

He watched her preparing Oliver's meal for him—cutting the larger pieces of popcorn chicken in half and moving fries around to cool them off. She popped one of the French fries into her mouth, and he laughed when she immediately ate a second while very obviously avoiding looking at him.

"I told you the fries are unmatched," he said, pointing one at her before putting it in his mouth.

"I don't know about unmatched, but they're very good." Once she was satisfied Oliver's food was cool enough, she squirted a dollop of ketchup next to the fries and slid the plate to him.

After centering her own plate in front of her, she took a bite of the popcorn chicken and smiled as she chewed and swallowed. "Okay, *these* might be unmatched."

He nodded, but he knew his return smile was forced as the distraction the food arriving had offered faded and his mind returned to his ex-wife. "Speaking of your sister, since it may or may not be relevant in the near future, where is Kelly living these days?"

"I don't know." Skepticism must have shown on his face because she held up her hand. "I swear. I tried to call her the first day at the campground and her number's no longer in service."

"When was the last time you heard from her?"

"The day we finalized the adoption. Once that was done, she was gone and I haven't seen her or heard from her since."

"If there are documents to amend, they'll probably need to serve her."

She stared at the chicken on her fork without raising it to her mouth. "Anything we do to amend his birth certificate will lead back to the original, which could nullify the adoption because Oliver wasn't his to surrender."

He blew out a breath, running a hand through his hair. "But Kelly's still his biological mother and, since I'm his biological father, you and I should be able to adopt him together. Both states do second parent adoption."

"I think that's for unmarried partners who live together, though."

"We need a lawyer, Siobhan," he said, even though it was hard to watch the fear that settled into her features. "Do you know if she and the other guy are still together?"

"I don't know, but I doubt it. He didn't seem like the long-term type."

"So what happens if they void the adoption and Kelly decides to keep him and get child support and health care from me until Oliver graduates from college?"

Siobhan's chin lifted. "She wouldn't do that."

"Really?"

"If you're going to go into bitter ex-husband mode and trash my sister, I'm going to leave and you can walk back to the campground. By the time you get there, we'll be gone."

Brian didn't believe for a second Kelly deserved that kind of loyalty, but he also had three brothers of his own and knew he had to tread carefully. Sibling relationships could be messy, but they ran deep.

"I'm not trying to trash her," he said. "But she lied to you, Siobhan. She lied about the possibility I could be Oliver's father and she lied to you about our marriage."

"Using a child she didn't want to raise and hurting me just to get money out of you is different than lying to get out of a relationship she didn't want to be in anymore. And we need to stop talking about this right now because he's only two, but…you know."

"Okay. I'm just trying to say that you and I are on the same page, but we're not the only people involved."

"We would be if we just leave it alone. You and I can figure it out like reasonable adults, without involving lawyers and courts."

Not when it came to his son. And Brian knew Siobhan didn't believe it, either. She was reacting out of fear, and nothing he could say was going to mitigate that. They needed professional advice on how to go forward.

"I think you and I have a lot of misconceptions about each other," he said, and she nodded. "You've handled this with so much grace and generosity, and I know we can do this together. But I've exchanged promises before and then had the future I'd envisioned ripped away with no warning. If this goes the way I hope, I need it to be made legal."

She looked at him for a long time, her eyes searching his, and then the corner of her mouth twitched. "The way you *hope*?"

He looked at Oliver, who grinned at him with ketchup smeared halfway across his cheek, and his heart squeezed like a fist in his chest. "Yeah."

"Time for ice cream!" Oliver declared, and as far as Brian was concerned, it was the best way to put an end to the conversation.

He groaned and put his hand over his stomach. "I forgot until just now that I have to play volleyball this afternoon. I'm probably going to regret those French fries."

"So no ice cream for you?" Siobhan said, cleaning up the small amount of mess Oliver had made and depositing it on his plate.

"I didn't say that. I just said I'm going to have regrets."

Her laughter lightened his mood, as did the joy of watching a toddler thoroughly enjoy a bowl of soft-serve vanilla ice cream with chocolate jimmies. Oliver even offered him a bite and being fed melting ice cream from a spoon that trailed vanilla and jimmies across the table and down Brian's chin filled him with a quick burst of happiness he hadn't felt in a long time.

By the time Siobhan dropped him off at the front of the campground so she could go give her sticky son a more thorough scrubbing, Brian was looking for a few minutes to decompress. Rather than heading for where he knew they'd be putting the volleyball net up or going into the store, he let himself into the house.

He was hoping for a few minutes alone, but he should have known better. Joey was rummaging around in the fridge, and he looked up when he heard Brian come in. "Hey, you're back."

"Whatever you're looking for, we don't have any."

"Too late." Joey held up a jar of pickles and closed the fridge. "I'd warn you that you were the number one topic of conversation over lunch, but you probably know that already."

"The kid wanted popcorn chicken."

"Taking a right out of the campground and driving a few minutes up the road doesn't seem like tough directions to give." When Brian flipped him off, Joey leaned against the counter and set the pickles down so he could cross his arms in big brother mode. "This is one of the messiest situations anybody in the family's ever gotten into, and everybody's just afraid you're going to do the one thing that would make it a whole lot messier."

A familiar anger triggered by his family being up in his business rose up, but he didn't allow himself to react until he had it under control. If ever he'd been in a situation that affected all of them, it was this one.

"I was talking about their fries and she said I could join them, so I did. I'm super grateful everybody's handled this so well, but it was nice to have a break from the goldfish bowl."

"And that's it?"

What, exactly, was Joey getting at? There was no way he could be implying it was some kind of date. "We talked a little. Kelly came up, and that was tense."

He sighed, wondering where his dog was. Stella either hadn't seen him come home or she was getting so spoiled by belly rubs or food she didn't care.

"She came up in what capacity?"

Brian snorted. "She's a pretty central character in this drama we've found ourselves in. But to answer your question, I asked where Kelly lives now and Siobhan doesn't know."

"She doesn't know where her sister lives?"

He could understand the skepticism, but not every family was like theirs. "She said she hasn't seen her since the adoption was finalized and my gut says Siobhan hasn't lied to me. And before you ask, yes, there's a chance we might have to involve her, but that's a next week problem. This week's about the wedding."

"Yeah, the bride's been walking around with the ball

for twenty minutes, trying to get people to show up at the playground."

He snorted. "She probably thinks she's going to win because nobody can play rough with the bride three days before she walks down the aisle."

"She's a Kowalski. She should know better." Joey chuckled. "But still, dibs on being on Team Bride."

Chapter Ten

"Who are you rooting for?" Mary asked as she settled into the chair next to Siobhan's. The spectators were lined up along the tree line, where they'd be safe from wayward balls. Hopefully, anyway. Siobhan assumed they wouldn't let the ball hit the matriarch of the family, so the closer she sat to Mary, the better.

She smiled at the woman who was probably her son's great-grandmother and decided not to admit that of course she'd be rooting for Brian's team. "I don't know. I heard Evan's in charge of the grill tonight and that he makes an exceptional homemade marinade, so I might root for his team."

"Plus, nothing drags down the wedding photos like the father of the bride nursing a broken nose."

She winced. "Does that happen a lot? It seems like you must have a lot of experience with broken bones."

"There have been a few over the years, I guess. I had kids who played hard and they had kids who play hard, but there probably haven't been as many injuries as you'd imagine. They learned all the rules and boundaries before they started testing them, and they look out for each other."

Like the pool, Siobhan thought. Chaos, but a controlled and safe chaos. "Who are you rooting for?"

Mary shrugged. "All of them, of course, but I'll cheer for whichever team Leo's on because he'll be grumpy if I don't."

"Leo's playing?"

Lisa, who was in the process of setting up a chair on the other side of her mother-in-law, laughed. "Try to stop him."

Terry leaned her chair against a tree, opting to sit on the blanket with Oliver and Stella—probably because they had a bag of Goldfish crackers. "Dad is the unbeaten champion of The Annual Kowalski Volleyball Death Match Tournament of Doom, so they can't play without him."

"Wait. His team wins every year? Does he cheat?"

They all laughed, but it was Mary who explained. "His team doesn't win every year, but as the patriarch of the family, he claims the glory trickles down so all wins are traced back to him."

"Mom, please don't say *trickle down* when talking about the family gene pool."

"Teresa—" Mary was interrupted in the process of middle-naming her daughter by the fact that Lisa had almost choked and spit water all over her legs. "So much for trying to impress Siobhan."

"Wait, that's been you all *trying* to impress me?" she teased, and Lisa and Terry dissolved into fits of laughter.

Mary's mouth curved in a reluctant grin. "I knew you'd hold your own."

"Now I know where Steph gets her sense of humor from." All the personal drama aside, this time getting to know this side of her friend and her family was a blast. "If it's a tournament, do they play multiple games? Are there rounds?"

Mary shook her head. "They just play until they can't

play anymore. Lisa's boys named it when they were really little and didn't know what all those words actually meant, but liked the way they sounded together."

Hannah, Ellie and Nora showed up then, and the little girl immediately planted herself on the blanket while the other women added their chairs to the line. It looked less like she was excited to join Oliver and Stella, though, and more like a sulky flop because she couldn't play.

With a groan, Terry pushed herself to her feet and retrieved her chair. "Sitting on a blanket on the ground is fun in theory, but not so much in practice."

"None of you are playing?" Siobhan asked, thankful it wouldn't only be her, the little ones and the family matriarch on the sidelines.

"It's a grown-up game and I'm too little," Nora said, definitely pouting.

"Ellie's out because this game is definitely not on the recommended activities list for expectant mothers and I'm not in the mood," Lisa said. "Fair warning, Siobhan, we'll be expected to act as line judges and referees at times."

"I don't really know the rules of volleyball."

"Nobody does," Mary said. "Feel free to annoy or reward family members at will. The 2019 tournament absolutely was decided by the fact that the previous Thanksgiving, Evan suggested I try changing up my gravy recipe, just to keep things fresh."

Mary said it with a straight face, but a smile lurked in the corners of her mouth, so Siobhan wasn't sure if she was serious or not. She probably was and Siobhan laughed, watching as players emerged from different parts of the campground to converge at the net. When Kyle and his family showed up, she was surprised. She hadn't thought they'd join in what was sure to be a melee, especially his grandfather. "Ron is playing?"

"If Leo's out there, Ron's gonna be out there," Mary said, and the other women made a sound that Siobhan translated as *men*. "They'll probably divide the teams under the two grandfathers, which would also be the bride's team versus the groom's team, I guess."

And that seemed to be the case as Leo and Ron took positions on opposing sides of the net that had appeared while Siobhan and Oliver were at the restaurant.

"So now it's a schoolyard pick?"

"It's more like everybody roaming and crossing back and forth under the net until both teams are satisfied," Terry said. "They try to pit siblings against each other, of course. To keep things interesting."

Siobhan watched Leo yell at Cat to get on his side of the net, and the girl taunted her teenage brother as she went. "That's sweet of Leo to choose her over her much taller brother."

Lisa scoffed. "Johnny's tall and fit, but he's very chill and might sneak off with a book at any moment without warning. Cat's not big and she's the sweetest thing, but when it comes to competition, she's practically feral and there's not much she won't do to win."

Siobhan chuckled, and then watched in silence as the family sorted itself into two teams, complete with a lot of yelling, taunting and movement. The women on the sidelines with her kept up a running commentary, occasionally heckling or shouting out suggestions.

Having never experienced a large family—especially such a close-knit and dynamic one—she was fascinated by their interactions with each other. They were loud and didn't pull many punches when it came to hurling insults about athletic ability, but it was all taken with good humor because the family foundation was so strong.

And the laughter. There was so much laughter. Growing up, she and Kelly might laugh at a funny show or an amusing story, but it wasn't baked into everyday life the way it was with the Kowalski family. Janelle Rowe was bitter and resented that she didn't have the things she felt she deserved in life, and if Siobhan heard her laugh, there was a good chance she was trying to charm somebody she thought she could get something out of.

The charm worked, as a rule, because there were very few men able to resist Janelle's manipulation. She'd run off for a night or a weekend, or even weeks at a time once her daughters were teens. Kelly didn't seem to care, but Siobhan would be a ball of stress, trying to keep her sister in line so nobody found out they were alone. Then Janelle would return, angry her latest dream didn't come true and resenting her life. It was no wonder Siobhan envied the bond and the humor the Kowalski family shared.

There was a good chance this was her son's family, she thought, and that reminder sent a shiver through her entire body. If the test confirmed Brian was his father, Oliver would grow up a part of this family. On one side, he'd have a mother who loved and provided for him, and with whom he shared a love of books and puzzles. On the other side, all of this.

She pressed her hand over the ache in her heart and told herself in no uncertain terms to stop. Oliver loved her. She was his mother and nothing would change that bond between them. And if it turned out he was a Kowalski by birth, his time with them might be more fun than his time with her, but that was okay.

And the more people who loved and supported Oliver through life, the better.

"It's going to start getting intense soon," Lisa said, and Siobhan refocused her attention on the game.

"That wasn't intense?" Hannah asked incredulously, reminding Siobhan it was also *her* first time watching them play volleyball.

Just as her gaze landed on Brian—which seemed to be an involuntary habit she couldn't break—he peeled off his T-shirt and used it to wipe sweat from his face before flinging it away. Then he ran both hands over his hair, giving her a lovely view of his arm muscles flexing, as well as an unobstructed view of his taut stomach. No rippling abs, which she didn't care for anyway, but it was clear he spent a lot of time working outdoors.

Thankfully something happened elsewhere in the game that made everybody start yelling, even from the sidelines. That was good, because Siobhan was pretty sure the noise she made low in her throat when Brian took off his shirt might not have been silent.

At least everybody on the sideline was watching the players, so nobody would notice she couldn't take her eyes off of Brian. They probably couldn't even tell it was him she was looking at—she hoped.

Because she was watching him, she saw him point at Cat and then make some kind of hand gesture. The girl grinned and nodded before resuming her laser focus on the ball.

Kevin served and as the ball soared high and fast toward the net, Brian crouched. Cat was there, stepping into Brian's locked hands. Siobhan had maybe two seconds to appreciate the way every muscle in his body rippled and flexed as he launched Cat into the air before she spiked the ball straight into the groom's head and chaos erupted.

"Not his face!" Steph screamed.

"Foul!" Kevin yelled.

"It's okay," Kyle called out, rubbing the side of his head. "It didn't get my face."

"Still a foul," Ron grumbled. "You can't use other people to hit the ball."

Siobhan was still watching Brian with wide eyes. He'd caught Cat around the waist and set her on the ground before pointing at Kevin and laughing. His uncle was pointing back, but he wasn't amused and she thought it was probably a good thing everybody was yelling, so she couldn't make out what he was saying.

"Buckle up," Terry said. "This one's coming our way."

Siobhan wasn't sure what that meant until everybody on the grass seemed to turn in their direction at the same time. Right. It was line judging time, or whatever they called it. The other women seemed content to shout out their opinions, so she just sat quietly, hoping they'd go back to playing before she had to say anything.

"Siobhan's the tie-breaker, then," Leo boomed, and all eyes turned to her.

"Oh. Oh, no." She knew nothing about volleyball. She had no idea what the score was or how important this ruling would be. She didn't even know if there *was* a score being kept.

Her gaze flew to Brian, who was her best hope for getting some help, but that was a mistake. He was the one being ruled on, of course, so just a little bit of bias there. But also, he seemed to land on a judge manipulation tactic pretty quickly.

He gave her that smile. Those blue eyes crinkled and

that crooked grin asked her how she could possibly say no to him. Her pulse quickened and she folded her hands in her lap to keep from crossing her legs as heat pulsed between her thighs. The man's charm was potent. She'd give him that.

But she wasn't giving him the point. "That's totally not legal."

As his team groaned and the other cheered, Brian put his hand over his heart and gave her a wounded look.

She grinned. The man had underestimated her ability to say no to pretty blue eyes and cheeky grins. But right before he turned back to his teammates, she saw something else in his expression.

Amusement. And a challenge. There was going to be some kind of payback for this, and a thrill of anticipation sizzled through her.

"Well done, Siobhan," Hannah said with a chuckle. "That'll keep them riled up for a while."

Riled up was a good expression for it, Siobhan thought. And they weren't the only ones feeling it. She probably should have let Brian score the point.

"Do you need help with that?"

Brian looked down to see Siobhan standing near the foot of the ladder, watching him. She was wearing a loose V-necked T-shirt, and he guessed she wasn't aware the angle gave him a generous glimpse of cleavage. Clearing his throat, he lifted his gaze to her face and was thankful she was looking at the lights he'd finished stringing and hadn't caught him staring.

Not that she had a lot of room to talk when it came to staring. He had exceptionally good peripheral vision and Siobhan had done her fair share of staring at him during the volleyball game. Playing an extreme version of the sport on a warmer-than-forecast day wasn't the only reason he'd left the field hot and bothered.

He cleared his throat and started down the ladder to derail that train of thought. "I'm about done, but thanks."

She turned but didn't walk away. Instead she looked at the fairy lights they'd strung through the trees on either side of the dirt road leading from the field where the wedding would take place to the bride and groom's cabin. "Your brother will be able to get beautiful pictures of them here."

"That's what we're going for. Of course, the first time we didn't get enough lights, so we had to wait for more to arrive and then redo the whole thing. And we did all that without really testing them, so *then* we learned we couldn't get the solar collectors in a good enough spot to power them. Emma's now the proud owner of a ton of barely used solar-powered fairy lights, and these plug in to the outlets in the site on the corner, which means we have to credit the camper for the power we use. One of the many aspects of this wedding that sounded simple in the group chat, but turned into a pain in the ass for me and Rob."

"It's worth it. They're magical."

He believed her, because standing here in the dark with the tiny lights warming her face and reflecting in her eyes did feel magical. His fingers twitched, desperate to touch her, and he curled his hands into loose fists.

"Ellie went and got Nora a little bit ago and she said Oliver was out like a light on Steph's bed," she told him. "I was on my way to get him earlier, trying to avoid that, but then Emma was telling me how she and Sean met and that's not really a story you can walk away from."

"Once the family stories get rolling, there's almost never a good time to duck out, but I think everybody will head inside early tonight. The volleyball game took a lot out of us." He arched an eyebrow at her. "Especially those of us who didn't win."

"I think the word you're looking for is *lost*," she shot back, and her grin lit a fire in his blood.

"I thought we were friends," he said. "The fries, Siobhan. The unmatched popcorn chicken. I introduced you to them and then you go and rule against me?"

She started to laugh before stifling the sound with her hand. It was quiet in this part of the campground. And dark. And about as private as they could get outside with most of his relatives around them.

But he wasn't thinking about that. Not at all.

"You tried to charm me," she said, and maybe it was his imagination, but did she move closer to him? To be able to keep her voice low, he told himself. "The smile. The eyes. I saw what you were doing."

"In my defense, it usually works."

"I bet it does. But apparently you forgot that, whether it's cold leftover pizza for breakfast or sticking things in electrical outlets to see what will happen, I say no to pretty blue eyes and cheeky smiles on a regular basis."

And there it was—a reminder of the thread already connecting them. Even though there was no official confirmation yet, on some level they'd both accepted they shared a child. And he didn't need any kind of official documentation to know that any kind of intimacy between him and Siobhan should be avoided at any cost. His best move was to go back to his original plan for dealing with her—ignoring her presence entirely.

But the version of him that had come up with that plan

was gone and he'd never be that guy again. There might be some question as to whether he was a father now, but there was no question about the fact that this version of him knew Siobhan was sweet and funny and sexy. Now he knew that her laughter immediately lifted his mood, even from a distance.

And he knew that magic was the reflection of fairy lights dancing in her hazel eyes.

"Just remember, when it comes to losing, a Kowalski can really hold a grudge," he said, injecting a lightness he didn't feel into his tone.

"Oh, I saw the look you gave me when I lost you the point," she said, her eyes sparkling. "It promised payback."

The way he remembered it, a *lot* of looks had passed between them during that volleyball game, and most of them hadn't been promising retribution. Every time their eyes met, he felt singed by the sparks arcing between them, and he didn't think he was imagining it.

Then Siobhan rested her hand on his forearm and instantly it felt as if the blood in his veins had been replaced with lava.

"Promise me that payback won't come in the pool, though," she said earnestly.

Nothing could stop him from touching her, and he smoothed wisps of her hair back from her face before cupping her cheek. "I wouldn't do that to you."

Siobhan leaned into his touch, her fingers sliding down his arm to circle his wrist. He trailed over her cheekbone as their gazes tangled and caught, neither of them looking away. Her lips parted as he closed the distance between them. She didn't back away, and as she tipped her head back, her anticipation-quickened breaths matched his.

Finally whispered through his mind as he lowered his mouth to hers.

He slid his hand from her cheek to the back of her neck as she released his wrist. For a second he thought she was pulling away, but then he felt her hands on his back and groaned against her lips.

Brian lost himself in the kiss, everything fading away as his tongue danced over hers. Siobhan's hunger matched his own, and he kissed her harder and deeper as her fingernails bit through his T-shirt.

The jingling brought him back to reality. He broke off the kiss, backing away from her as the sound of Stella's metal tags bouncing off each other grew closer. *Please don't let anybody be with her*, he thought as he looked into Siobhan's eyes and saw his awareness of what they'd just done reflected back at him.

"I'm sorry. I shouldn't have—" Stella reached them, thankfully alone, and bending down to greet her with a good back scratch gave Brian an excuse to have somewhere else to look besides Siobhan's eyes. He cleared his throat. "I'm sorry."

"Me too. That was…" She didn't say what it was, instead letting the words fade away. "I should go get Oliver and wrangle him into bed."

Now that he'd had a minute, Brian forced himself to straighten and look her in the eye. "Do you want me to carry him for you?"

He watched her consider it, knowing she'd probably rather see the last of him for the night. But Oliver was heavy and the walk from Steph's cabin would be even longer than from the playground.

"I'd appreciate it. Thank you."

They walked in silence to Steph's cabin. She opened

the door before they could even knock and put a finger to her lips before waving them in. Kyle was as deeply asleep as Oliver, and neither of them stirred when Brian scooped the little boy into his arms and lifted him.

Stella walked with them until they got to Siobhan's camper, and then she ran off to find somebody more interesting to hang out with. Once he'd navigated the steps, he laid Oliver down on the edge of the bed.

"Thank you," Siobhan said quietly, not meeting his eyes.

"No problem. Good night, Siobhan."

He left without trying to say anything more. He wasn't even sure what he *could* say. Kissing her had been a mistake. He knew it. She knew it. The only thing he could do was promise he wouldn't do it again.

But that wasn't a promise he was sure he could keep, so he just kept walking.

Chapter Eleven

She'd kissed Brian Kowalski.

It was the first thought to pop into Siobhan's head when she opened her eyes, which was extra annoying because it was the thought running on a constant loop when she'd finally fallen asleep.

Rather than sliding out of bed and enjoying a quiet cup of coffee before Oliver stirred, she pulled the blanket over her face in an effort to hide from the world. She knew it would fail. Oliver certainly wasn't going to spend an entire day hiding under the covers with her. And as the actual wedding part of the wedding trip crept ever closer, she'd promised Steph they'd focus on preparations today.

There was only so much they could do since Brian's brother wasn't arriving with the bigger stuff from the rental company until later in the afternoon. And it was going to be a simple ceremony, so there wasn't a lot of fussy stuff to do. Steaming the outfits. Preparing the vines they were going to wrap around the arbor.

The memory of Brian stringing the fairy lights flashed through her mind, followed swiftly by the remembrance of his lips on hers as his hand cupped the back of her neck.

Nope.

Suddenly too warm, Siobhan pulled the blanket off her

face. That wasn't enough, so she pushed it off entirely, careful not to nudge Oliver in the process. He was getting restless and she knew he'd be awake soon, but she'd take every minute she could get.

Unfortunately, there was no way for her to think about the wedding preparations without thinking about Brian and those lights, so her mind kept returning to the kiss over and over.

The fact that her first instinct to call Robin and tell her everything was immediately followed by a resolve to tell Robin nothing was like a flashing neon sign telling her she'd definitely done the wrong thing.

They commiserated regularly about the sad state of their sex lives—Siobhan too tired to care and Robin too picky. If Brian was a man she was supposed to be kissing, her best friend would have been her first call.

Instead, she was desperately hoping nobody would ever find out. Not Robin and especially nobody with the last name of Kowalski.

When Oliver finally opened his eyes, Siobhan was almost relieved he was awake because she needed the distraction. Rather than popping out of bed and hitting the ground running, her son snuggled against her and she recited one of his favorite board books from memory. In a few places, she deliberately substituted a different animal or color, and Oliver would giggle and correct her, calling her silly.

When she suggested some oatmeal, she half expected him to remember the Kowalski family would be gathering for the big breakfast buffet and jump out of bed, but he didn't seem to have a lot of interest in them today. She got him dressed and then started the oatmeal while the Keurig brewed.

She'd just sat down when her phone buzzed with a message from Steph. Breakfast is ready!

Siobhan didn't even have to look at Oliver to know it was going to be a while before they emerged from the camper. He was content to be leisurely this morning, and anytime he was content, she was.

We just woke up. Oliver's feeling lazy, so we're going to have a quiet breakfast inside today.

Lazy mornings are best! See you in a while, then!

A few minutes later, her phone buzzed again, this time with a text message from a number that wasn't in her contacts.

You're not leaving, are you? I'm sorry. It won't happen again, and I'll work in the store today if it makes you more comfortable.

Adding to the "that's so wrong" list, the assurance there would be no more kissing triggered a deep sense of regret—maybe even loss. She'd liked that kiss a lot.

This is Brian, by the way.

Siobhan laughed at the second message, and then she laughed again at Oliver's look of sleepy confusion. His mom laughing at seemingly nothing over her first coffee of the day was a new experience for him.

After taking a long swig of the coffee and thinking for a moment, she typed in her response. I'm not leaving and you don't have to hide. We're adults, it won't happen again, and we're not at breakfast because Oliver slept in and he's having a quiet morning. We'll be out in a bit.

Even though he sent back a smiley-face emoji, Siobhan suspected Brian might make himself scarce today. They might be adults who knew kissing couldn't happen again, but they were also adults tangled in a family drama who didn't even like each other a few days ago, but kissed last night.

There was no way around *that* being awkward.

Several hours later, with the clouds gathering to deliver the brief showers in the forecast, Siobhan left Oliver in the care of Mary, Ellie and some of the other women, who were going to put on a movie for the little ones and do some of the wedding baking.

Alone with Steph in the bride and groom's cabin, Siobhan sat on the edge of the bed, trying to get as much of the downdraft from the ceiling fan as possible. "I can't believe they're going to bake in a camper."

"I know, right? But they always have. I told them baking stuff ahead of time and freezing it was fine, but it's my wedding. And the guys offered them the kitchen in the house, but Gram's used to her oven, whatever that means."

"I'm not a baker, even when I'm not in an aluminum box, so I have no idea."

Steph pulled a hand steamer out of a bag she'd been rummaging through. "I'm so glad you were able to come Wednesday instead of waiting until Sunday. I was afraid if you just came for the wedding part, things would still be awkward at the ceremony."

"It was smart to dangle a free vacation in the woods of northern New Hampshire with my son in front of me. And you're also lucky, because you called on a day I was so over the city I wanted to curl up on the floor of my shower and cry. Excellent timing." She laughed. "I've had fun."

Of course, if she'd only come for Sunday and Monday, she probably would have left Oliver with Robin. Her friend would have watched him for overnight and then gotten him off to daycare with little disruption to his schedule. And if she hadn't brought Oliver with her, Brian and his family wouldn't have seen him and nobody would know.

But she would have. At some point, she would have seen Brian smile in that way the Kowalskis had and the resemblance was so strong, there's no way she wouldn't have missed the connection. And then what would she have done?

Probably nothing at the time, she decided. But once she got home, it would have eaten at her. She would have tried to contact Kelly, of course. But as terrifying as this all was, she didn't think she could live with herself if she chose to hide him from Brian. That was a choice her sister had made, not her.

"You okay?"

Siobhan blinked away the what-ifs and smiled at her friend. "Of course. I was just lost in thought for a minute."

"Anything juicy?"

Alarm jolted through Siobhan at her friend's choice of words. Had she and Brian been seen last night? "Juicy? Hardly. I was thinking about the best order to steam the clothes in, actually. And speaking of, I can handle this myself, you know, freeing you up to relax. I'm pretty sure taking stuff off your plate is in my job description."

"Listen, I had to fend off pretty much all of the women in this campground right now to get this time with you. I feel like we've hardly had time to talk since you got here and I feel bad. You dropped everything to be my maid of honor."

"Don't worry about me. We're having a great time." Not the part where she accidentally found her son's biological father—maybe—and then kissed him, but she and Oliver were enjoying themselves for the most part. "It must be nice to spend time with your whole family like this."

Steph beamed. "It really is. It's exactly what Kyle and I wanted. Bringing our families together and just wallowing in the love and happiness is the perfect way to make it official."

She couldn't hold back her laughter. "Wallowing?"

Before Steph could respond, there was a light knock on the door and then it opened. Brian stepped in, blinking as he crossed from the bright sunshine into the dim cabin.

"Hey, Steph, do you need—" He spotted Siobhan and froze for a second. "Sorry. I heard you were steaming stuff and figured I'd see if you need an extension cord."

"Glad I wasn't in the middle of trying my dress on," Steph said, and then she laughed. "And Brian Kowalski, are you actually *suggesting* I plug something with a heating element into an extension cord?"

"There's a big difference between a hand steamer and a space heater." He snorted. "And that was Bobby that almost burned down the garage, not me."

"I'm going to get you a T-shirt that says *It Was Bobby* for Christmas."

"I'd wear it every day." He looked at Siobhan. "Did she tell you Rob used to be Bobby until his voice changed and he thought a new nickname would make him sound older?"

She laughed. "Rob told me about the nickname, actually, although he left out the part about his voice changing."

Brian grinned, his blue eyes crinkling, and Siobhan smiled back. Their gazes held until her heart was pounding in her chest. Then she realized she was twirling the end of her hair around her finger and shoved her hands into her pockets. One ill-advised kiss and she was acting like a dreamy teenager.

"We're all set, I think," Steph said, and they both looked at her without responding. "The extension cord you were talking about? We don't need it."

"Oh, right," Brian said. "Text me if you change your mind."

When the door closed behind her cousin, Steph put her hands on her hips. "What was *that*?"

"What was what?"

She waggled a finger between Siobhan and the door. "That. You and Brian. There was…something going on there."

Siobhan snorted, but she could feel the heat in her chest and cheeks. She was absolutely *not* going to confess there had been a kiss between them, and she could only hope nobody had seen them. "Trust me, there's nothing at all going on there."

"I'm pretty sure there are rules about maids of honor lying to brides. I've known him my whole life, obviously, and he's into you." She pointed at Siobhan. "And you're into him back. How did I not see this coming?"

"Because there was nothing to *see* coming. Steph, he's my sister's ex-husband." Talk about needing something written on a T-shirt. Maybe cross-stitched on a pillow. Written on her mirror in lipstick.

"That's one way to look at it." Steph's hands went back to her hips. "But he's also the father of your child."

"That's…not how that works." She frowned. "Okay,

technically that's true—maybe, I mean, pending the paternity test results—but not even remotely in the way you're insinuating."

"Sure. Whatever you say." She picked up the hand steamer and gave it a test blast. "But I'm not wrong."

Since the steamer was ready and Siobhan would take any distraction she could get in that moment, she lifted the plastic off Steph's dress. It was a gorgeous pale yellow, with a fitted sleeveless bodice and a flared skirt that hit midshin. It was summery and shimmery and she was definitely letting Steph do the actual steaming. She'd hold the hanger and offer moral support.

"I can't believe how perfectly your dress complements mine," Steph said as she gingerly steamed the few wrinkles in the dress from traveling.

"Right?" Hers was similar, though not quite as fitted in the bodice, and the skirt was knee-length. The pastel floral pattern included yellows that matched the bride's dress perfectly. "You'd almost think they were bought together."

Steph stood back to give the dress a final looking over, and then glanced sideways at Siobhan. "I should tell Rob to get a photo of Brian's face when he lays eyes on you."

"Stop!" Her cheeks were so hot, it felt as though Steph had given her a shot of steam in the face. "My former brother-in-law does *not* have a thing for me. He's barely come around to even liking me."

"Oh, he came all the way around to liking you and then kept right on going."

"And don't you *dare* say anything to Rob. Or anybody else, for that matter. The last thing I need is to be the center of more drama."

Steph rolled her eyes. "Of course I won't. But people

will notice on their own because it's like a miracle to see him like this again. He's been so…flat."

"Flat?" Siobhan finished smoothing the plastic over the freshly steamed dress and hung it back up. Then she grabbed the groom's pants.

"Emotionally, I mean. He was pretty wrecked when Kelly left him. He never saw it coming."

Siobhan was silent, focusing all of her attention on the pants. Not only because there was nothing she could say to defend her sister, but because she wanted to hear Brian's side of the story, even if she didn't get it from him.

"I mean, I didn't see it myself. He's not great at letting people see how he's feeling, but he's super close with his brothers and word filters around the family, you know?" Steph sighed, running the steamer over one of the legs. "Brian loved her so much and he didn't see it coming. One day he came home and she told him she was in love with somebody else and was leaving him."

"He didn't fight for her," Siobhan said quietly. "He just let her go. When I went to pick up her stuff, he just opened the door and ignored me. He didn't ask about her or anything."

"If it had just been her being unhappy, he would have. He would have done anything for her. But she'd been cheating and was in love with somebody else, and there's no coming back from that, so he just…shut down. Everybody was relieved when they bought this place, even though it was stressful, because they were afraid he was turning into some kind of angry hermit guy. Except for Stella, of course. I think getting her kept his heart from totally shriveling up."

"She's a great dog." Siobhan wasn't sure what else she could say.

"So Brian lighting up when he sees you? Yeah, we're going to notice, but I'm probably the only one who's going to say anything to you. I'm the bride and you're my maid of honor, so I get to be nosy."

Siobhan laughed, even though the idea of his entire family watching them made her mildly uncomfortable. "Was there a wedding etiquette book I missed? I don't remember that chapter."

"Maybe you'll start dating. That would be perfect, wouldn't it?"

On the surface, Steph sounded like a woman who thought her cousin dating her friend would be fun, but Siobhan didn't think that's what she meant. Oliver was probably the reason she thought them dating would be a good idea, because them being a couple would make things easier for everybody.

Right up until it didn't work out and then it was ten times worse. She snorted. "Like I'd date a guy who's still hung up on my sister."

"I don't think he's still hung up on her so much as he was grieving the life he thought he'd made for himself."

And having Siobhan and Oliver would be an insta-family to fix that? She didn't want any part of that. On a conscious level, anyway. Clearly on some subconscious level, she was attracted to Brian because she'd kissed him under the fairy lights.

But they'd both known that was a bad idea and they'd been right. They didn't need anybody else's opinion on it.

"Getting this campground ready to open and then running it snapped him out of it, really," Steph continued. "He's been a lot more like himself all summer, and Rob said he's actually seemed happy."

She felt a pang of guilt over having been a part of what

Kelly did to Brian, but she forced herself to acknowledge it and then dismiss it. Yes, she'd had Kelly's back through the divorce and been cold to Brian because they were sisters. That's what was expected of her. But she hadn't had all of the facts—and the few she did have had been outright lies—so it wasn't really her fault.

What she could do, though, was make sure that another Lowe sister didn't put him through the emotional wringer again. No more lingering looks. No more small yet sizzling touches.

And definitely no more kissing.

Brian was alone in the store, pretending he needed to deal with a vendor issue while actually just hiding from his family, when his brother Danny arrived. He was towing a trailer with stuff for the wedding, so he pulled alongside the pool. Even though Brian knew he probably wanted to know where they wanted the stuff before heading into narrow campground roads with the trailer, he'd hoped he'd keep going.

While he might be good at hiding his feelings from most people, he wasn't sure he could hide *I kissed the mother of the child I didn't know I had last night* feelings from his brothers.

He wasn't even sure what they were himself, so he certainly couldn't explain them to anybody else.

"Hey, Danny," he said when his brother walked in. Brian knew from the way he looked at him—concerned and with a dash of amusement—that he'd been filled in on the news already. "I guess you've heard."

"This is one of the few times I don't even need to ask you to be more specific. How are you holding up?"

"Honestly? I don't know. Nobody's avoiding me or,

on the flip side, fussing over me, so I must look like I'm doing okay."

"I'd say you didn't answer the question, but I feel like you did. How are things between you and Siobhan?"

"I knew her being here was going to be hard, but this? Didn't see it coming." That was an understatement, and he had to actively concentrate on not spilling everything, either verbally or with his face. "I guess we're doing okay, all things considered. I appreciate that she didn't take Oliver and run home that day because being here can't be easy."

Danny nodded. "Showing up to be your friend's maid of honor and having your sister's ex-husband and former in-laws lay claim to your kid? I would have run."

"I'm laying claim to *my* kid," Brian bit out. "Probably."

His brother's eyebrow shot up. "Are you going to try to have the adoption overturned?"

"Not if she doesn't make me do it." His shoulders dropped as he shook his head. "No. That's shock and fear and I don't even know what talking. Siobhan hasn't given me any reason to think she'll keep Oliver from me once the test makes it official, and I certainly don't want to take him away from her."

"So you'll share custody, basically, like if you were a divorced couple with a child."

"Something like that." He wasn't sure why that made him sad. It was the best he could hope for, really. They both knew the kiss had been a mistake, and this was a big reason why. Whatever was between them just made a messy situation messier. "I try not to think about the future too much because there's still the very, very slim possibility it's just a coincidence and he's a dark-haired kid with blue eyes."

"Mom and Gram both said it was like looking at one of us, and it's not as if they were looking for it. It was just there and they couldn't miss it."

"We're holding off on the hard discussions until after the paternity test, obviously, but that's basically a formality as far as everybody's concerned." He sighed. "And then? We'll take it one step at a time, I guess."

Danny chuckled. "The easiest solution might be getting married and then adopting him as your stepson."

"No." If last night had taught him one thing, it was that he and Siobhan could definitely not live in the same house platonically, no matter what they might tell themselves and each other going into an arrangement.

"Why? Then you get divorced, but because you adopted him, you'll do a standard custody agreement, which is essentially your end goal, anyway."

"Again, *no.* There's nothing easy about that. One, we'd all have to live together for at least six months after the wedding before they'd do it, and then we'd have to turn Oliver's life upside down all over again when we split." He paused and blew out a breath. "And two, there would be new paperwork, but that guy's name would still be on the original and I want him erased."

"You've looked into it already, then."

"Of course. Not a lot because we're busy and I'm only using my phone because one of the things we do in the store when we're bored is dig through the computer's search history and give each other a hard time."

"You need to accept that no matter how the paperwork gets accepted, that original will probably still exist. Maybe you just need to keep your eyes on the road ahead and not look in the rearview mirror."

"That's good advice," he said grudgingly.

"I'm offended by how surprised you sound." Danny sighed and looked out the window at the truck and trailer. "Where am I dropping this stuff, anyway?"

"You can drop the trailer in any empty site for now. Most of it isn't getting set up until tomorrow, and we can move the trailer with the tractor when it's time. Rob and Joey were able to do some mowing and trimming because we only got a quick shower and then the sun came out with a vengeance."

"With Dad and Gramps supervising, I imagine."

"Of course." Brian closed the binder he'd been flipping through, and stowed it under the counter. There wasn't any sense in even pretending to work anymore. "How's the writing going?"

"I'd rather talk about the septic system. Or things you've skimmed out of the pool. Or almost anything else."

Brian winced. That didn't sound good. "You were really excited about this one."

"They're all exciting at first. Then the initial burst of inspiration fizzles out and there are still a lot of pages to fill, but you managed to write your way into a giant plot hole you can't figure out how to get out of."

"Maybe a couple of days away from your desk will do you good."

"Maybe." Danny shrugged. "Have you gone up to the restaurant lately?"

He asked the question casually enough, but Brian was pretty sure his older brother's interest in Corinne's Kitchen had more to do with Kenzie than the menu. "I was there with Siobhan and Oliver yesterday. For the popcorn chicken."

"It *is* good popcorn chicken."

Brian narrowed his eyes. "There's no way you didn't already know I went out to lunch with them."

"Yeah, I guess somebody probably mentioned it. But there have been a *lot* of texts in the last few weeks, which you know."

"Sure. I mean, not this week because mostly they're just yelling things to each other across the campground. If you want to ask me about Kenzie, just ask."

Danny crossed his arms, stubbornness setting into his jaw. "Or maybe I was looking for an opening to find out why you and a woman whose name you were cursing a week ago went on a lunch date together."

They stared at each other for a few seconds without speaking. Brian knew Danny wasn't going to admit he was infatuated with Kenzie yet, and he didn't want to talk about Siobhan more than he had to. Especially with Danny, who sometimes seemed a lot more perceptive than his other two brothers. If any of them were going to guess he and Siobhan had gotten up to no good by fairy light, it would be Danny.

"We should get that trailer dropped and the truck parked before the rest of the family decides to *help* and there's an hour-long debate on where to put it," he said finally.

Danny chuckled. "Excellent plan. And then I'm going to meet my maybe-nephew everybody's been talking about."

Chapter Twelve

"Sorry. I'm doing it again, aren't I?"

Siobhan smiled at Danny, who'd definitely been watching Oliver with an intensity she hadn't seen since their first day at the campground. "A little bit."

"It's uncanny. I'm only three years older than Brian and five years older than Rob, but I have some fuzzy memories of them at that age. And there are a ton of pictures, of course." He winced, pressing his palm to his forehead for a moment. "Sorry again. Brian threatened terrible things if we made your stay awkward."

She liked Danny. They'd met for the first time when Brian married Kelly, and he'd gone out of his way to socialize with her and Janelle, as well as the smattering of acquaintances Kelly had lured to the wedding with free food to balance the bride's side of the aisle with the groom's.

"Trust me, day one was probably the most awkward day of my life," she said. "We got past that, but you just got here and, like you said, it *is* uncanny."

"Notice how I timed my arrival for *after* The Annual Kowalski Volleyball Death Match Tournament of Doom," he said, giving her his own version of the endearing Kowalski grin that had blown up her life.

"You'll notice we saved you plenty of potato salad, though."

When he groaned, she laughed and he joined in. Oliver, who was a few feet away, painting a rock with what Terry had assured her were washable paints, laughed with them even though he had no idea what was happening. He just knew laughing with Mommy was fun and made her happy.

Danny pointed at the streaks of green in Oliver's hair. "Not only making the rock into a frog, but himself as well, is dedication to the activity."

"I figure once he's done painting himself green, I'll just dunk him in the pool." As expected, Brian and Rob—who were in conversation not far from them—both turned to face her, and Rob was actually about to say something when she laughed. "I'm kidding."

After his brothers returned to their conversation, Danny gave a low whistle. "You really picked up quick on how to push their buttons."

"It's almost too easy."

They lapsed into silence, watching the rock painting activity. It looked as if it was wrapping up, with the teens and some of the adults already cleaning their brushes. Most of them had chosen to paint flowers, which would be set around the bottom of the rented arch. A few of them had gone rogue, including her son, and painted whatever struck their fancies.

Because it wasn't something she could stop no matter how often she lectured herself, she shifted so Brian was in her peripheral vision. He'd been standing with his brothers Rob and Joey for about ten minutes, with his hands in his pockets. There was something in one of his pockets because she could tell he was fiddling with something. A pocketknife, she'd thought, but now he pulled it out and rubbed his thumb over it.

It was a small gray rock. And after a moment of watching him turning it in his fingers, she realized it was the rock Oliver had given him before running off to play their first day in the campground.

There had been a lot of clothing changes between then and now, which meant it was a treasure he was deliberately keeping, and she had to blink away a sheen of tears.

It had to be so hard for him, falling for a child who might or might not be his. For all of them, actually, but especially for Brian. And yes, even Siobhan had to agree there was *almost* no chance Oliver wasn't his biological son, but until the test was done, there was a very slim chance it was just the worst coincidence of physical features ever.

Siobhan knew that very slim chance her son wasn't Brian's was the best case scenario for her. She and Oliver would be free to resume the life they'd been living and this would just be a memory of a strange vacation she didn't want to revisit. But she couldn't wish that kind of heartbreak on Brian or his family. Even though he'd only known Oliver for a few days, he would be devastated.

They'd managed to avoid being alone for even a second today, and moving through different family conversations so they were always talking to other people was a dance they'd mastered the steps to.

And it held for the remainder of the evening when Brian was tasked with helping move the rocks to the makeshift table in the garage they'd made with a sheet of plywood across two sawhorses. Because Oliver had gotten as much paint on himself as he had the rock, she had a good reason to excuse them to get cleaned up.

When they reached the site, she had him sit on the step while she got the worst of the paint off with a cloth and plain water. Washable or not, she didn't want him leaving smears and handprints all over the interior.

By the time she scrubbed all of the green paint off of Oliver and then off of herself and then out of the shower in the camper that didn't belong to her, Siobhan was exhausted. Luckily, Oliver was worn down, as well, and he didn't seem the least bit interested in getting re-dressed and going back outside.

"Where's my frog?" he asked once they were in pajamas.

"It's going to dry in the garage while you're sleeping, and then they'll put a clear spray on it to keep the paint safe."

"Then I can have it back?"

"Yes. You'll get to bring your froggy home with you."

He rubbed his eyes, and she wondered if he'd make it through a single story tonight. "Home?"

Siobhan ran her hand over his dark hair. "We'll sleep here three more times, and then we'll go home and you can show your froggy to Auntie Robin."

He grinned. "And go to school?"

"You can probably bring it to school. We'll see." Siobhan knew her life was made immeasurably easier by the fact that Oliver loved his daycare program. He wanted to share everything with his teachers and friends, but it was a big rock. "Which book should we read tonight?"

"Beep beep!" Oliver yelled, grabbing the book out of the pile, and heading for the bed.

Siobhan knew going to bed early meant getting up early, but Oliver was going to drop into sleep one way or another. He might as well be in bed for the night when it happened.

Sure enough, it was barely full light when Siobhan sipped her coffee the next morning, listening to her very excited son talking about his frog rock. And she tried not to think about Brian running his thumb over the small rock he kept in his pocket.

Hours later, when breakfast was over, the men headed out with the ATVs and side-by-sides for a day on the trails. Today was serving as the bachelor and bachelorette parties, with the men taking the groom out into the woods, apparently.

For most of the women, the fact that the men would be gone all day was enough of a party, but there were some fun activities planned. Robin had helped Siobhan pull together a few basic bachelorette party games last-minute, and with a few family traditions and an impressive mimosa pitcher added in, it promised to be a good day.

"We're definitely playing Scrabble," Terry announced when they were all gathered together with nothing to do but enjoy themselves while Cat played with the younger kids on the playground.

Siobhan looked at Steph, wondering what her friend's reaction would be to playing a board game at her bachelorette party, but judging by the grin and bouncing on her toes, she was excited about it.

That didn't make any sense to Siobhan, but she had to admit a bachelorette party probably landed differently when your mother and grandmother were in attendance. And when it came to word games, Siobhan usually crushed her competition, so she was in.

"Wait," she said, holding up her hand. "Do you mean *actual* Scrabble? Or is this some kind of Kowalski-fied

Scrabble of Doom where we use a slingshot to pelt each other with letter tiles and have to spell out words with the ones we can catch before they take our eyes out?"

They all stared at her for a minute, and then Emma laughed. "That actually sounds super fun. We should try that some year."

Siobhan held up her hands. "Did you miss the part where they take your eyes out?"

"We'd wear safety glasses, of course."

"It's the board game," Steph said.

Keri nodded. "The actual game, with standard Scrabble scoring, along with a bonus double word score for any word you shouldn't say in front of the kids. Any if there's a word you can't bring yourself to say out loud at all, even if there aren't any kids nearby, you get a bonus triple word score. We've changed it a bit, though, as the kids got older, and you also get a bonus triple if it's a word Gram would smack you with a wooden spoon for saying in front of her."

Siobhan nodded, considering. "Does she *actually* hit us with a wooden spoon?"

They all laughed when Mary very slowly reached down and adjusted the tote bag on the ground next to her, folding over the top so nobody could see inside of it. Siobhan doubted she actually had a wooden spoon in there— though she wouldn't have bet against it—but she loved the woman's sense of humor.

"Oh, we do have one somewhat coed activity, too," Siobhan added. "Low risk of personal injury, I think, though I make no promises because…well, you know. And I'm not going to tell you what it is, but just so you know to leave a time slot."

It was a game Robin had suggested, but Siobhan hadn't

been sure how it would go over with people she hadn't met. But she'd gotten to know the Kowalski family pretty well and they were exactly the right players, so she'd mentioned it to her counterpart, the best man. Wes had immediately been on board, but they were both a little out of their element as far as supplies, so they had to get Brian involved. When she'd explained it to him, he'd laughed and said they would absolutely make it happen.

"I'm intrigued," Steph said, leaning forward. "Can we get a hint?"

"Nope."

"When are we doing it?"

Siobhan laughed. "Not yet, since the guys aren't even back yet. And based on the last time they went riding, they'll probably need some time to clean up. So approximately…later. Brian will text me when they're ready."

"So Scrabble first, then," Lisa said.

"More mimosas first," Keri corrected. "*Then* we play Scrabble. I found a website that taught me lots of new naughty words and my spam ads have taken quite a turn, so I intend to win."

"This is the most ridiculous thing we've ever done," Danny grumbled before blowing out a breath that made the toilet paper hanging in his face quiver.

"You look radiant," Rob said as he snapped photos as fast as his camera's shutter could fire.

"Stop fidgeting," Joey ordered, trying to get Danny's veil fixed.

The toilet paper bride pageant had been Siobhan's idea, but she didn't exactly have to twist Brian's arm to get him on board. Especially since the two of them, as the hosts of the pageant, were excluded from participation. Technically Wes should be hosting, as the best man and brother of the groom, but he was a quieter introvert type and he'd privately told Kyle and Brian that he'd have a much better time if the Kowalski brothers stepped in for leading the festivities.

Since Siobhan had come to Brian with this party game, he'd called dibs.

Several heated rounds of Rock, Paper, Scissors had Kyle and Danny as brides for Team Groom. And Steph and Amber—sister-in-law of the groom—were representing Team Bride. The goal was to fashion wedding gown finery from toilet paper, and the most fashionable bride would win.

"Easy," Rob cautioned Joey. "You're going to rip it again."

"Whose idea was one-ply?" Kyle asked. "If I was in charge, I would have sprung for two-ply."

Danny snorted. "You can't be in charge because you're the groom. And we got one-ply because we needed a lot of it, and this was the cheapest we could find at the store after Brian here thought he'd raid the campground supply."

"You make us buy it in bulk," Rob pointed out.

Danny started to turn his head, but a growl from Joey stopped him. "It's all fun and games until we run out of toilet paper and our campers are flushing who knows what down the toilets."

"Okay." Joey backed away from Danny. "Are we done?"

Brian had to admit they'd done a good job. Kyle's looked more like a hula skirt than a gown on the bottom and they'd wrapped the toilet paper around his torso like bandages for a bodice.

Danny's flowed from where the ends had been tucked into the neck of his T-shirt, with a sash tied just below his chest to hold it all in place. He had a traditional veil, though they'd finally given up on covering his face.

"We're done. Team Bride?"

"We're ready," Kevin called back from the other side of the tarp they'd strung to divide the store into two "dressing rooms."

"Texting Siobhan now," Brian said.

I hope you're ready because they're going to sweat and we'll have a ton of papier-mâché on our hands.

Ready. I'll count to ten and start the music.

Even though he was in the back, trying to keep Stella from grabbing at the trailing toilet paper, he heard the women's laughter and knew the men had been spotted. He wasn't surprised the chosen brides threw themselves into their roles, walking regally across the grass to the tinny rendition of "Here Comes the Bride" coming from Siobhan's phone.

The women—who were wound up from a lot of mimosas and a rousing round of dirty Scrabble, based on the shrieks of laughter coming from that end of the grass—clapped and cheered throughout the pageant.

It was all fun and games until somebody pointed out Steph's headpiece was anchored with rolled up paper towels and not toilet paper. The accusations of cheating got heated, somebody wearing a toilet paper gown got too close to the campfire, and *whoosh*, they segued straight into a game of Stop, Drop and Roll.

Brian was pretty sure the flash fire was fully out by the time his uncle Joe tossed the contents of the water dispenser from the picnic table onto them, but he didn't begrudge anybody a good time. If he could have gotten to the hose in time, he might have joined in the fun.

In the aftermath, when their stomachs ached from laughing and the brides were a slightly charred sodden mess, it was Danny who asked the question. "So who won?"

More debate and laughter ensued, while everybody voted. Somehow it came down to a tie between Danny and Amber and, once again, it fell to Siobhan to vote.

"Nope," she said, holding up her hands. "I was one of the emcees, so I don't get a vote. I think it's just a tie."

"A tie?" several people echoed at the same time, and Brian chuckled at Siobhan's expression. His family did win and lose, but not so much with draw.

"I think I should get an extra point for not setting myself on fire," Amber pointed out.

Danny snorted. "I should get the point because I was more entertaining."

"There *was* a lot of screaming, which your family seems to enjoy," Siobhan said. "And you whipped that T-shirt off so fast, you were practically a stripper, which was one thing this bachelorette party *didn't* have."

They all laughed again, and Brian knew Danny being the stripper at Steph's bachelorette party was already part of the Kowalski family lore. Then Siobhan turned to face him and his breath caught. She was so beautiful when she was laughing, her eyes sparkling with mischievous amusement.

How could he ever have thought this woman was cold?

The win finally went to Team Bride after a tiebreaking round of Rock, Paper, Scissors, and then Johnny somehow convinced Nora and Oliver that a race to pick up toilet paper would be the most fun game ever. They rushed over from the playground and started gathering it up.

"We could have reused some of that," Leo grumbled.

Mary rolled her eyes. "He saw some show years ago, and the husband had the wife buy two-ply toilet paper, unroll it, peel the layers apart, and then reroll that into two rolls. He looked over at me and opened his mouth, and I'm not sure what my expression was doing, but he snapped his mouth shut and changed the channel pretty quick."

"Then that guy probably used twice as much of the one-ply rolls, making the entire thing a waste of his wife's time with no money saved," Lisa said, and then everybody started talking about the financial aspects of toilet paper.

Brian moved closer to Siobhan, who was hovering to make sure Oliver didn't get too close to the fire. "It was a fun game. I'm sorry it went sideways like that."

"Oh, it went about like I suspected it would." She chuckled. "Maybe not the fire, I guess. That was an unexpected twist."

Once the toilet paper was cleaned up, the two parties blended into one. There was the usual storytelling and laughter. Conversational groups changing as people got up to refill their mimosa glasses, grab another beer or get a snack. At one point, Brian and Steph made eye contact, and the smile she gave him made all the headaches from the planning and group texts worth it. She was beaming, and as long as tomorrow went off without a hitch, he and his brothers would have pulled off the wedding of her dreams.

When he spotted Ellie ushering Nora and Oliver into the tots' tent with water bottles and coloring books, he looked over at Siobhan. She looked uncertain for a moment, as if she thought she might take Oliver inside, but then Steph said something and she laughed, relaxing into her seat.

From that moment on, Brian's body felt as if it was on high alert. Most likely, Oliver was going to fall asleep in that tent and Siobhan was going to need help carrying him to her camper again. The boy would be sound asleep. Brian had a few beers in him. She'd had a few mimosas.

They'd be alone.

It was going to be very, very hard not to kiss her. *Very* hard.

Two hours later, when Nora stumbled sleepily out of the tent looking for her mom, Siobhan stood and he knew it was time. He pushed out of his chair, and she smiled at him as they approached the little tent.

"I tried to balance mimosas with food and water," she whispered. "But at some point we started running low on juice and the ratio was adjusted."

He chuckled. "Funny how the Kowalski women can calculate the exact amount of peanut butter the entire family needs to get through a week at camp, but they can never bring enough mixer for the alcohol."

She giggled and then slapped her hand over her mouth. "Shh."

He pushed aside the netting and smiled at Oliver, who was sound asleep with a blue crayon in his hand. It took some maneuvering, but Brian got the crayons into the cup and closed the coloring book before lifting Oliver out of the tent.

He was able to concentrate on not tripping over rocks in the dirt road, but the click of Siobhan closing the door behind them clanged like alarm bells in his mind.

There was no way he could kiss her again, he reminded himself as he laid Oliver down. He'd told her it wouldn't happen again. Right now, Oliver waking up and demanding Siobhan's attention would be the best case scenario.

But of course he didn't. The kid was out like a light.

When he turned, Siobhan was leaning against the counter by the door. The heat in her eyes when she smiled did nothing to cool him off, and he wasn't sure he was capable of getting past her without touching her.

Especially when she pushed away from the counter and took a step toward him, holding up her index finger. "Just one more."

"We both agreed it wouldn't happen again," he pointed out, using every last scrap of willpower he could summon.

"Then we can both agree it'll happen just one more time." And then she hooked her finger in the neck of his tee and tugged.

He was lost.

When their mouths collided, he wasn't sure which of them moaned, but he felt it through his entire body. The fingertips of one of her hands bit into his upper arm while she slid her other hand up the nape of his neck. When her fingers tangled in his hair, he groaned and deepened the kiss.

It was gripping her hips and pulling her hard to his body, making her gasp against his lips, that broke through the hunger and reminded him this was just a kiss. One more kiss, and nothing else.

With a reluctance he hoped she could feel, he released her hips. Then, pressing his hand to her cheek, he planted a final quick kiss to her mouth. Then more *absolutely the last* final kiss.

"I have to go," he whispered, and his voice was so hoarse, they were barely words.

"I know. I wish…"

With every fiber of his being, Brian wanted her to finish that sentence, but he knew pushing her would only end in more frustration for both of them. Their situation was what it was.

He also knew some of the nosier members of his family were probably still sitting by the campfire, counting how many minutes he was inside Siobhan's camper. They'd given his family more than enough to talk about this week already.

"Good night, Siobhan," he said, moving past her.

"Brian?" When he turned back, she gave him a grin that was going to keep him up half the night. "Sweet dreams."

Chapter Thirteen

The one thing no number of group chat text messages or checked-off tasks on lists could control was the weather, so Brian couldn't have been happier to wake on Monday morning to a gorgeous August day.

According to the forecast, which had a history of being close but not exact for their location, it would be warm and sunny, but not humid enough to trigger a late-afternoon thunderstorm. It looked as though that was going to hold true, and he knew he wasn't the only one breathing a sigh of relief.

Of course, there was a lot left to do between now and the vows, including the rest of the guest list arriving from Maine. Also, setting up the arch and wrapping it with the vines and flowers that had been made for it. The chairs needed to be set up.

"You're making that growling sound again," Rob said, and Brian spun, not realizing his brother had come into the kitchen.

Usually Rob and Hannah stayed in a camper on site twenty-nine, leaving Brian and Stella alone in the house unless Joey or Danny showed up to help for a weekend. But since Joey had his wife and daughter with him, they were staying in the camper, and Rob and Hannah had moved into the house. If Danny hadn't begged for the pull-out sofa in their parents' RV, he'd be sleeping on the lumpy couch.

"Last time you growled like that, it was because Siobhan would be showing up," Rob continued. "Just a wild guess, but this one's not about her. Or, if it is, maybe for a different reason?"

His brother was fishing, and it wasn't subtle. "Just thinking about all the stuff on the to-do list today, and how hard it's going to be to keep everybody on task when the cousins from Maine start rolling in."

"I think we'll all be glad when this week is over."

No.

The word surprised Brian, and he was thankful he didn't say it out loud. But it felt true. He wasn't going to be glad when this week was over because everything would change.

He recognized that he, Siobhan and Oliver were in something of a bubble right now, removed from real life. Tomorrow that bubble was going to pop and they were going to have to learn how to navigate the situation they'd found themselves in all over again.

With one hundred percent less kissing, he reminded himself, and he must have growled again because Stella bumped his leg, looking for pets. He scratched her head, hitting the sweet spot behind her ears, and let it soothe away his aggravations of the morning.

It was going to be a good day.

Two hours later, it had become a mantra he repeated to himself through clenched teeth. *It's going to be a good day, dammit.*

The family from Maine had arrived and, as expected, the schedule went out the window. While there were more hands to help, all of the greetings and the lightning rounds of catch-up had to be done.

Of his dad's cousins from Maine, Sean stayed in New Hampshire after he met Emma, and Ryan lived in Massachusetts with his wife, Lauren. The rest were still in Maine. Ryan and Lauren's son, Nick, was about Brian's age, he thought, but he wasn't able to make it. The rest of the cousins had teens ranging from thirteen to fifteen. Mitch and Paige brought Sarah and Charlotte. Liz, the only female cousin on that side, and Drew had fourteen-year-old Jackson, and Josh and Katie brought Nate and Bella with them. Rosie, who'd always run the Northern Star Lodge and had practically raised the Kowalski kids there and was tight with Mary, had brought her husband, Andy. She'd always been an honorary aunt. Other than that, Brian had given up trying to keep everybody straight and they were just collectively the family from Maine.

Luckily, Siobhan was spared the awkwardness of an entire new pack of Kowalskis meeting Oliver. He'd been handed over to Ellie and Nora while Siobhan focused on getting the bride ready for her big day. And Brian actually overheard his mother start the whispering to hold off on letting Steph know they'd all arrived until they'd all had their chance to remark that yes, it was so clearly obvious the little boy was one of them.

Brian finally made his way to Rob. "If we're going to have time to shower and change so we don't show up all sweaty in shorts and T-shirts, we need to get going on setting stuff up."

"I'll give Mom and Gram the heads-up to start moving social hour over to Gram's site. I know she's got lemonade and a light lunch in the works to perk them up after the long drive, plus they can socialize out of our way."

Once the majority of the family was lured away by snacks, Brian hooked the tractor to the trailer and pulled it over alongside the grassy area they'd chosen for the ceremony. They'd had to relocate some of the playground equipment and Rob would have to digitally remove a power line from some of the photos, but the background beyond the arch would be the pond and trees.

Steph and Kyle had opted out of bride-side and groom-side seating. For one, her family vastly outnumbered his. But also they just didn't want to start their life as a married couple with a vibe of family separation. They still left an aisle for Steph to walk down, but the only reserved seating was the front row, for parents and grandparents, as well as one chair that would hold a photo of Kyle's parents together and a single rose.

They got the arch up so Hannah, Emma and Keri could decorate it with the vines and flowers, and then they managed to move the entire thing three times without breaking or knocking the flowers off as Rob adjusted and readjusted the angle for photos. Brian was about to bodily drag his brother to the edge of the pond and shove him in when he declared it good.

They didn't want to ask too much of the guys who'd come over from Maine, since they'd arrived already dressed in their summer outdoor casual wedding attire, but Brian and his brothers needed a hand with the massive white canopy they'd rented. They were erecting it a ways behind the chairs because Steph wanted the open air ceremony. But they'd not only needed a backup plan for rain, they'd also want the shade during the reception. With the rain panels down on the side facing the arch, it also offered a place for Steph to enter from, and they could remove them later.

By the time they finished, they were already running late for getting dressed, but Brian took a moment to admire the culmination of so much planning and work, and so many text messages. Fingering the smooth rock in his pocket, he looked at the venue they'd made for his cousin's wedding and felt a rush of pride.

It was simple without being plain. Elegant without being fussy. A perfect backdrop for the couple who'd shared their first kiss here. It was everything Steph wanted, and they'd actually pulled it off.

Movement in his peripheral vision made him turn in time to see Ellie and Nora, with Oliver between them holding their hands, turn the corner toward the camper Joey and Ellie were using. She was probably hoping he'd take a quick nap, Brian thought. Or at least have some quiet time before the wedding started.

"You okay?" Danny asked, having appeared at his side at some point while he was watching Oliver. "You look… off."

He chuckled. "I look like I've been sweating my ass off and now I have to go put on a shirt with buttons. You know I hate those."

"Unless they're flannel."

"Good point."

"But you're okay?"

"Yeah. I think putting all this together kept me distracted from the fact that the last wedding I attended was my own. I don't love thinking about that, especially…" Brian had decided to respect the concern in his older brother's voice by being honest, but maybe not *that* honest. He didn't want to talk about Siobhan. "There's Oliver, which is messy and brings up that time, too. There's a lot going on, but nothing *bad*, you know?"

"That's understandable. As long as you're good." Danny blew out a breath. "You should shower, though."

They started walking toward the house together, and Danny slapped his arm. "Good call on vetoing Stella being the ring bearer, by the way. Brianna wanted to see if she'd hold the ring pillow and it was a shredded mess of satin and stuffing before she could get it back."

Brian laughed. "Stuffed toys have about a thirty-second lifespan around here. Please tell me the rings weren't tied to it."

"No, but there was a panicked moment when we weren't sure and we thought the ceremony might have to be pushed back while we followed your dog around with a poop bag and rubber gloves."

"I guess that explains why I heard everybody yelling *not it* about twenty minutes ago?"

Danny chuckled. "Stella's probably one of the most beloved dogs this family's ever known, but in that moment she was undeniably *Brian's dog.*"

"Thank goodness we don't have a full glam squad because there are no outlets in this cabin at all," Terry said, looking around with a scowl on her face.

Siobhan smiled because there actually *were* outlets in the cabin. There just weren't very many. But she wasn't about to correct the mother of the bride when she was clearly venting about the electrical situation to keep from crying.

Steph's dress was still hanging on the rack in the corner, and the bride herself was pacing the floor of the cabin so intensely, Siobhan had finally given up and sat on the edge of the bed. If she tried to keep up with her friend's nerves, she'd be worn out before the ceremony even started.

"You talked to Dad, right?" Steph asked, pausing to stare at her mother for a few seconds. "He's not going to try to be funny or anything, right? If he pretends to trip going down the aisle or refuses to give me away or something, it won't be funny."

"Yes, honey, I did. But I didn't need to because I know it doesn't always look like this family takes anything seriously, but this is the most special day of your life and every single person here is one hundred percent dedicated to making it beautiful for you."

"Oh. Okay, I know that." She blew out a breath and resumed pacing. "Why am I nervous?"

Siobhan smiled. "Because we started getting ready too early and you've had too much time to pace around making up things to be nervous about."

"Have a peanut butter and jelly sandwich," Terry said. "There are some already made and cut in that insulated bag by the door."

Siobhan already knew from the days they'd spent together that Steph's favorite comfort food did, in fact, make her friend feel better, so she didn't give her a chance to say no. She pulled a sandwich out of the bag and handed it to Steph. Then, after a nod from Terry, she handed her one before taking another for herself.

"Did they send you a picture?" Steph asked her mom after she'd eaten half the sandwich. "They hadn't finished setting up when I went down to say hi to everybody who got here today. Did they get it done?"

"Nobody sent me a picture, but it's done and Gram says it's perfect."

Steph beamed. "If Gram says it's perfect, it must be."

"When I went down to check on Oliver, Ellie said it's beautiful," Siobhan added.

Considering how hard they'd worked on the fairy lights just to make the walk from the lower part of the campground to the cabin beautiful, Siobhan had no doubt they'd made the ceremony site just as magical.

Of course, thinking about the fairy lights made her think about kissing Brian. Her cheeks heated and when Steph cocked a questioning eyebrow at her, she took a huge bite of her sandwich, filling her mouth with sticky peanut butter and jelly.

"How was Oliver doing?" Steph asked, thankfully letting her off the hook. "I know he hasn't gotten to see you a lot today."

She swallowed the lump of sandwich and took a swig of water before answering. "He's doing great. He's pretty happy as long as he's with Nora, and Ellie's been an absolute dream with him. I can't thank her enough for watching over him like she has."

"Well, he's…" Terry let the sentence fade away, and Siobhan knew she'd been about to say Oliver was family. "Such a sweet boy. He's so happy and smart, and we've all enjoyed spending time with him."

"Thank you." Siobhan looked at Steph, wrinkling her nose. "I can't absolutely guarantee he won't try to get to me while I'm standing next to you, though."

"He can if he wants to. There's a big difference between Oliver wanting to be with you and somebody in my family doing something embarrassing." She licked jelly off her thumb and smiled—a genuinely happy and content smile. "I don't know why I even worried. No matter what happens, I'm marrying my true love today surrounded by my ridiculous but amazing family I adore, with you by my side."

Terry's phone chimed, and she popped the last bite of her sandwich in her mouth before reading the message. "The officiant just arrived. The men are in the house to get dressed. Everything's in place."

"Now it's time to get ready," Siobhan said.

It didn't take long. Because it was an outdoor wedding in August, their makeup was simple—tinted moisturizer with lip gloss and waterproof mascara. Anything more would probably melt down their faces by halfway through the reception and nobody wanted those pictures.

Also simple was their hair. Steph's thick, dark hair was pulled into a ponytail, which they looped through itself to make a little pocket. Terry tucked some daisies and baby's breath into that space—artificial so they wouldn't wilt and/or attract insects—and pinned them in place. Siobhan's hair was pulled back in a simple ponytail.

Once they'd put on their dresses, all that remained were the shoes. Siobhan wore ballet flats that complemented the floral pattern of her dress. And after many discussions within the family about high heels and grass, and the feasibility of some kind of platform or carpet, Steph had found cute summer flats with hand-painted daisies to match the ones in her hair and bouquet.

The bouquet was currently waiting in a vase—fresh daisies, white roses and baby's breath. And Emma had made a smaller version from artificial ones. Terry had told Siobhan earlier the plan was to press and save the real bouquet and toss the artificial one, which Siobhan would walk down the aisle with, during the reception.

"Okay," Terry said, clearly trying to hold back tears as

she took a photo of Siobhan doing a final fiddling with Steph's hair. "Do you have the ring?"

Siobhan nodded and put her hands in her pocket to pull out the ring box. "I do, because my dress has *pockets.*"

"So jealous," Steph said. "Mine doesn't."

"It's my job to hold all your stuff anyway."

"I have no stuff." She frowned. "Am I supposed to have stuff?"

"It's not like you need your car keys," Siobhan said. "I'll take your lip gloss for touchups, though."

"The car's coming around now," Terry said.

The plan was for Paige to pick them up in her car—one of the few vehicles in the campground that wasn't an SUV or truck—and drive them around to the canopy. Once they were in place, the men would walk down from the house. When everybody was ready, Johnny would start the music.

Steph took a deep breath, clasping Siobhan's hands. "Okay. Wedding of Doom time. Let's do this."

Chapter Fourteen

Brian was thankful everybody was looking at the maid of honor when she stepped out from between the white panels—being held open by Jackson and Nate—because he was pretty sure everything he felt when he set eyes on her would show on his face.

And he couldn't stop it because she took his breath away.

The dress hugged her beautifully, showing off skin that was sun-kissed from days outside, despite the copious amounts of sunscreen he'd suffered through watching her rub into that skin. Her hair had been in a messy and wispy ponytail more often than not, but this ponytail was smooth and sleek, showing off the curve of her neck and the small pearls gracing her earlobes.

But it was her expression—soft and joyful—that captivated him as she slowly made her way between the chairs.

"Mommy looks pretty," Oliver declared from his perch on Leo's lap. Her cheeks flushed a deep pink, but Brian agreed with the boy wholeheartedly.

Once she'd taken her place in front of the officiant, opposite Kyle and Wes, and Johnny switched the music to the orchestral piece Steph had chosen, he was forced to tear his gaze away from her to watch the bride. There was a rustle as everybody stood, and then the boys parted the curtains again so Evan could escort his daughter to the arch.

Steph was beautiful today, as well, with tears glistening in her eyes as she made her way to the groom. Brian basked in his cousin's emotions, but once she'd handed her bouquet to Siobhan and Evan had taken his seat next to Terry, his gaze was drawn straight back to the maid of honor.

He'd seen her standing next to a bride before, and he couldn't stop the memories of the first time from flooding his mind. Siobhan had been expressionless the day she served as Kelly's maid of honor. She'd smiled a few times through the day of course, managing to fake being happy for the bride and groom. But when all eyes were on Kelly and Brian, and he could see her over his bride's shoulder, her face had been carefully and deliberately blank.

Her face wasn't blank today. Her smile never dimmed, even when she had to discreetly dab tears from her cheeks. Watching her as she watched Steph say her vows, he finally understood what Siobhan had meant before. Her reservations about him marrying Kelly hadn't been about him. The coldness had come from her complicated emotions regarding her sister and an inability to throw herself into the joy of a wedding she knew shouldn't be happening.

Shaking off the unpleasant memories that had no place here, he watched Steph and Kyle exchange rings. There were more words and happy tears, with a lot of sniffling in the audience, and then—finally—the groom could kiss his bride.

Brian joined everybody else in standing as the newly joined husband and wife made their way down the aisle together. And then it was Siobhan's turn, on Wes's arm. She blew a kiss to Oliver, who had been so well-behaved through what must have seemed to him to be the boring parts.

Then her gaze landed on Brian and she gave him a smile that warmed him to his core. Being so close to Siobhan while she was wearing that dress and they were in front of literally his entire family was going to make for a very long day.

After everybody filtered through a makeshift receiving line, the bride and groom walked to the edge of the pond alone. It gave the couple a few minutes together to just breathe, and Rob had switched to a zoom lens—with Steph's blessing—to get some sweet shots without intruding on their moment.

While that happened, the guys took the rain panels off of the pavilion canopy. Everybody grabbed a chair, so shifting them into casual groupings in the shade didn't take long. Then Brian grabbed his brothers and they moved the flowered arch to a spot centered behind the bride and groom's chairs at the head table.

The head table, of course, being the same rugged plywood across the sawhorses they'd used for drying the rocks, but now with a white fabric tablecloth hiding it. The edges were weighted down with the flower rocks they'd painted.

And one frog, Brian thought with a smile.

Rather than spacing things out over the course of a typical reception, they'd be front-loading the wedding-related things so the family from Maine could head home. It was a long drive to make twice in one day, and in appreciation, Steph and Kyle wanted to make sure they didn't miss anything fun.

There would be toasts and then the cake first. When tinkering with the schedule, nobody had objected to eating dessert first. Plus, if things ran long, the Maine crowd could take finger sandwiches for the road, but eating wedding cake while driving was messy.

Brian missed the toasts while he and Joey went to retrieve some of the camp chairs leaning against his grandparents' RV. Once the formalities were over, they'd set them out because rented folding chairs got very uncomfortable after a while. He did catch the very end of Siobhan's, though, when Steph hugged her maid of honor and then they wiped away each other's tears.

More photos were taken. The cake was cut. More photos. Brianna and Lily, Kevin and Beth's teenage daughter, took charge of serving the slices. More photos. Laughter when Siobhan bent down to talk to Oliver and he cupped her face in his hands to tell her she was pretty, leaving smears of frosting on her cheeks.

And Brian did his best not to watch her. Not to watch Oliver. To not even think about them because that shutter sound was constant and he didn't want Steph's wedding album to be a highlight reel of Brian's yearning.

After the cake plates were cleared and the family had settled into mingling and chatting—which was something that could go on for hours—Steph clapped her hands. "I'm going to toss the bouquet now!"

She led the way to the open grassy area next to the tent, gesturing for everybody to come along. The younger girls were excited, jockeying for front row positions even though it would be at least a decade before their turns came.

A look passed between Steph and Siobhan, and Brian felt as though a boulder had been dropped into the pit of his stomach. He knew his cousin, and something in her expression told him she was teasing Siobhan. And when her gaze flicked to him, the big lump of dread did a slow roll. Whether Siobhan had said something—she was Steph's maid of honor, after all, so they were close—or Steph was fishing, that bouquet was going to her and it was about him.

Siobhan was shaking her head, and Brian thought he heard her say Oliver's name as she looked around. Unfortunately, her son was happily ensconced on Ellie's lap and unavailable to act as a human shield against tossed flowers.

Terry clapped her hands. "Is everybody ready? Wait, Siobhan, get in there. And Hannah, Rob hasn't gotten you to the altar yet, so you get in there, too."

There weren't a lot of single ladies in the group, and Brian saw the wink Steph gave Siobhan before she turned around. He also saw another quick shake of Siobhan's head, and the way she was trying to fade backward without attracting attention. She clearly didn't want to be in that kind of spotlight, but there was nothing she could do without bringing the mood down.

So he'd handle it himself, Brian decided. As Steph lowered the bouquet in front of her, he snapped his fingers. The sound was mostly drowned out by the buzz of excitement in the crowd, but Stella heard it and snapped to attention.

Brian watched and, at just the right second, made his move. "Catch."

The bouquet was the only thing being thrown, and it was arcing high in Siobhan's direction. Stella sprinted through the women and launched herself, snatching the bouquet out of the air as if it was her favorite stick.

And the crowd went wild.

* * *

Siobhan laughed and backed away as the bouquet toss turned into a melee. The men and a few of the women were howling with laughter, while the rest of them were screeching at the dog who'd saved her from being Steph's target in this ridiculous wedding tradition.

Maybe because her senses refused to ignore the man, she'd heard Brian's quietly spoken command to his dog, and as the dog raced around playing keep away with the flowers, she turned to look at him over her shoulder.

"Dogs, am I right?" he mouthed with a shrug, and then he winked.

Then Stella pivoted and for a moment she thought the dog was going to blow everything by returning the prize to her human. But a young female voice rose above the rest. "Stella, wanna treat?"

The dog veered off to Lily, dropping the flowers at her feet in exchange for an unfrosted sugar cookie Brian's cousin must have snatched off the dessert table. She grabbed the bouquet and raised it over her head. "I win!"

Brianna laughed at her. "You know that means you're next to get married, right?"

"I don't think so," Kevin growled. "She's nineteen."

"Ew." Lily tossed the bouquet to Hannah, who probably *would* be the next to go down the aisle. "I just wanted to win."

Siobhan laughed with the others, relieved that *she* wasn't in the spotlight as the next bride-to-be. She trusted Steph to keep her suspicions about Siobhan and Brian to herself as a rule, but that would have been a lot of temptation. And there was champagne in the mix.

There was a short break in the festivities, and Siobhan took Oliver back to their camper. She freshened him up and gave him a few quiet minutes with a book. Then she touched up her light makeup and made sure her hair still looked okay. They'd be doing family photos soon, and she guessed she'd be roped into some of them as part of the bridal party. Most of them she could sit out, but as the maid of honor, she needed to get out there and make sure Steph was touched up—especially since she had her lip gloss in her pocket.

There were so many photos, going well beyond the wedding party. There were family photos in every configuration. Some with all of the cousins together. Some of grandkids. She and Oliver were in several of them because she was the maid of honor.

Then Leo and Mary sat side by side in chairs. Joe, Terry, Mike and Kevin stood spaced out behind them, and then Joey, Danny, Brian, Bobby, Brianna, Steph, Lily and Gage all squeezed in between. Nora stood next to Mary's chair. There were no spouses in this one. Just, thanks to Nora coming into the family, four generations.

She caught the sad look Mary sent Oliver's way before Rob called for their attention, and the emotions in the older woman's eyes hit her hard. In Mary's heart, there was a great-grandchild missing from the photo and nobody knew what the future held. They might never get this moment back. And asking Siobhan might put her in an awkward spot, so they weren't going to do it because Brian had asked them not to.

There was a good chance these were her son's great-grandparents and that already meant something now, but someday a photograph would mean everything.

Siobhan waited, uncertain, while Rob took several shots of the family. Then, when he started to lower his camera, she stepped forward. "Maybe one more? You know, just in case."

Before she could lose her nerve, she walked over and set Oliver on Leo's lap. She smoothed the boy's hair the best she could, though there wasn't much she could do about it. As she started to move away, Leo took her hand and squeezed it for a few seconds, clearing his throat. She smiled at him and then at Mary, who was blinking away the moisture in her eyes, before backing out of the picture.

Because she was standing near Rob, she could hear the shutter go off, so she knew in the first shot, Brian was looking at Oliver, his lips curved into a warm smile. The second time, he was looking at her with warmth and gratitude shining in his eyes. Then he shifted his attention to the camera and Rob fired off a few more shots.

Once Rob announced he'd gotten every shot he could possibly think of, Siobhan started to move, but Brian was already there—lifting Oliver into his arms and talking to his grandparents for a moment. Then they headed for her.

Siobhan's heart cracked at the sight of the two of them. Oliver looked so much like Brian, and the two of them smiling and talking to each other about something was almost too much for her to bear without crumpling into an emotional heap on the grass.

But Oliver grinned and kicked at Brian to be put down so he could run to his mom. "I said cheese, Mommy."

"I heard you. You did a great smile, honey."

"Thank you for that," Brian said. Then he paused to clear his throat. "It meant…"

"You're welcome," she said, because he wasn't going to get through explaining what it meant to his family without choking up. "If…after, you know, I'd love copies for Oliver's room."

"Of course." He blew out a breath. "The family going back to Maine will start leaving soon, so I should go wander around and make sure I say goodbye to all of them."

"The ones that are staying to drive the campers back tomorrow," she said before he could walk away. "Did you find places for all of them to sleep? The dinette in mine breaks down if somebody needs a bed."

When heat flared in his eyes, she came to the same realization he apparently did in that moment—maybe Oliver could camp out on the dinette, freeing up room in Siobhan's bed for Brian, and his bed in the house for somebody else—and her body responded in kind. A tangled, sweaty goodbye on their final night together, something deep inside of her seemed to whisper.

His ears turned as pink as her cheeks felt, and then he shoved his hands in his pockets and rocked back on his heels. "I appreciate that, but we got it sorted. It took a lot of sticky notes and whoever got stuck with the couch is going to feel it tomorrow, but we're good."

"It's time to dance," Steph yelled over the buzz of conversations around her, and everybody groaned. "Oh, no, we're dancing. You all nixed my wedding karaoke idea, so you're going to dance instead."

"The farmer across the street told us that the last time we did a family karaoke night here, all his cows dried up for like two days and he had no milk."

"You're lying."

Joey shrugged. "That's what he said. I didn't ask the cows personally, though."

"Hopefully the cows can't see this far," Rob said. "If they see Brian dancing, they might never give milk again."

A memory flashed through Siobhan's mind of Brian dancing with Kelly to a slow, romantic ballad shortly after they vowed to be man and wife until death did they part. That part didn't work out so well, but she couldn't forget the way he'd looked at her sister that night. He'd been a man so utterly in love, it made her stomach hurt to think of it now.

Of course, Brian chose that moment to flash his Kowalski grin and lean close. "I won't be able to dance with you tonight because there's no chance I can put my hands on you in front of my family and retain any dignity at all. But just know I want to."

Chapter Fifteen

Despite the wedding festivities running late into the night, Siobhan woke early again on her final day at the Birch Brook Campground. She slid out of bed and made a cup of coffee to take to the dinette. A peek through the curtains told her nobody was out and about yet, and there was no sign of Brian.

Just know I want to.

Yeah, she'd wanted that, too.

It had been the most fun wedding she'd ever attended—one of the most fun weeks she'd ever had, actually, even with the paternity bombshell that had kicked it off. But throughout the rest of last night, she'd known in some other place and time, under other circumstances, she and Brian would have left that party together.

There was one final group breakfast planned, with Steph and Kyle leaving for Bar Harbor right after. Then, according to Mary, who'd been overseeing these vacations for decades, the real chaos would begin. A week of roaming from site to site and communal meals meant sorting and returning things and, according to her, nothing ever went back into the campers and RVs the way they came out.

Her own packing wouldn't be too bad, but her laundry

when she got home would be daunting. She also wanted to give the camper a thorough cleaning to thank the owner for lending it to her and Oliver.

The hardest part was going to be saying goodbye to Brian. Once she drove out of this campground, the surreal limbo they'd been existing in would be over. The days of getting to know each other while a definitive answer and the accompanying headaches were delayed had been a gift.

And if she was honest with herself, she was going to miss the entire Kowalski family. Her life was quiet and structured. It worked for her—and was necessary to juggle work and single motherhood—but she'd miss their loud, loving chaos.

Growing up, she'd moved around a lot, with Janelle relocating them on a whim for an opportunity that never worked out. Siobhan made friends in school, but never with the degree of closeness that led to sleepovers and being exposed to various family dynamics. Other than wishing Janelle would tell them who their dad was—if she even knew—because he might offer stability, Siobhan had only known a self-involved mother and a sister who followed her example.

Robin's stories about her large family had always sparked a wistfulness in Siobhan, but being a part of the Kowalski family for the last week had triggered a yearning so strong it made her heart ache.

A week ago, she never would have guessed this day would stir up so many mixed emotions.

"Mommy, are we going home today?"

The sleepy voice broke Siobhan out of her thoughts, and she opened her arms as her son crossed the camper to her. After moving her coffee mug out of harm's way, she wrapped her arms around him and kissed the top of his head.

"Yes, we're going home today." She realized he might not actually want to do that, so she kept talking. "You can tell Auntie Robin all about your adventures, and we'll make sure we get your froggy, too."

"Can Nora come?"

Siobhan closed her eyes for a moment, wishing being a parent came with a book of all the right things to say for every occasion, organized by age. "Nora's going to go home to her house, but you'll probably see her again soon."

He seemed to accept that, so she started the process of getting them ready for the day. The more Oliver woke up, the more excited he got about seeing everybody again and then finding his frog, which transitioned straight into being excited to see Auntie Robin and go to school again. Siobhan managed to get an entire coffee into herself, but she would have liked another cup. Or two.

The rest of the morning passed in a blur. Steph was understandably not even in the ballpark of being ready to leave, so Siobhan and Hannah helped her pack while Ellie took Oliver and Nora to find their rocks. Then came the big newlywed sendoff, which took about forty-five minutes from start to finish. Steph was yelling goodbyes out the window as Kyle pulled out onto the main road.

"Okay," Mary said, hands on her hips once the bride and groom were seen off, looking over the mess remaining from breakfast. "We'll wash everything all together, and then we can sort out what belongs where."

Siobhan helped with the washing, but she had no idea which utensils and containers belonged to which camper, so it felt like a good time to pack up her stuff. Though she hadn't been specifically told who her camper belonged to, she suspected it might be going to Maine and she didn't want to hold up whoever was hauling it back.

She was on her way up the road, holding Oliver's hand with one hand while his frog was in the other, when Terry caught up with them. She fell into step beside Siobhan, slightly out of breath.

"Things just get more chaotic from here, so I wanted to make sure I get to thank you for being here for Steph. My daughter had the wedding of her dreams and you were a big part of that." Her voice was heavy with emotion, but she took a deep breath and continued. "I know there was a lot to navigate, but you were wonderful and I want you to know that no matter how things turn out, you and Oliver are always welcome to join us for family things."

"Thank you." Siobhan suddenly felt a little emotional herself. "This week with your family has been one of the best of my life, even with navigating this little situation next to me. You all made that so much easier for me."

"Keep in touch," Terry said, touching her arm lightly. "Now, I need to go referee because my husband and my brother are trying to micromanage my nephews and that never goes well."

Siobhan turned as Terry walked away, and saw Evan and Joe on one side of a trailer and Brian and Joey on the other. From this distance it looked as though all of the rented items weren't going in the trailer the same way they'd come out and she was right. It was getting heated.

It was probably for the best. Brian being wrapped up helping his family leave and her getting herself and Oliver ready to go would keep the goodbye from dragging out.

In an hour or two, she and Oliver could do a quick round of goodbyes and then hit the road. They'd be home before supper and for the first time, Siobhan would get to be alone and process in just how many ways this week had changed her.

Brian was aware that Siobhan's car was packed and she was taking Oliver around to say goodbye to everybody.

He kept his focus on the landing gear of the camper that wasn't cranking up the way it was supposed to. Doing a drawn-out goodbye with Oliver and Siobhan would kill him. And he didn't want to witness his family saying goodbye, either. It would be tough for them, not knowing when or if they would see Oliver again. Genetics aside, he'd secured a place in everybody's heart already.

"Are you sure you're cranking that the right way?" Sean asked, and Brian glared over his shoulder at his dad's cousin.

"I'm sure," he snapped, though he looked at the setup for a second before resuming his efforts because his head wasn't totally in the game this morning.

But the closer Siobhan got to her car, the less attention he gave it. Finally he stood and brushed off the knees of his jeans. "Fine. You do it."

By the time he got to Siobhan and Oliver, only his mother remained at her side. As he got close, he watched her place her hand on Siobhan's arm and say something. Then she kissed Oliver's cheek and turned away. She was wiping tears from her cheeks when Brian passed her, but she managed to summon a weak smile for him.

"Hey," Siobhan said when he reached her. "I was about to text you and let you know we're ready to go. I wasn't going to leave without saying goodbye and I figured somebody would tell somebody who'd tell somebody else who would tell you that we're leaving."

"The roots of my family's grapevine run deep," he said, giving her what he felt was a ghost of his usual smile.

He wanted to touch her—to pull her into his arms and hold her. They couldn't leave if she was in his arms. And he was afraid if he looked down at Oliver, who was patiently holding her hand, he might cry.

Siobhan inhaled deeply and then blew out a breath. "I guess we've run out of time to not talk about it, so which one of us is making the appointment?"

"I don't mind doing it—and I'll pay the bill, of course— but I know your schedule must be a lot tighter than mine, with work and Oliver and everything, so it might be easier if you set the time and place. I can make anything work."

"That makes sense, and I appreciate it."

He hated this stilted, awkward conversation. "So just let me know where to be and when, and I'll be there. I'm going to head home, probably tomorrow, so I'll be closer. I own a place in Northfield, so I can be in Boston in an hour and a half or so."

"Sounds good."

He reached down and ruffled Oliver's hair, taking a second to get his emotions under control. "Be good, little man."

"Going home now," Oliver said.

Brian put his hand in his pocket and felt the small gray rock. "Do you have your frog?"

Oliver nodded, grinning. "Gonna show it to Auntie Robin."

"She'll love it."

"Okay," Siobhan said in an overly chipper way. "Time to get buckled."

Brian stepped out of the way while she put him in his car seat and gave him a water bottle and some books to keep him happy. Then she moved and Brian gave Oliver a little wave before softly closing the door.

"Can you just shoot me a quick text to let me know you got home okay?" He wondered too late if the request was out of line, and he braced himself for her telling him he was overstepping.

Instead, she smiled. "I will."

"Thanks."

Her fake smile crumpled and her words were a whisper. "Please don't stand here and watch us leave. I'll be able to see you in the mirror and…"

"I won't. Can't have you driving into the pool," he said, and got the pleasure of hearing her laugh one more time. He hoped it wasn't the last time. "Drive safe."

Then he spun and walked away. He didn't have a destination other than away, and he didn't look back when he heard her car door close. Or when she started it, or when he heard the crunch of her tires on the gravel in the dirt road. He didn't even turn back when she called a goodbye to the family waving as she left.

Once he could no longer hear the small engine of her car accelerating up the road, he threw himself into the work of getting everybody out of the campground so he and Stella could sit on the couch and mope. Well, he'd mope and Stella would sleep because she found moping too boring to watch.

His family gave him a wide berth, letting him work. There was comfort in physical movement, and going through the steps for hooking up campers to trucks and double-checking the RVs were ready for travel. It was so familiar to all of the men in the family that they didn't really need to talk. They could just do the work.

Saying goodbye as each unit was ready to roll was

hard. Over and over, he reassured family members he'd let them know as soon as he knew anything. And his mom cried into his T-shirt for a solid three or four minutes before his dad was able to detach her and get her in the passenger seat.

Several hours later, when it was finally just him and Rob and Hannah, his phone buzzed and he pulled it from his pocket. As expected, it was from Siobhan and he caught himself smiling as he swiped to open the message.

We're home. I got lucky with traffic and Oliver napped a good chunk of the way. Thank you for a wonderful week, and I'll be in touch as soon as I make the appointment.

Questions started flying through his head. Was Oliver glad to be home, or did he miss being with the Kowalski family at the campground? Had Siobhan been sorry to leave at all? Would she think about him the way he was undoubtedly going to think about her?

Glad you made it home. I'm happy you both had a good time, and I'll talk to you soon.

After a long moment passed with no response and no dots to indicate she was typing, he locked the phone and slid it back into his pocket.

All he could do now was wait.

Chapter Sixteen

One week later, Siobhan swung Oliver onto her hip before stepping through the glass door Brian held open for them. The humid heat hit hard after the almost two hours they'd spent waiting in the heavily air-conditioned clinic and she knew it was going take forever to get her car to cool off.

Though the actual process hadn't taken long, several callouts had left them short-staffed, leading to all of the appointments getting backed up. The long wait had been fraught with tension, but they'd both turned down the offer to reschedule. Besides the travel logistics, they needed the results.

Siobhan had spent the last week in a state of emotional turmoil that she wasn't accustomed to. Anxiety about the paternity test. Fear of the legal consequences if Brian was Oliver's father, and pre-results empathy for him and the family if he wasn't. And, the entire time, missing Brian on a level that existed separately from Oliver. She thought about him constantly, and it was wreaking havoc on her sleep.

Now, finally, the swabbing was done. In as little as three days, *maybe* would become *definitively*, one way or the other.

Brian shoved his hands in his pockets and smiled at Oliver before looking at Siobhan. "Are you up for some *i-c-e c-r-e-a-m*?"

It was thoughtful of him to spell it out, giving her the option of saying no without disappointing Oliver, which she appreciated. Not getting ice cream once the idea was put in her son's head would definitely kick off an impressive meltdown.

She'd had to leave work around lunchtime for this appointment, which hadn't pleased her boss coming so soon after a short-notice week off, and she'd planned to spend any remaining time in the day to go through the clothes and toys Oliver had outgrown.

"It's okay if you don't have time or whatever," Brian said when she didn't answer right away. "I just thought it would be a nice treat for him after having to wait in there so long."

"No, you're right. I think we've all earned a treat."

Was it a good idea? Probably not. While they were probably going to have to co-parent together, the three of them spending time together wasn't necessary. And after the sparks and kisses between them at the campground, it wasn't advisable.

Just know I want to.

The memory of those words, spoken in his low and husky voice, still played on a loop in her mind at the most inconvenient times.

But they had ice cream at a cute little shop Brian found on his phone. Oliver dominated the conversation, talking about daycare and Auntie Robin and a dog he saw that looked like Stella but was kind of mean.

It felt to Siobhan as if they were both deliberately focusing all of their attention on Oliver. There were a few glances between them, but no lingering. No cheeky grins and no flirtation. They were in the real world now, and in this world, they were now in a waiting game to see if their lives were changed and bound together forever.

Brian walked them back to where she'd parked, which she expected, and he was the one who lifted Oliver into his car seat. She watched him do the buckle, which he did correctly. After bopping his fingertip on Oliver's nose to make him giggle, he looked at Siobhan over the roof of her car.

"So we'll talk soon, I guess."

She nodded, not sure what else there was to say. "Thank you for the ice cream."

When he walked away, his hands were in his pockets and his shoulders slightly hunched, and she wanted to run after him. He looked like a man who needed a hug, but it wasn't her place to comfort him. And Oliver was getting impatient in his car seat. She drove home and tried not to think about Brian.

It didn't work.

She was in the tiny break room designated for people who weren't dedicated enough to eat at their desks, about to put a forkful of a slightly sad-looking salad into her mouth, when she opened her email app and her gaze caught on the name *Brian Kowalski* in a message between an email from a retailer promising her twenty percent off and a newsletter from the library. It was a forwarded email from the lab.

Her gut response was that she didn't want to know right now—not when she still had half a day of work to get through. And there was no way she could claim she didn't feel well and leave. She was already on thin ice there.

But sitting at her desk all afternoon with the email hanging over her, unread, wasn't going to happen, either. She needed to know. After setting down her fork, she clicked on the email.

Brian had not only forwarded the email and the report with the results, but he'd added a note.

Hey, Siobhan. I wanted to call you and talk to you in person, but I know you're at work and it didn't seem like the sort of thing for a text. I assume if you're going through your email, you're not in the middle of something, and I know you'll want to see the results for yourself. I guess we should talk, so if you could give me a call after work, I'd appreciate it. Brian.

With trembling hands, she scanned the report that confirmed Brian was, in fact, Oliver's biological father. Even though it was the expected result, it shook her and she spent the rest of her lunch break staring at her uneaten salad, trying to process how their lives were going to change now.

Unable to wrap her head around it, she sent back a simple reply—I'll call you around six—tossed her salad, and went back to her desk. Maybe she should have congratulated him or something. *Surprise, it's a boy!* But the more it sank in that she was actually going to have to share her son with Brian forever, the more the numbness settled in.

Brian had no idea what to do with himself. He couldn't sit still, but he also screwed up everything he touched. Even though the campground was busy, with a lot of campers arriving early for the long Labor Day weekend, Rob had told him to stop helping after he directed a long camper to a short site and they'd played hell getting it back out.

Leading up to the moment he clicked on the report, he'd thought he was prepared for the results. Believing something and having it proven beyond a reasonable doubt landed differently, he guessed, because he'd ended up sitting with his head between his knees, trying to breathe while Stella anxiously licked his face.

He'd told Rob and Hannah first, since they'd been in the store and were the reason he'd been sitting in a chair and not lying on the floor. Then he'd called his parents. His mom had put him on speakerphone so he could tell them together.

She got a little weepy, but they both stayed calm for the most part. And they agreed his next step should be a conversation with Siobhan, away from the rest of the family. There was a legal process in their future, but ideally, they'd go through it as partners and not as adversaries.

Once he'd informed his parents, he told the rest of the family via the massive group chat.

He'd followed Rob's advice and let the conversation run its course. Once the notifications slowed to reasonable, he read them all and sent a blanket thank-you and a promise to keep them updated.

With that done, there was nothing to do but wait for Siobhan to call.

"Maybe you should start heading south." Rob flopped in the chair and took a long draw from his tumbler's straw. "You said she's going to call around six? If you leave now, you'll be home by then. If you wait too long, you'll be on the road when she calls."

"I'm not going home. It's a long holiday weekend."

"Hannah and I can handle the campground. She can

manage the store and I'll run around and deliver firewood and yell at people who break the rules. It'll be fun."

Brian sat in the chair facing his brother, and Stella curled up on her bed with a sigh of relief. "I know you *can* handle it. But with Joey not coming up because they're getting Nora ready to start school and Danny writing, you'd be doing all the heavy lifting and that wasn't the idea behind the four of us buying the campground together."

"Do you remember when I was going to let Hannah walk out of my life for that exact same reason—my responsibility to you guys and this campground—and you told me you'd all let it go under before you let me throw away my chance at a future with her?" He leaned forward, resting his elbows on his knees and looking Brian in the eye. "You have an almost two-year-old son, Brian. A *son*. It's going to take you a minute to process that, and you and Siobhan have a lot to talk about. It's okay to step out for a bit. We've got you."

Brian nodded slowly, knowing his brother was right.

"And think of Stella," Rob continued. "She hates it when the campground's totally full of strangers and she'd much rather hang out at home."

"When I went home after the wedding week, I think she slept about twenty out of the first twenty-four hours. The family wore her out."

"They wore us all out." Rob took another sip of his water before pushing himself to his feet. "Hit the road."

He and Stella pulled up in front of his garage with fifteen minutes to spare. The dog was elated to be home and immediately started a grid search, searching for any smells that hadn't been there when she left.

Brian had time to carry some stuff inside and use the

bathroom, and then his phone vibrated in his pocket. He took a deep breath, checked the caller ID to make sure it was Siobhan and not his mother or grandmother, and answered it.

"Hi."

"Hey," she replied, and then they were silent for a long moment. "You okay?"

"I think so. You?"

"I think so." Her sigh was loud in his ear. "I mean, I think we all knew it. But somehow it being official is just so…"

"Official?"

"Yeah. So what now?"

She asked the question he'd been asking himself since he read the results, but still didn't have an answer for. "I don't know. But I do know I'd like for us to get together. I need to see him again."

"There's no way I'm driving all the way back to the campground on a holiday weekend," she said. "I don't know if you want to make the drive this weekend, either."

"I'm not at the campground. I came home today, so I'm a little over an hour north of you now. Maybe an hour and a half with traffic. I can come to you if you want."

"We can drive that, and Oliver and Stella would probably have more fun at your house than in my apartment. And I should probably see where you live, I guess?"

Because of visitation, he thought, his stomach tightening. So much was going to change. "Any day that works for you."

She was quiet for a moment, and he let her think. "I told Robin we'd go out with her on Sunday, and I have Monday off, but that's a big traffic day. Is tomorrow too soon?"

"Tomorrow's perfect." One night. He probably wouldn't

sleep at all, but it was only one night until he saw them again. "I know he's little, but did you tell him anything yet?"

"No, I didn't. I think it will make more sense to him if you're physically there to associate the word with."

Daddy. Brian put his hand over his stomach and blew out a breath. "Yeah. That makes sense."

"Just text me your address so I have it in my phone. And he usually likes nuggets as a long-drive treat, so if we get there around noon, he'll have eaten and be in a good mood."

"That sounds great. The GPS on my house is pretty accurate so your phone should bring you right here, but if you have any issues, just call me."

"Okay. We'll see you tomorrow, then."

Once they hung up, Brian sat on his back step and watched Stella run around the yard. She'd found the trail of something she didn't think should have been in the yard, and she was sniffing the grass furiously.

It made him smile, but it wasn't enough to quell the turmoil churning inside of him. He was somebody's father. Oliver's father.

Daddy.

Chapter Seventeen

Brian loved his house. It was small—a two bedroom cape built before his grandfather was even born. It only had one bathroom, and it was upstairs between the two bedrooms. The ceilings up there were sloped, following the roof line, which made the bedrooms feel even smaller. The kitchen was a decent size, but it was badly in need of updating, and other than refinishing the hardwood floors, he hadn't done much decorating in the living room.

But the house had a deep front porch and it sat on forty acres of land. As far as he and Stella were concerned, a shady spot to sit and acres of their own woods to explore were all they needed.

Now he stood in the driveway, arms crossed, trying to see the property through Siobhan's eyes. To him, it was rustic. Would it look shabby to her? She might think he was lucky to have been able to grab some great land because he took on the fixer-upper residence. Or she might think he was a loner type living in a shack in the woods.

"It's not a shack," he said out loud. Then he looked down at Stella, who was gazing up at him with her usual blend of curiosity and adoration. "It's comfortable, right?"

Stella's head whipping around was Brian's first warning. Then he heard the distant sound of a car engine. His driveway was off of a dirt road that was off of a back road, so they didn't get much traffic. Siobhan and Oliver would turn the corner and come into view any second, so he took a few deep breaths to clear any residual worry from his face.

He ran his thumb over the rock in his pocket, trying to soothe himself, but that was a lost cause. His skin was hot and prickly, and it was hard to take a full breath. Anxiety wasn't something that he'd dealt with a lot, but since Oliver had come into his life, he felt so out of his depth, he couldn't remember what standing on solid ground felt like.

And Siobhan. Everything was different now and there was too much at stake for them to risk messing it up, but he missed her so much he couldn't really wrap his head around it.

He was thankful he was still on his feet and hadn't passed out when her car came into view. She smiled when she saw him, and he returned it as some of the anxiety melted away. He'd worked himself into quite a state, but it was as though he saw her face and his body relaxed. *Oh, it's her. We really like her and it'll be okay.*

"Did you have any trouble finding the place?" he asked when she'd turned off the engine and climbed out.

"No, even though you're really out here in the middle of nowhere. It must be fun in the winter."

He waved a hand toward the pole barn, under which he kept the three-quarter-ton truck he used for plowing, along with the plow, sand hopper and a pretty impressive tractor. Not that Siobhan would find it impressive, he thought. But it was. "I don't usually have a problem getting in and out."

"Mommy!" a small voice yelled, and Siobhan hurried around the car and opened Oliver's door. "Stella!"

It was hard to tell who was more excited—the boy or the dog—but the two immediately started running around the yard. Oliver's laugh echoed through the trees, and Brian chuckled. It was impossible to be tense while watching the two of them play.

"There's nothing in the yard that can hurt him. Stella has an area she's limited to without me, and she'll keep him in it, too. We'll just make sure he stays out of the pole barn." He turned to face her and caught her looking at him. "You want to sit on the step? The front porch is nicer, but they've got more space back here."

"Sure. He always has a burst of energy after being in the car for a while."

Once they were seated side by side on the step, with enough space between them so their arms and legs wouldn't brush each other, Brian rested his elbows on his knees. "So is there a certain way we should explain this to him? I don't want to traumatize him or anything, so even though it would suck, if we should wait and ask somebody, we can. Like a therapist or something."

"If he was older, I'd say that was necessary. But at this age, I think he'll roll with it, to be honest."

It wasn't long before Oliver found a colorful leaf on the ground and came running back to show it to his mom, Stella right beside him. "Look, Mommy."

"It's so pretty!" She took the leaf and twirled it between her thumb and finger. "Oliver, do you remember when you asked why you don't have a daddy?"

Brian's breath caught in his chest when he nodded. "Colton has a daddy and Abby has a daddy, but I don't."

"We didn't know you had a daddy, but we found out you do. Brian is your daddy, so we came to visit and you'll get to visit him and Stella a lot now."

Oliver leaned on Brian's knee and looked up at him with blue eyes that reflected his own, and the eyes of his brothers and father. "You're my daddy?"

He thought he said yes, but his throat was so clogged with emotion, he wasn't sure the word was recognizable, so he nodded.

The boy tilted his head, and then grinned. "Do you want a leaf, too?"

Brian watched Oliver—*his son*—run off and then scrubbed his hands over his face. His body vibrated with emotion and he didn't think he could have spoken in that moment if he had to. His throat and his chest felt as if they were being squeezed in a vice.

In a flash, Oliver was back, holding out another leaf. "Here you go, Daddy."

Brian sucked in a shaky breath, and then managed to take it with a trembling hand. "Thank you. Can I have a hug?"

Oliver reached up and wrapped his arms around Brian's neck as he lifted him off the ground. He was careful not to squeeze too hard as he closed his eyes. Tears slid down his cheek, probably landing in the boy's hair, but he didn't let go until Stella nudged his leg.

He managed to swipe his cheeks with one hand while setting Oliver on the ground, and then he gave Stella's ears a good scratch.

"I like leaves," Oliver said, still leaning against his knee. "Do you like leaves?"

"I do. In the fall, I make piles of leaves and Stella plays in them."

He giggled. "Mommy does that for me at the park sometimes. We don't have our own grass. Is this your house?"

"It is. Do you want to see inside?"

* * *

Something had shifted in Siobhan, and she couldn't quite put her finger on it. While she'd known Oliver would adapt easily to Brian being his father because he was still young enough not to know how things usually worked, hearing him call Brian *Daddy* had wrecked her.

No, that wasn't it, she thought. Hearing that had rocked her, but it was Brian's reaction that had totally wrecked her. It had been a humbling and emotional experience watching a man be profoundly changed by a single word.

But change him it had, the same way Siobhan had been changed when Kelly put Oliver in her arms and told her to keep him. Now she was afraid that moment might also have him rethinking all the things he'd said when being Oliver's father was a hypothetical. Maybe now that he'd felt those arms hugging him and heard the word *Daddy*, he'd fight to keep him.

No, she told herself firmly. She knew Brian better than that. She knew his family. None of them wanted to cut her out of his life. But as she followed them into the house, she looked at Oliver's tiny hand tucked into Brian's much bigger one and her chest felt tight.

His house was small and she wasn't sure if rustic or just old was a better description, but it was clean and cozy, with great light from the big windows. The kitchen needed updating badly, but the floors were gorgeous. She took for granted he'd been chipping away remodeling when he had the time and money, and buying the campground with his brothers had probably taken a lot of both from him.

They only got as far as the living room, where Oliver spotted the wicker basket of books. "Beep beep!"

Brian chuckled at her expression and shrugged. "I ran to the store this morning and got a few things. I probably asked a dozen different parents with little ones with them which books had that phrase in them before a guy with a daughter about his age took pity on me. There are also some classics I remember from when I was a kid, and other ones the dad recommended."

"That's sweet, though he's going to bail on the tour now because some of those he hasn't seen before." Oliver was already sitting on the floor, pulling books out and showing them to Stella, who stretched out beside him.

"That's okay. Maybe we can sit at the kitchen table and talk for a few minutes. I installed a baby gate at the bottom of the stairs, and we'll be right there."

"Okay." He sounded serious again, which refired her nerves.

He pulled out a chair for her, and then walked around to the other side of the table. She sat, her mind spinning as she tried to anticipate what would come next.

Oliver's favorite books. There was already a baby gate. He was making this house into Oliver's home.

"Hey, are you okay?" She heard Brian's voice, but it sounded like it was coming from some far end of a tunnel. "Siobhan, what's going on?"

Siobhan couldn't say the words out loud. Even if she managed to come up with a way to phrase the question, fear closed her throat.

Kelly and Steve lied on the birth certificate and they lied on the adoption papers. Brian Kowalski was Oliver's biological father and he could fight to have the adoption overturned.

And he'd win.

Nausea rolled through her stomach, and she brought her hand to her mouth as things got fuzzy. The lights seemed to dim slightly and she placed her other hand flat on the table in a feeble attempt to steady herself. As though from that same end of the long tunnel, she heard the scrape of chair legs on the floor, and then hands were helping her to the floor.

The laminate flooring was cool and it helped, as did the cool, damp cloth on the back of her neck. He lifted her head slightly before lowering it onto some kind of lumpy pillow, and when the scent of him filled her senses, she realized it was his sweater.

"Siobhan," he said, his voice very close to her head. "Look at me."

She reluctantly opened her eyes and found Brian lying on the floor next to her, his head rested on his outstretched arm. Siobhan looked into his blue eyes, oddly comforted despite the power this man had to break her heart and destroy her life.

"I don't want to take Oliver away from you."

Her breath caught and a tear slipped out, running down into her hair. If she hadn't already been on the floor, she might have collapsed as relief sapped the strength from her body. Untangling the mess Kelly had made of their lives was going to be a tough process, but she could get through anything as long as she had Oliver.

"You're his mother," Brian continued, and the words helped calm the storm of emotions inside of her. "But I'm his father, and *that's* what we need to figure out."

Siobhan wasn't sure if he intended for his words to be an ultimatum or not, but she heard one. As long as she didn't stand in the way of his parental rights, he wouldn't mess with hers.

"Okay," she whispered hoarsely, barely managing the single word.

She knew she should get up. The dizziness was gone

and she felt steadier. But Brian's face was relaxed and lying on the floor together felt so much less adversarial than facing each other across the table.

Then Stella crawled in between, her belly low to the ground, and Brian laughed. The dog licked his face and then wiggled her back against Siobhan. She smiled as she ran her fingers through Stella's soft fur, and then her hand stilled when her fingertips brushed Brian's.

He just smiled and kept rubbing his dog. Siobhan shifted her hand to scratch between the dog's ears and for a few minutes, the three of them were just content to hang out on Brian's kitchen floor. By tipping her head, she could see Oliver's feet and the book he had propped open on his legs. He was still lost in the picture book, oblivious to the goings-on in the kitchen.

"I'm sorry about that," she said after a while. "I don't know what came over me. It's been so much and now it's actually *official* and this is happening. Forever."

"It's a lot. I've had to sit down and put my head between my knees a few times myself." He paused, rubbing Stella's belly. "And I get that I'm overwhelmed by what I'm gaining, so I can't even imagine how it feels to worry about what you stand to lose. So I just want to say again, right up front, that what I really *want* is for you and me to find a way to co-parent Oliver and nobody loses anybody."

Even after the week they'd spent together, it was so hard for Siobhan to wrap her head around this Brian lying on the floor with her and offering reassurance being the Brian her sister had been married to. How had Kelly given this man up so easily? It didn't begin to make sense to her.

She slowly pushed herself to a sitting position, not at all surprised when Brian leaped to his feet to help her up.

Once she was back in the chair, she gave him a sheepish grin as she accepted a glass of water.

"I'm not usually this dramatic," she told him.

"This is all extremely intense. I get it. But I also think part of why it's so intense is not knowing what lies ahead, so we're both going to be off-kilter until it's settled. I'll ask around and get some recommendations for a decent lawyer who's as affordable as possible so we can start getting an idea of our next steps."

He sounded sincere, but alarm bells went off, drawing attention to the little voice in the back of her mind that remained skeptical. Perhaps it was being raised by a manipulative mother, but she couldn't be sure Brian wasn't trying to make her drop her guard. If she believed they were going to happily share Oliver, she might not pay attention to him pursuing legal options behind the scenes with a lawyer who technically worked for him. She didn't want to believe that, but when it came to Oliver, she couldn't just go on faith.

"I hope you won't be offended, but I'll have my own lawyer."

He thought about it for a few seconds and then nodded. "I understand that. But maybe I can pay one to do the initial consult and get an idea of what we're working with, and then you'll know what you need from yours. Save some time and money, perhaps."

"Okay."

"Okay. In the meantime, I want to show you something." He stood, so she did the same, and he went to the living room first. "Oliver, do you want to see the upstairs?"

Of course he did, so Siobhan took him by the hand. He was pretty good at stairs, but he was also excited about exploring a new place. And Stella was pretty excited, too. They didn't need a fall.

It took Brian a minute to get the baby gate open, and then they were held up again by the second baby gate at the top. She tried not to laugh at him, but some amusement squeaked out and he rolled his eyes at her.

"I'll get it eventually." Once they were in the hall and he'd secured the gate behind him, he pointed. "That's my room and there's the bathroom. But in here."

Siobhan stepped into a room that was very clearly Oliver's bedroom. There was a box with a picture of a toddler bed frame, complete with side rails, on the label. A small mattress wrapped in plastic leaned against the wall. There was a toy box with some plastic trucks and stuffed animals in it, and a low bookshelf with more brand-new books on it.

There was that gut punch again, but this time she was able to shake it off quickly. Of course he'd need a room for Oliver. "This is amazing. You got all of this this morning?"

"Yeah. I figure after you've been here a few times, maybe we can try a sleepover. You know, when he's ready. But this is what I wanted to show you."

Siobhan turned, and that's when she saw the framed photos on the wall. The family photo, with Oliver sitting on Leo's lap. There was also a small picture of Nora and Oliver, their heads bent in concentration as they painted their rocks. Next to that was Oliver in the grass with Stella, pointing to something in his book while the dog looked on eagerly. There was an 8x10 photo of Brian helping Oliver toast a marshmallow.

And right next to that one, an 8x10 of Siobhan and Oliver taken during the reception. She'd been holding him—

dancing, so to speak—and Oliver had his hand pressed to her cheek while they laughed.

"I wanted him to have family photos in his room, so Rob sent them to me and I had them printed and bought frames this morning." He smiled at Oliver and then at her before turning back to the wall. "This is who Oliver's family is to me and there's no world in which that doesn't include you."

She breathed in slowly, taking in the images of all the people who'd fallen in love with Oliver over the course of a week, and who'd never once tried to push her out. It calmed her fears in a way no words ever could. "Thank you."

"Let's have a day of hanging out and just making this a comfortable place for Oliver. Then the rest, we'll get through it together."

Chapter Eighteen

There were very few things Siobhan enjoyed less in life than calling her mother. Talking to Janelle drained her on every level, and other than Christmas, her mother's birthday and Mother's Day, she kept contact to a minimum.

It wasn't hard to do. Her mother only called her when she needed something, and she'd decided years ago her older daughter had little to offer. Working hard and paying bills weren't exciting to Janelle, and she complained about Siobhan's lack of *generosity.* Janelle had always been much closer with Kelly, and Siobhan hoped that was still true.

She'd finally found a lawyer who had the time to talk to her before snow fell again. She didn't have space to take on Siobhan's case, but she was willing to do a brief consult about next steps. Step one was to find an attorney she could afford, and it seemed as though she had a better chance of finding Sasquatch than an affordable family lawyer taking on new clients.

Step two was finding Kelly. The odds of them sorting through the adoption mess without needing her involvement weren't great, and since her number was disconnected and an online search hadn't turned up anything, the only way Siobhan could get to her was through Janelle.

She waited until Oliver had eaten his supper and settled

into his little bean bag chair with a picture book that had him hunt for objects in a busy picture. It would keep him quiet and occupied for long enough to make the phone call, and she was out of excuses.

Janelle answered on the third ring. "Siobhan. Haven't heard from you in a while."

"I'm sorry," she lied. "I've been busy."

"Or you want something," her mother said, because that was really the only motivation for reaching out to somebody that Janelle understood.

Siobhan didn't bother denying it. "I need to get in touch with Kelly and the number I have for her isn't good anymore."

There was a long silence on the other end, and Siobhan guessed Janelle was choosing between inserting herself into the situation or trying to make Siobhan feel guilty for only calling her because she wanted something from her. "What do you need her for?"

She'd spent a lot of time thinking about how she was going to answer this inevitable question. Telling the truth led to too many variables. Janelle might try to protect Kelly by refusing to give up the information—assuming she even had it. And if anybody was going to whisper in Kelly's ear about taking Oliver back and fleecing Brian for child support, it would be her. Unfortunately, that was just how her mother's mind worked.

And then there was Kelly herself. There was a good chance if she found out Siobhan wanted to talk to her about Oliver, she'd change her number again. Because she wasn't quite as selfish as their mother, she might not think about how much monthly money she was missing out on, but she definitely shied away from anything that smacked of *responsibility*.

"I was going through some stuff to donate and found a necklace of hers," Siobhan said. "It's not really my style or I'd keep it because I think it's valuable."

"It might be mine," her mother said without hesitation. "I've lost a necklace or two over the years."

Even though she'd known Janelle would try it, Siobhan was still disappointed by how quickly dishonesty came to her mother. Of course, she was being dishonest, too, but for a good reason and she'd had to practice before she made the call. "I'm sure it's Kelly's. I remember her wearing it. If I can get her address, I'll drop it in the mail from work tomorrow."

"I don't know her address, but I'll tell her to call you."

"Just give me her number and I'll call her and that way I can check returning it off my to-do list."

"I'll have her call you." A door slammed in the background and Siobhan heard a female voice that sounded a lot like her sister. "My food's here. Gotta run."

The call disconnected before Siobhan could ask if Kelly was staying with her. After writing *Janelle's address* on the back of an envelope, she circled it twice. If she could prove her sister was staying with her mother, maybe that address would suffice if legal service became necessary.

Before she even set down the pen, her phone buzzed and she saw an unknown number on the screen. After underlining *Janelle's address* with a bold line, she answered it.

"Mom said you have something of mine?"

"A necklace," Siobhan replied, pushing down the disappointment that swept through her when Kelly didn't even say hello. They'd been reasonably close before her sister married Brian, but the conflict between them during the marriage and divorce had put a dent in their relationship.

Siobhan adopting Oliver had essentially ended it. "Tell me your address and I'll drop it in the mail tomorrow."

"Just keep it."

"It looks valuable."

There was a long silence, and Siobhan was looking at her screen to make sure the timer was still ticking off seconds before her sister spoke again. "What do you really want, Siobhan?"

"Did you know Brian is Oliver's biological father?"

Kelly sighed, as though she was annoyed at being bothered. "Maybe."

"You knew his cousin and I are friends and I might be around his family at some point."

"I was hoping the kid would look like me."

"He doesn't. Why did you lie?"

"Because I know you and you would have sided with *him*, and then I would have had to deal with that man for the rest of my life just because we shared a kid."

A kid. Siobhan took a deep breath, glancing at Oliver to cool her flash of temper. "You could have still gotten the divorce while you were pregnant, and given him to Brian instead of me when he was born. You didn't have to raise him, so it doesn't explain the lying. And the *fraud*, Kelly. You and Steve signed legal documents and I don't know about him, but *you* knew they were false statements."

"Steve thought the kid was his, but then he didn't want to be a dad anyway, so it worked out okay."

Okay? Except for paperwork that had made Siobhan Oliver's mother being fraudulent. "Where are you now?"

"Why?"

She pinched the bridge of her nose, praying for patience. "Because we have to straighten this out, and we'll probably need a signed statement from you."

"For what? Just let him see the kid if he wants to."

The words were thrown out casually enough, but Siobhan knew her sister well enough to hear the underlying fear. Kelly wasn't sure what the penalties for lying on birth certificates and adoption papers were, but she didn't want any part of paying a price.

"It's more than just seeing Oliver and you know that. To have his paternal rights protected, the paperwork has to be done."

"I have a different boyfriend now, Siobhan, and he's going to propose," Kelly said, and there was a hint of panic in her voice. "He owns a house on the water in Connecticut and you should see his cars. But he doesn't know I had a kid before and that kind of thing matters to him."

It didn't surprise her at all that his money was the most important attribute for Kelly to share. "If that's a deal-breaker, he's probably not a great guy."

"Don't mess this up for me, Siobhan."

"For you? What about the mess Oliver and I are in now?"

"It's not my problem. I gave him to you, so that's *your* problem. Deal with it."

Siobhan closed her eyes for a moment, reminding herself she couldn't force Kelly to feel compassion or empathy. She'd certainly tried over the years, but her sister only cared about herself. Something she'd inherited from their mother, apparently. "Okay. I'll figure it out. I always do. Just give me your address, though, and I'll send you the necklace."

"You and I both know I've never owned a necklace worth the cost of mailing it."

The call disconnected and Siobhan forced herself to set her phone down on the table instead of throwing it across the room. One, she had to set a good example for her son and, two, she couldn't afford to replace it or have any damage to the wall patched.

She knew if she called back, Kelly wouldn't answer. By tomorrow, her sister would have a new burner phone, and Siobhan would have no way of contacting her again. And if she *was* staying with Janelle, there was a good chance her mother overheard at least Kelly's end of the conversation and wouldn't take Siobhan's calls for a while, either. She wouldn't want to miss out on an opportunity to have a son-in-law with a beach house.

Looking at the note she'd written on the envelope, she felt despair creeping in. Even if Kelly was staying with their mother temporarily, Janelle would deny it. Siobhan definitely didn't have the money to hire a private investigator to prove she was there, nor did she have the time or means to do it herself. She'd have to hope, if it came to that, the court system or law enforcement would be able to help.

Rather than wallowing, she stood and went to look at picture books with her son. Oblivious to her anxious state, he pointed out all the objects he could find in the photo of a busy playground, and she smiled when he started counting the flowers he could see on the page.

As she felt some of the tension easing from her body, she wished Brian was there to talk to about her conversations with her family, and that brought a whole new surge of tension.

He couldn't be the person she leaned on. He was her son's biological father, and that relationship between them came first for the rest of their lives. He was also her sister's ex-husband. Her former brother-in-law.

No, Brian Kowalski could definitely *not* be her person.

* * *

"How do you devote your life to running a true crime podcast and not be able to come up with a plan for getting away with murder?"

Brian paused in the doorway of the store, Stella at his heels, pondering the question he'd walked in on Rob asking Hannah. Then he continued on, making sure the dog's tail was in before pulling the door closed.

"I *can* come up with a plan for getting away with murder," Hannah was saying. "I'm just not going to tell *you* how."

"Dave again?" Brian asked, dropping into a chair.

"There seems to be some confusion about who actually owns this property," Rob said, and Brian knew the interaction must have been a bad one because their roles were usually reversed—Brian had a shorter temper and Rob was his voice of reason.

"Dave and Sheila have been camping here for decades," Hannah said, clearly stepping into the peacemaker role. "It's like a second home to them, so of course they're going to have feelings about things changing."

"I was trimming back the branches that scrape down the side of their neighbor's truck because I don't want us on the hook for repainting it if it gets scratched up and Dave accused me of trying to make it so there's no shade at all in the campground."

They'd taken some trees down before the campground opened for the season because taking down an unhealthy or dead tree was always better than having one fall on an RV or one of the guests. One of them had been a disease-weakened tree that had still offered shade to one of the campsites—not Dave and Sheila's—and it seemed they would have to hear about it forever now.

Hannah sighed. "Only six more weeks or so and then you won't have to worry about them again until spring."

Brian chuckled. "You sure you want to spend the winter alone with this guy?"

She looked at Rob, her expression softening in a way that Brian envied. He'd like to have somebody in his life who looked at him the way Hannah looked at his brother. "I'm looking forward to it."

"With fall coming and a list of things to do before we can close up, there's a lot going on," Brian said, mostly to distract himself. "Maybe I should tell Joey to come up next weekend."

Rob frowned. "For what? I mean, last I knew, Ellie's had some morning sickness, except it's also midday sickness and evening sickness, so Joey's been taking Nora to school and picking her up. He said something about maybe working Saturdays to make up for the lost hours."

"I'm not going to be around next weekend, and he hasn't spent as much time here, so he probably has a higher Dave tolerance than you do."

"Sure, because *you're* the tolerant one of the bunch." Rob snorted. "And did I know you wouldn't be around next weekend?"

"I told you. And it's on the calendar."

After a few seconds of thinking about it, his brother's face lit up. "Oh, the sleepover. I can't believe that slipped my mind."

On the other hand, it never *left* Brian's mind. No matter what he was doing, some part of his brain was thinking about the fact that his *son* would be sleeping in his house next weekend. It was surreal and exciting and terrifying.

Hannah laughed. "I won't let Rob kill off any of the campers while you're gone, Brian."

"Speaking of killing off campers." Rob sighed and held up his phone. "Some jerks rode through the pasture again and tore it up. Somebody passing by got a picture from the trail, but it's not great. Do these look like the machines from site thirteen to you?"

Brian took the phone from Rob so he could see the photo filling the screen. His brother was right about it not being great, but he knew whoever had sent it to the lodging establishments—either the conservation officers or the local ATV club—would send the best they had. After zooming in as far as he could, he squinted. "It's hard to tell, looking at the machines, but see here?"

He pointed to where there were some lighter pixels along the helmet of the guy on the four-wheeler, and then he panned over to a decal on the storage box of the side-by-side behind him. "We talked about the custom decals when they checked in, remember? Are they at their site right now?"

"No, I checked a few minutes ago and they were still out riding."

"Call it in and give them the details we have. If they catch up with them out there or when they're back and confirm it's them, we'll throw them out and blacklist them."

Most of the ATV trails in NH were on private property, used with permission between the landowners and ATV clubs. But when people disrespected the property and the landowners got mad, they could close the trails. That was bad for everybody who loved the sport respectfully, but especially for businesses—like Birch Brook Campground—that depended on the trail system financially. Sometimes Brian felt like he spent more time helping law enforcement ferret out jerks than anything else.

"Oh, and site twenty-two," Hannah said. "There's the beginning of a nest in the water hookup. Bees or wasps or I don't even know, but I noticed it when I was chasing a plastic bag around in the wind."

"Another day in paradise," Brian muttered, and they all chuckled. "I'll go take a look at it. Stella, you stay."

The dog gave him a look before settling onto her cushion. Brian knew she was bluffing. She loved being outdoors, but she also loved taking long naps in the store. It wouldn't have mattered. During their early days, there had been a very expensive trip to the emergency vet after Stella decided wasps were just flying snacks and Brian didn't want a repeat of that.

He was halfway to the site when his phone rang. Because the signal could get sketchy once he crossed into the wooded part of the campground, he sat on a picnic table in an empty site and pulled it out.

Then he frowned. Kevin never called him. He got frequent text messages from his uncle—joke memes and sports news, mostly—but never phone calls. "Hello?"

"Everybody's okay and nobody's sick or hurt or lying in a ditch somewhere," Kevin said, and Brian chuckled. They'd all been trained well. "I don't have the patience to type everything out, but I heard you'll be down in this part of the state for a bit. Any chance you can swing by Jasper's in the next few days?"

"I don't know. Siobhan and Oliver are coming up—to my house, I mean. Not to the campground. That's why I'm heading south. For the first time he sleeps over, it makes sense for her to be there just in case he has a hard time."

"Or you do."

Brian chuckled. "Yeah, there's also that."

"It's even better if you bring her with you, actually."

That was strange. "What's up?"

"I'm still waiting to hear back on something later today or tomorrow morning. But come to Jasper's this weekend and I'll talk to you then. Drop Oliver off at Mike and Lisa's because you know nothing would make them happier and come have a meal on the house. It'll be good to see you both and, honestly, you could probably both use a night out."

Brian wasn't one to turn down a free meal and he was intrigued by whatever Kevin was being vague about, but he hesitated. That sounded a lot like a date night and he wasn't sure that was a good idea. Siobhan might have agreed to an ice cream after the testing appointment, but that had been for Oliver's benefit. "I'll pop by, for sure, but I'm not sure about Siobhan. I'll have to ask her."

"Sure. Ask her, and if she decides she's up for a meal she didn't have to cook in a very fine establishment, if I do say so myself, just text me and I'll reserve a table."

"I'll call her when she gets out of work and then shoot you a text."

He still had a couple of hours before that would happen. She'd mentioned the only almost-guaranteed time to catch her on the phone for a chat was between the time she left work and arrived at Oliver's daycare. Thanks to hands-free tech and being the only person in the car, it was her best time to chat.

"Did you set an alarm?" she teased when she took his call. "Exactly two minutes after I got in my car."

"I did set an alarm," he confessed. "I didn't want to miss the window while destroying wasp condos and redoing the signs telling campers what they can and cannot flush in the bathhouse toilets, but this time in bold font and italics and some red ink."

"Campgrounds are a lot more fun when you're a camper."

He laughed. "You're not wrong. So anyway, Kevin called me today and wants me to stop by his bar this weekend to talk to me about something quick. When I told him you and Oliver were coming up, he said he'd love to see you, too, and suggested we let Oliver visit my parents for a bit and go get a free meal."

"Um. You mean just the two of us?"

"He has something to talk to me about and when I told him you guys were coming up, he said to bring you." Brian pinched the bridge of his nose, knowing how it sounded. "It's just a good chance to have a meal we don't have to cook *or* pay for, and for my parents to have a visit with Oliver."

"They haven't seen him since being his grandparents became official, I guess."

"They'd love to see him. But there's also no pressure. You and Oliver can hang at my place and I'll run over for a few minutes." He paused, but she didn't fill the silence. "Or I can tell him I can't make it and I'll see him another time. Whatever works best for you and Oliver, of course."

He heard her exhale over the phone, as if she'd been holding her breath while she thought it through. "No, it's fine. He adores your parents and I know how hard it was for Mike and Lisa to wait for the results. Oliver would love to spend some time with them."

"Great. I'll let Kevin know to hold us a spot. How's Oliver doing?"

"Good. One of his favorite things now is looking at the pictures from camping on my phone. Over the course of the week, I guess I managed to get almost everybody, even if they were in the background, so I zoom in and he says their names and fun things about them."

"You're amazing," he said, the words slipping out without thought, and he winced. It was true, but it was also a weird thing to say.

Her chuckle sounded tinny through the hands-free on her end. "Thank you. It seemed like an easy way to kind of transition into family. I noticed the younger ones tend to call their grandmothers Grammy and Mary is Gram, so I've been sliding that in there. I think it's easy for him because that's what Nora calls everybody, so it makes it less overwhelming, I guess."

"Family Tree of Doom," he said, and they both laughed.

"Okay, I actually have to run into the market before I get Oliver and I'm here now. But a meal I don't have to cook or cut into toddler-sized pieces sounds good. We'll see you Friday."

"I can't wait."

He was smiling when they hung up, already looking forward to spending the weekend with them. Before he left, he'd check off as many things as he could on the campground to-do list because he still didn't love leaving Rob and Hannah holding down the fort.

And then he was going to have a great weekend with Siobhan and Oliver. Just the three of them—and Stella, of course—and it felt right.

Chapter Nineteen

It was surprisingly easy to leave Oliver with Mike and Lisa for a couple of hours, Siobhan mused as Brian steered his truck out of their neighborhood. He'd been thrilled to see them again and happy to have a new house to explore.

After quick hugs, Lisa had given her a quick tour of the house, which was lovely. The yard was securely fenced, there were toys and puzzles thanks to Nora, and they had dinosaur chicken nuggets in the freezer. "Also some ice cream," Mike had added with a wink. They were fully in grandparent mode.

They made small talk about the family during the drive, mostly about Steph and Kyle's trip to Bar Harbor. They'd stayed offline during the honeymoon, but Siobhan and the Kowalski family group chat had gotten photo dumps when they got home. They had a beautiful time, though Steph claimed it would have been even more fun if the entire family had been with them.

"We don't do Family Honeymoon Trips of Doom," Brian said when he repeated that, and Siobhan laughed. "It might not look like it, but we do have limits."

Once he'd found a place to park, they walked a short distance to Jasper's Bar & Grille, and Siobhan smiled when she walked through the door. Even to a non–sports fan, it was very obvious this was a haven for New England sports fans. There was memorabilia hung up, much of it autographed. New England Patriots. Boston Bruins. Boston Red Sox. Boston Celtics. Connecticut Sun. The New England Revolution. It was everywhere. Along with, of course, the required television screens. But they had the sound muted and closed-captioning on, and the overall vibe was comfortable, not super aggressive.

A young person waved to Brian, obviously recognizing him. "Kevin set you up in the back corner."

Siobhan followed Brian in that direction, which led to a small table holding a cardboard sign that declared it reserved. The television closest to it was off, and because the lighting was designed around being supplemented by bright LED screens, it was dim and quiet.

Romantic, she thought. Hopefully his uncle wasn't trying to play matchmaker. She and Brian didn't need any help in that department. Their struggle was keeping things platonic.

A server dropped off a pitcher of ice water and two glasses, along with two menus. "Kevin's dealing with something, but he'll be over as soon as he can. Do you want a beer while you wait?"

"Sure. Whatever the most popular on tap is right now." When he looked at Siobhan, she nodded. One beer was okay. "Make it two."

Siobhan wasn't usually the sports bar type, but this really was a nice place with a relaxed vibe and not as loud as she'd feared. "How long has your uncle owned this place?"

"I'm not sure, actually. At least since I was a little kid because I don't remember him *not* owning it."

"Okay. Next question, then—why is it called Jasper's Bar & Grille?"

"According to my uncle, that's what it was called when he bought the place and keeping the name was a lot cheaper than buying new signs and napkins." He shrugged. "And you know how it is. No matter what he changed the name to, the locals were still going to call it Jasper's, and that would just confuse people who aren't from around here."

"That actually makes sense, and it's pretty funny. It's a great place."

Brian nodded and looked around, and she could see the nostalgia in the way he smiled. "It really is. All of us kids did some time working here at some point. It wasn't for me—I need to be outdoors too much—but it was a good experience."

"Which one of you was best at it?" she asked, and then she paused while the server dropped off their beer before holding up a hand. "Wait. Either Joey or Rob, I think."

He chuckled. "Probably a tie between those two, for sure. Danny was good at a lot of it, but he didn't love the interactions with customers as much. But Steph was definitely the best. Now the younger kids are starting. Lily's great behind the bar, but it's the family business for her. She was upstairs in the office with Beth from the time she was born, and Kevin used to bring her down here when it was quiet. Johnny just started bar-backing, so it's too soon to tell. And Brianna made it through two and a half shifts before a customer said something out of line to her and she said something back he didn't like, and he said something *way* out of line and got punched in the face by another customer and then…well, there was some broken furniture and a *lot* of broken glass to clean up."

"Oh." She winced. "Did he have to fire his own niece?"

Brian chuckled. "Nope. Kevin always sides with his staff and nobody who works here—family or not—is expected to take any crap from anybody. But when the fight was broken up and the cops were on the way, she stood in the middle of the room with her hands on her hips and told him this was not her vibe and she quit. Just walked out."

"Good for her."

"And then she had to come back in and ask Kevin for a ride home because she'd been dropped off."

Siobhan laughed. "There's nothing worse than having a grand exit ruined. Did he give her a ride?"

"Of course." He took a sip of his beer and then leaned back in his chair. "And most of us took a turn working for Emma, too—landscaping, or building with Sean—and that was definitely more my thing. I still do a lot of work for them, actually, as a subcontractor. Joey's full-time with them since he quit playing ball, and Danny can't tell a dandelion from an orchid, but he's good with a hammer."

Siobhan leaned forward and fiddled with her napkin, wondering how to best phrase the question forming in her mind. "So was it mandatory?"

He tilted his head. "What do you mean?"

"Did you have to work in the family businesses? Like, whether you wanted to or not?"

"Are you asking if our parents forced us and if I'm going to try to make Oliver wash beer glasses and haul bags of mulch?"

Her cheeks grew hot. "Maybe a little bit."

"We all had to work, of course. Working for family gave us the ability to have a first job with a boss who wouldn't hesitate to give us a kick in the ass if we needed it, but also cared about stuff going on in our lives. Plus, they're our family's businesses. They built them and having the next generation learning the ropes means something. Nobody *has* to stay. There's no legacy stuff, like my father built this and now I run it and you have to and so on. Joey stayed on with Emma. There's a good chance Lily's going to run this place someday, but it'll be because she wants to, though my dad talked her into getting a business management degree so her dad will have to pay her more. I think it was just an opportunity to be taught to be out in the workforce by somebody invested in how we turned out as human beings."

"That makes sense."

They lapsed into a comfortable silence, which was okay with Siobhan because it all sounded great. Except for the fact *their* son lived almost an hour and a half south of here. Oliver could only take his place in the Kowalski family business rotation if he was staying with Brian.

Maybe he would be, she thought, and then she took a big swig of beer. If a teenage boy had a choice between living with his mom in an apartment in the suburbs or living up here, with all the family and opportunities they had to offer, why wouldn't Oliver choose Brian?

"Hey, you okay over there?"

She blinked away the moisture in her eyes before it could coalesce into actual tears and smiled. "Of course. Just lost in thought for a minute."

"While we're *still* waiting on Kevin, I wanted to talk to you about Oliver's birthday. My family would like to be there, of course."

"*All* of them?"

He chuckled. "No. But a lot of them."

"Fair warning—besides me and Oliver, I can fit maybe one and a half more people in my apartment before sitting on laps comes into play."

"We'd love to throw him a party at the campground. I know it's a lot to ask and you might not believe this, but they really are doing their best to give you space. But birthdays are a pretty big deal in our family and we missed his first one."

Siobhan struggled to keep her smile. Coming on the heels of her worrying about the possibility of Oliver choosing him over her as a teenager, Brian's words landed differently than they may have any other time. But she knew it was her own insecurity talking, and she took a deep breath before responding.

"It would have to be on a weekend, obviously," she said. "I can't miss more work, and I know you guys are busy on the weekends."

He nodded. "Yeah, ideally it would be on a Saturday afternoon and be a day trip for my family because we definitely can't put them all up again. But you and Oliver could spend the night and go home Sunday since it's farther for you and a lot of car seat time for him."

"And Robin. She'd come up with us, so she'd be staying, too. Oliver can't have a birthday party without his auntie Robin."

Brian grinned. "Of course. I'd love to meet her. So would my family."

There was nothing she could really object to. And she had to admit Oliver would love to spend his birthday at the campground with room to run. "He'll be upset it's too cold for the pool."

"Rob will have it covered by then, so he won't be able to see the water. That might help him understand it's gone to sleep or whatever until next summer."

Kevin walked up to the table, grabbing an empty chair from a nearby table to sit in. "Hey, sorry to make you wait. Our new server grabbed a basket of jalapeño poppers thinking it was the stuffed mushrooms for his table and let's just say I had to sign off on a pretty big gift card."

"This isn't a bad place to wait," Siobhan said. "I'm a homebody by nature, so being home with Oliver isn't a struggle for me. Plus, my friend Robin comes over and we do movie nights. But it's nice to get out once in a while."

Like a date. No, it wasn't a date.

"Thanks. We're pretty proud of this place, and we have a second location up in the northern part of the state, too, though friends run that one."

"I've never really paid attention to sports, so I imagined a grubby bar with angry men yelling obscenities at televisions."

"Only during the playoffs." Kevin's laugh echoed through the dining room, and then he slid a napkin across the table. "My friend Paulie—well, and her parents, I guess—they know a lot of well-connected people in Boston."

Siobhan frowned. "Like the mob?"

"No." He paused, tilting his head. "I mean, *maybe*. But in this case, no. She explained your situation to a very close family friend who happens to be a family court judge."

Siobhan's skin prickled as she leaned closer to Brian, trying to see the napkin he'd picked up. There was a name and address, along with a date and time, scrawled across it.

"Bring the paternity test results with you to that meeting, and be prepared to answer a lot of custody-type questions and do a lot of talking. Bring a written co-parenting plan. Both of you need to be there, and you can bring your lawyers even though you won't need them, and she'll sign off on amending the birth certificate and adoption so you're both legally Oliver's parents."

It sounded too good to be true, and Siobhan took the napkin from Brian. "And she can do that? It'll be legal?"

"Yes. She's not doing anything she wouldn't do eventually, anyway, but it'll save you a lot of time and money and headaches waiting for hearings and all that." He shook his head. "Somebody dropped the ball here because Kelly should have had to prove paternity before the adoption because she was legally married to Brian at conception so he was, by default, the presumed father. It's right there in the dates. Hell, she shouldn't have been able to put that other guy on the birth certificate without a test. The divorce shouldn't have been finalized without one. There was a glitch in the system somewhere, and the judge is going to make *their mistakes* right without dragging it out. That's all."

"I don't understand," Brian said, shaking his head. "Just like that?"

"Just like that, though it's not really that simple. It's a favor called in on behalf of family by somebody the judge knows and trusts."

A tear slipped down Siobhan's cheek and she thrust it at Brian. "Take this before I accidentally wipe my eyes with it and smear the writing."

Kevin laughed. "I have a text from Paulie with the info, too. She sent it to me and I'll forward it, but we just like writing important things on napkins around here."

"I noticed the framed napkin with lipstick kisses over the bar," Siobhan said.

"Beth and Lily, back when Lily was tiny," he said with a smile full of love and nostalgia.

"And my brothers and I wrote the business plan for buying the campground on the back of a Jasper's napkin," Brian said.

Kevin snorted. "Playing pretty loose with the words *business plan*."

"Hey, we own Birch Brook Campground and it's going pretty okay."

Kevin laughed and then nodded at Siobhan. "See? That's the magic of a Jasper's napkin. Now how about we introduce you to the magic of a Jasper's burger?"

"That was amazing," Siobhan said, pushing her empty plate away. "I can't believe I ate all of it."

Brian gestured at his also empty plate. "I know how you feel."

"I think knowing that everything's going to be okay—legally, I mean—was this huge weight off and I'm not even worried at all about Oliver because he's with your parents. It's been a long time since I've felt this relaxed."

"It does feel good. Every time I think about the mess we were in, it drags up a lot of stuff for me and I'm looking forward to being able to close that door forever." He held up a hand. "No, I won't say more because she's your sister, but it'll feel good to not have to revisit that anger again."

"No, my relationship with my sister is over. It was never great, but now… I'm angry, too. When I asked for her help to sort this out, she told me it's my problem. And I'll never forgive her for what she stole from you and Oliver. Never."

He reached across the table and laced his fingers through hers. "I'm trying to forgive her."

"She doesn't deserve it. Especially from you."

"Maybe not, but if she'd been honest from the start—whether Kelly stayed in a marriage that made her unhappy or we divorced—you wouldn't be Oliver's mom and that's not a trade-off I'd ever make."

She sniffled, squeezing his fingers. "I hadn't thought about it like that."

"I have, because I don't want to spend any more of my life being mad at a woman who's not even part of it anymore. I missed out on Oliver's baby years, but I have him now and he won't even remember a time I wasn't his dad. And you're his mom."

His phone buzzed in his pocket and he let go of her hand to pull it out and read the message. "Speaking of moms."

"Is Oliver okay?"

"He's fine. He's getting sleepy and Mom says they'd be happy to have him spend the night if we'd like to stay out late and have fun." It wasn't until after he'd repeated the message that he realized how it sounded, and his gaze flew to Siobhan. His mother wasn't even trying to be subtle.

Her cheeks were pink, but she was trying not to laugh. "You can tell her we appreciate the offer, but the entire point of us being here is for Oliver to get comfortable with sleeping at your house, so we'll be there shortly."

He knew there was no way Siobhan had missed what his mom was getting at, but at least she wasn't offended. If she wanted to pretend she was amused that his parents were missing the point of the sleepover, he'd let her.

Honestly, he wouldn't have minded taking his mom up on her offer, but that was Siobhan's move to make. Yes, they'd held hands across the table for a minute, but that had been more of a comfort gesture than a romantic one. Other than that, there had been no hot looks, no touching and definitely no kissing.

Oliver was still awake when they arrived, but barely. And Siobhan had to work hard at keeping him awake during the drive back to his place. She didn't want him to just wake up there, which was a possibility considering how hard he slept. It was important for him to go through the process of getting ready for bed and doing the routine, according to her, and she was probably right.

"How about I give you kisses down here and Daddy puts you to bed tonight?"

Brian wondered how long it would take before hearing himself called Daddy didn't hit him with a surge of emotion. He hoped it was never.

Oliver blinked at him, and he smiled back. "I'm pretty good at reading stories."

"Okay."

"Do you remember what you do at bedtime?" Siobhan asked, pulling Oliver onto her lap.

"Get changed and brush my teeth and get a story and then night-night."

She ran her hand over his hair, and Brian saw a hint of sadness in her smile. It couldn't be easy for her to share him, and every day he appreciated her more. "Good job. Give me night-nights now."

After Oliver squeeze-hugged her neck and gave her a smacking kiss, Oliver took his hand and they went up the stairs together. Brian had been practicing with the baby gates and he was pretty proficient at this point. Stella wasn't a fan of them, of course, but they were only closed when Oliver was here.

It probably took him longer to go through the routine than it did Siobhan, but Oliver didn't seem to mind. At this point, he was so sleepy, he probably didn't even care. He sighed contentedly when Brian tucked him into bed, and by the time he finished a story about a train who was learning not to be naughty and ignore caution flags, he was surprised Oliver was still awake.

Barely, but he was awake enough to open his arms for a hug. "Night-night, Daddy."

Brian closed his eyes as the little arms wrapped around his neck, and for a moment he just breathed in the scent of his hair. Then he kissed him on the forehead. "Night-night, son."

After turning on the little night-light, he turned back. "Mommy will be in that room right there and I'll be downstairs, so if you need anything, just holler, okay?"

He made a small sound of understanding, almost out. Brian turned off the light switch and partially closed the door. Not totally, but enough to block out the television or conversation from downstairs.

Siobhan was still on the couch, her legs drawn up so her feet were tucked under her. Stella was sprawled next to her, her head on her lap. When he'd first brought Stella home as a pup, he'd tried to tell her she wasn't allowed on the couch or the bed. She'd disagreed.

The television was on, and Siobhan had the remote in hand, flipping through channels. She paused when she saw him, giving him a smile. "I'm nosy and wanted to see what channel you'd left it on."

He made an exaggerated *uh-oh* face that made her laugh. "I don't even remember what I was watching."

"There was a show about game wardens on."

"Oh, yeah. Stella likes to watch that and cheer on the K-9s from the comfort of her couch. I'm not a big TV watcher, so go ahead and choose anything you want."

She shrugged, setting the remote down after putting it back on the original channel. "It was a long day that ended in a big emotional rush and a large dinner, so I'm not far behind Oliver. How did that go?"

"He went down surprisingly easy," he said, dropping into his battered leather recliner, which had been a hand-me-down from his uncle Joe.

"After extra outside time at daycare because it's getting cooler and a long car ride and then being at your parents, he's exhausted. But he's never had a problem going to bed, as a rule, and he's really comfortable with you."

"It feels miraculous, honestly."

She shrugged. "He's a pretty open, loving kid which obviously can be a concern as a parent sometimes, but also spending a week with both of us helped. Even though you weren't as hands-on, his subconscious probably recognized that I trust you and your family, so he can."

"Is he always so easygoing?"

"Honestly, yes. He's very chill most of the time. He can get whiny and stubborn when he's overstimulated—that's why we were leaving the campground to get lunch that day—and we've had a few temper tantrums, but mostly he's a sweetheart."

They fell into a comfortable silence, both of them looking at the television screen, though he didn't think either of them were particularly watching it. As the minutes ticked by, though, the silence grew heavier.

With Oliver presumably sound asleep, they were as good as alone and they had a history of hot kisses when nobody was watching.

But that had been during their week in that bubble, with the real world on the outside. And he couldn't decide if the happy bombshell Kevin had dropped on them tonight would make it easier or harder to keep their hands off of each other. Now, as long as everything went okay with the judge—and there was no reason to doubt his uncle—sharing Oliver would be their life now. And while they'd had a wonderful dinner and would be sleeping under the same roof tonight, going forward, they would probably only cross paths during drop-off and pickup on his weekends. They might spend a few milestones and holidays together, but there was going to be a physical distance between him and Siobhan.

So did that mean spending a night together would get it out of their systems before the next phase of their relationship? Or would it just make that next phase messy?

Brian was willing to risk the messy if it meant keeping Siobhan in his life. Falling hard and fast for her wasn't something he had ever imagined happening, but here he was. He didn't know if *she* was willing to risk things being messy, though. It was simply a fact that she had more to lose because no matter what happened, Oliver was his biological child. He was never going away.

"I'm beat," Siobhan said after a few more minutes. "I think I'm going to turn in. And, fair warning, being in a new location means that child might get up at the crack of dawn."

He chuckled. "So I should probably turn in, too. Your bag's on the bed and I put a night-light in the bathroom so you don't have to look for the light switch if you get up in the night. If there's anything else you need, just let me know."

"Thank you for that. And for giving up your bed so I could be here for him the first time." When he nodded, she smiled and gave him a little smile. "Good night."

"Night."

He forced himself to keep his eyes on the television and not her butt as she walked up the stairs after expertly handling the baby gate. He heard her go into his bedroom, then into the bathroom. Stella was giving him questioning looks because this was definitely not part of their routine, and Brian decided it was a good time to let her out to do her business.

After flipping on the outside light and scanning the yard for random visitors that might want to fight Stella, spray her or give her a face full of quills, he opened the door and followed her out. Standing on the back step, he crossed his arms and tried to keep her on task as quietly as possible.

Once the dog had gone through her bedtime song and dance, he brought her in and tried to convince her to curl up on the recliner. She was having none of that and stretched out on the couch.

The creaking of floorboards above him told Brian Siobhan was finished in the bathroom and was moving around his bedroom. As quietly as he could, he went up the stairs and opened the baby gate at the top. There was no sense closing the one at the bottom when Oliver was upstairs, so at least there was only the one. He'd stashed a pair of sweats and a soft, well-worn T-shirt in the linen closet, so he was able to brush his teeth and get ready for bed without disturbing her. Then he crept down the stairs, making sure to close the top gate, and made himself comfortable in the recliner.

With the TV on and muted, and the overhead light off, he hoped it would hold his attention enough to distract him from the woman above him, but not enough to keep him awake.

An hour later, he was still awake, and so was Siobhan. It had been quiet for a while, and he'd assumed she was asleep. But then the floorboards had creaked and the thick rug probably muffled the sound for her, but the subfloor was old enough so he could follow her steps across the room and back by the various squeaky spots.

She was pacing.

He tried to ignore it. Whether she slept or did laps to get her steps in or whatever was none of his business. If she needed something, she knew where to find him.

Unless she assumed he was asleep and didn't want to wake him up.

What if the bedroom was too hot or too cold? Maybe she needed another blanket. His window stuck a bit. Maybe she was desperate for fresh air and couldn't get the window open. He didn't want to invade her privacy or overstep, but he also couldn't stand the thought of her suffering half the night instead of sleeping over something he could easily take care of.

He deliberated another few minutes before throwing off the lightweight fleece blanket and getting up. After giving Stella the command to stay on the couch, which she was more than happy to obey, he crept up the stairs— again with the gate that was already the bane of his existence—and tapped lightly on the door.

She opened it, looking at him with her lips pressed together. He tried *really* hard not to notice she wasn't wearing a bra under her baby blue sleep shirt and the matching shorts were definitely short. It wasn't easy, but he managed to keep his eyes on her face for the most part.

Then she turned and walked away, leaving the door open. She started pacing again, a shorter route this time, and he stepped over the threshold. After a moment of indecision, he opted for not disturbing the toddler across the hall and moved inside enough to close the door behind him.

"I can hear you pacing up here. Is everything okay?" She shook her head, but slowly, and with the way her lips were still pressed together, Brian got the impression she was mad about something. "Trouble sleeping?"

The slow shaking of her head shifted to a slow nod before she covered her face with her hands. "This room smells like you."

"I'm…sorry, I guess? I put fresh sheets on the bed. I could spray some air freshener around, but then it'll probably just smell like a tropical version of me."

To his relief, she was smiling when she dropped her hands. "Yeah, that would definitely be worse."

Brian wasn't sure how to ask what he could to help her because he wasn't sure he wanted to know why the room smelling like him would keep her from sleeping. While occasionally, after a hard day of work, he might get a little rank, his bedroom shouldn't smell that bad. Especially with fresh bedding and all of his laundry clean.

"Or maybe it's my imagination," she muttered, and he wasn't sure if she was talking to him or to herself. "In your bed with my head on your pillow, I just imagine it must smell like you and then it does."

He finally caught on to what was happening, and he had to bite back a smile at the realization that thinking about him was keeping her awake. "We can switch if you want."

She snorted. "You think your couch smells *less* like you?"

"Fair point. Although, I'd argue the couch is more Stella scented." He took a single step forward. "Is there anything I can do to help you sleep?"

She pressed her fingertips together for a moment,

slowly shaking her head, but he could see the amusement in her eyes. "I see what you're doing."

"I like to make sure my guests are taken care of."

Her arched eyebrow let him know that hadn't come out the way he'd intended. "Not that I have a lot of guests. Dammit. Is there something I can do to help you sleep, Siobhan?"

"Yes."

Chapter Twenty

The only thing Siobhan knew for sure in that moment was that she wasn't going to be able to sleep until she'd quenched some of her thirst for the man whose scent had been filling her senses since she came upstairs.

She'd thought being away from the campground and returned to her regular daily life would diminish her attraction to him, as though he was a summer fling during a holiday on a tropical island—not that she'd ever had one, but she'd watched her share of romantic comedies. She'd been wrong.

Now, because she wasn't capable of anything else and was sick of resisting, she stepped forward and let Brian haul her into his arms, his mouth claiming hers. He kissed her hard, letting her feel the hunger that matched her own, and slid her hands under his T-shirt so she could feel the hot, solid muscles of his back under her palms.

It wasn't until she was out of breath and her entire body ached with need for him that Siobhan realized he'd been slowly backing them toward the bed. The bump of the mattress behind her knees broke through the haze of desire and she put her hands on his shoulders to hold him still.

"We shouldn't do this." She didn't sound convincing, even to her own ears. "We can't."

"We can't do this," he agreed. But then he tucked her hair behind her ear and then trailed the backs of his fingers over her cheek and neck. "Can we keep seeing each other and being a part of each other's lives and *not* do this, though?"

Resting her forehead against his shoulder, she sighed. "Not without cold showers, buckets of ice cream and a lot of tossing and turning."

"Why should we both suffer like that?"

"Because we might mess everything up."

"We won't let it. I know you'll put Oliver first, no matter what. And I know I will," he murmured as he pressed a line of kisses down her jaw to punctuate his words. "This is separate. Ours."

"Maybe just this once, to get it out of our systems." She tipped her head back, baring her throat to his mouth. "Or twice."

She already knew this man was like potato chips. Just once wouldn't be enough.

It was as if consent lit a fire in Brian, and she gasped when his mouth closed over the soft fabric of her shirt, which did nothing to lessen the impact when he captured her nipple between his lips.

Everything faded away except his mouth and his hands on her body. He was ravenous for her, and it didn't take him long to make her sleep shirt and shorts disappear. Once she was naked on the bed, he stripped off his shirt and then gave her a look so hot it made her shiver.

"Damn," he said in a husky whisper. "You are so gorgeous."

Siobhan pulled him down, burying her fingers in his hair so she could kiss him thoroughly. Then she released him so she could run her hands over his arms and shoulders, and then skim her fingernails over his back. She was fascinated by the way his muscles rippled and flexed, reacting to her lightest touch.

Brian talked to her the entire time, letting her know how beautiful she was and how the feel of her turned him on. Her nails dug into his shoulders as he licked his way down her stomach, and she sank her fingers into his hair as he reached her thighs.

It wasn't until he'd gotten one orgasm out of her, the back of her hand pressed to her lips so she wouldn't cry out, that he kissed his way back up her body. He was briefly distracted by her breasts, but she wrapped her legs around his and nudged him to keep him moving.

It only took him a few seconds to don the condom he'd fished out of the bedside drawer at some point. Then he was inside her, moving with slow and measured strokes, as his blue eyes held her gaze captive.

Then she moaned against his mouth as he thrust deeper into her because she'd wanted this for so long, and his strokes quickened in response. She dug her fingers into his hips, wanting all of him as the need steadily built.

When Brian reached down and stroked her with his thumb, she raised her hand, biting down on her knuckle to keep from crying out. Siobhan heard him groan as her body clenched around him, and then he quickened his pace, thrusting deeper and faster until his orgasm shook him.

When he collapsed on top of her, his fast and hot breaths punctuating the kisses he pressed to her shoulder, she wrapped her arms around him and held him close. Neither of them spoke as their breathing slowed, and Siobhan was content to bask in the afterglow.

With a reluctant sigh, he withdrew, and Siobhan heard the rustle of the tissue box and then a plastic sound she

assumed was the lid of the small trashcan under the bedside table. A moment later, he pulled her into his arms
and kissed the top of her head.

There was no harm in cuddling, she told herself. But
only for a few minutes, and then they needed to go their
separate ways. Waking up naked and tangled together in
the morning was definitely not part of the *get it out of
their systems* plan.

But when his breathing slowed, coming in deep and
even puffs against her skin, she nudged him with her
foot. "Brian."

He made a vague questioning sound that told her he'd
been almost asleep, so she nudged him harder. "Ow.
What's the matter?"

"You need to go."

"Go where? I live here."

"Back to the couch."

For a long moment, she thought he was either choosing to ignore her or had fallen asleep, but then he lifted
his head. "Seriously?"

"Yes. This is all confusing enough for Oliver. I don't
want him finding us in bed together to make it even more
confusing."

He groaned and rolled onto his back. "He'll probably
call for you rather than roaming around."

"You put the baby gate at the top of the stairs pre-
cisely because he might come looking for a parent," she
reminded him.

"Good point," he admitted with obvious reluctance.
"I'm going."

But he kissed her again before sliding out of the bed
to retrieve his sweat pants, and Siobhan almost changed
her mind.

She wasn't wrong, though. Knowing what Oliver understood at this age was tough, but he could probably wrap his mind around the concept of mommy and daddy as a family unit, and she wanted to avoid making her and Brian a couple in his mind.

And herself, she thought as she listened to Brian wrestle with the unfamiliar baby gate before his footsteps receded down the stairs. She couldn't make them a couple in *her* mind, either, and waking up naked with him in the morning would be a giant step in that direction.

As she drifted off to sleep, she thought maybe she should have told Brian that instead of hiding behind her— *their*—son, but there would be so many tough conversations in their future.

Maybe they could just keep this one thing light and easy.

"Daddy!"

Brian jerked awake, the cycle of sleep to confusion to alarm racing through his head and circling back to the only important thing—Oliver yelling "Daddy."

His son needed him.

Hitting the lever on the side of his recliner too hard as he tried to get up got him launched onto the hardwood floor, knee first. After pushing himself to his feet, he struggled with the first baby gate—which he'd closed after Stella kept trying to go upstairs and he got sick of her nails clacking on the wood—and then took the stairs two at a time, ignoring the dog's panicked barking. The baby gate at the top of the stairs stuck and he finally just shoved it hard, ripping the screws out of the wood.

Siobhan stepped into the hall as he scrambled over the plastic and pushed Oliver's door open, practically falling into the room.

No blood. No tears.

No flames or smoke.

No man in a black ski mask in the corner.

He looked at his son, chest heaving and knee throbbing. "What's wrong?"

Oliver smiled. "I'm awake."

"Oh. Good morning," Brian said, and then he flopped onto his back on the floor, trying to catch his breath and hoping his heart wouldn't actually explode.

A high-pitched giggle echoed through the room. "Daddy's silly."

"Yes, Daddy is *very* silly," Siobhan said, looking down at him and clearly struggling not to laugh. "Are you okay?"

"Well, he's okay so I'm okay…but actually no. Not really." He put his hand on his chest. "Did that not scare you?"

She laughed. "If he's distressed, trust me, you *will* know. And also, I just rolled over and looked at that high-tech surveillance system you probably bought at a CIA garage sale and installed even though he's right across the hall."

He frowned. "A baby monitor is a totally typical thing to have. Even my parents had one."

"Did theirs have high-definition video and also track his temperature and heart rate?"

"They might have if it existed. Don't you have one?"

"Yes, I have a little baby monitor that's a microphone on his end and a receiver on mine so I can hear him. It doesn't double as a TSA body scanner."

Stella, having sniffed Brian all over and determined that either he was fine or, if he wasn't, there wasn't anything she could do about it, circled wide around him toward the bed.

He put out his hand. "No dogs on that bed, Stella."

She woofed once and veered just out of his reach before hopping up on the bed. Oliver wrapped his arms around her and she gave him sloppy morning kisses while he giggled.

"Since this is a test run, I'm going to go start a pot of coffee and leave you to it." She blew Oliver a kiss and then looked back at Brian. "Do you need help getting up?"

While he might be fresh out of dignity, he still had *some* pride left. "Nope. Just a few more seconds of oxygen and I'll be good to go."

She was still laughing when she walked out of the room, and he had to listen to her moving the debris of the baby gate so she could go down the stairs. He waited until she was on the first floor before rolling over and pushing himself to his feet in case he couldn't do it without some moaning and groaning.

Considering they got off to a fairly rocky start, getting Oliver up in the morning went surprisingly well. Brian got him changed and dressed with no problem. Because he'd been so tired last night, they'd skipped tubby time, but Siobhan said she'd given him a quick shower after daycare to get the sunscreen and bug spray off before the car ride. They brushed their teeth together, and Brian brushed Oliver's hair before running the brush through his own.

He'd jump in the shower…later, he guessed. He'd have to remember to ask Siobhan or his mother how an adult who was alone with a toddler got to go in the bathroom alone and be naked under running water and unable to hear what was going on in the rest of the house.

He walked sideways down the stairs, holding Oliver's hand while the child held the railing with the other. Brian wasn't sure his nerves could take it, but he knew navigating stairs was an important thing to learn. About a third of the way down, Oliver gave up and butt-bumped down the rest, still holding Brian's hand. That worked for him.

When he saw Siobhan sitting at the kitchen table, sipping her coffee in her pajamas, with her hair a messy cloud and one of his zip sweatshirts open over her sleep shirt, Brian's heart ached in a way he hoped never stopped.

This was what he wanted.

It felt so right, her smiling at him and then at their son, who was a lot more interested in what Stella was doing than the adults. This felt like home to him, and he busied himself taking Stella out so Siobhan wouldn't see the depth of emotion in his eyes.

Although, that would be hard for her to do since he realized once Stella was finished that Siobhan wasn't actually meeting his gaze. They made eye contact once, and she'd blushed and looked away.

Maybe it was just typical morning-after shyness. This was the space where they'd probably have a conversation about what happened, how absolutely perfect it was—in his opinion, of course, but he was sure she'd also enjoyed it—and where they went from here. But between his near-death experience trying to save his son from absolutely nothing and then going through a very new-to-him morning experience, there hadn't been a time for talking.

"I usually give him some water in his sippy cup when he first wakes up," Siobhan told him. "I'm going to get dressed now and then we can do breakfast."

She was gone before Brian could say anything, not that he had any idea what those words would be. They'd talked about a lot of things in front of Oliver because he was little and didn't grasp a lot of concepts, but there was a line.

Brian got Oliver's sippy cup from his bag and filled it

with filtered water from the fridge. Oliver thanked him in his little voice, making Brian smile, and then the boy toddled off to the living room, where he flopped down on the oversized dog bed that didn't get a lot of use. Stella joined him there, and Oliver ran his fingers through her fur while having his drink.

It took Siobhan longer than Brian expected to get dressed, but he supposed she might be enjoying having the freedom of Oliver being watched over. She smiled at him when she finally came down the stairs, but it didn't look like a smile to tell him she'd had a great time last night and wanted to do it again. It looked like an *I have a very amusing secret* smile.

"Oliver, what do you want for breakfast?" she called, again delaying any kind of adult conversation.

"Eggs!"

She looked at Brian and shrugged. "Usually he likes oatmeal, and I brought a box. But I guess today, he wants scrambled eggs."

"I can do that. How about you?"

"Scrambled eggs works for me."

They worked side by side, him scrambling a skillet full of eggs while she fed bread into the toaster and buttered it when it popped. Brian noticed after the first round, she nudged the dial toward darker toast a bit, but he kept his mouth shut. He could live with darker toast if that's how they liked it.

They'd just sat down, Oliver in a booster that was strapped to a chair, when his phone started blowing up. "Sorry. Usually I wouldn't have my phone at the table, but that's the family group chat and there's no reason why they should all be on right now."

She shrugged, that playful smile flirting with her lips again. "No problem."

That's when he realized hers was vibrating, too, almost in time with his, and he unlocked his screen to find a ton of messages that seemed to have come through *after* Siobhan posted a video link. He clicked on it and was treated to watching Oliver sitting up in bed and yelling for him. Then it sounded like a tornado swept through the downstairs, destroying everything in its wake—and oops, he hadn't meant to say that word out loud—before he stumbled into the camera frame. And it ended with his cute son telling him he was awake.

Realization struck that she'd taken so long upstairs because she'd figured out how to rewind the video and then captured the playback with her own phone. He lowered his phone, staring at his betrayer. "What did you do? How are you in the family group chat?"

Siobhan shrugged one shoulder, a sly smile curving her lips as she scrolled. "It's a new one with basically just your immediate family, so we can share Oliver updates. Like waking up for the first time in Daddy's house."

Brian opened a video message and immediately regretted it as he watched a video—taken from the doorbell camera at the campground—of Rob watching the video and then laughing so hard he dropped his phone and had to start it all over again.

He put his hand over his heart and sighed. "I can't believe you would do this to me. You're supposed to be on my side."

She snickered. "Oliver has some catching up to do when it comes to being a Kowalski. He's still little, but I can give him a head start."

He laughed. "Brutal."

"Yeah, I know. Kowalskis can hold a grudge forever. Blah, blah, blah." She pointed her finger at him. "Be honest. How long would it have been before *you* sent the video to the family group chat?"

He tried to scowl, but he couldn't hold it and chuckled. "I would at least have finished eating my breakfast in peace first."

Scrambled eggs weren't great cold, so they both silenced their phones and concentrated on breakfast. Once she realized toddlers weren't the cleanest of eaters, Stella fell even more in love with the small human. Unfortunately, Oliver figured out very quickly that the dog loved snatching up dropped bits of food and it became a game. Siobhan had to break out the mom voice to put an end to it.

"So that's a thing," Siobhan said once Oliver went back to munching on his toast. "I know you're going to want everything to be happy and fun because you're getting to know each other and you want him to love you, but you *will* create a monster if you don't set boundaries. There will be times you have to tell him no. He might cry. He might pitch a fit and need to sit quietly on his bed for a few minutes. But a no has to be a no, and he will still love you. I promise."

"Okay." He wasn't looking forward to that. "I know there's going to be a learning curve, but I have way too much respect for you to put us in a fun parent versus the stern parent situation with him."

Once they were finished, Oliver went back to hanging out in the dog bed with Stella, and Brian frowned. "Should I get one of those little stuffed couches for him? A beanbag? A little rocking chair?"

She laughed and shook her head. "Don't bother. He'll

still hang out on the dog bed. That's money better spent on lint rollers."

They were laughing together as they cleared the table, and he started filling the sink with hot, soapy water. He imagined starting every day this way—or at the least the weekends—and smiled as he dropped the plates and silverware into the water and turned off the faucet.

"That appointment's only like ten days away," Siobhan said, sounding serious again. "Should we just meet there?"

"It would probably be easiest because we can't meet at your place without you driving north and then turning around and going back into the city. But maybe we can take Oliver out after to celebrate?"

"That sounds great." She handed him the sponge she'd used to wipe the table down. "I'll be so happy when it's done, not just because we'll be settled with regard to Oliver, but I can't keep taking time off of work. Just the week of the wedding was a big ask because it was short notice, and since then, I've had to take multiple days and half days off, plus even when I'm there, I've had a lot on my mind. Obviously. But I'm going to lose my job if I don't get it together."

"You know, you and Oliver could move in here."

The words fell out of his mouth and they felt so natural to him, but Siobhan stared at him for a long moment as his heart pounded in his chest. "What?"

"If you think about it, it makes sense."

"It makes *no* sense."

Panic welled up in Brian's chest. He was blowing this. "You can get out of the city. Oliver will have a yard, and Stella. And you said you hate your job and the commute. You could find a job you want around here, and the child-care is so much less expensive. And he'd have both of his parents."

"Stop talking."

He stopped talking. Siobhan was so still, except for the rapid rise and fall of her chest. His heart was pounding in his chest, and he heard Stella's nails on the floor and then Oliver giggling. Siobhan's expression gave him nothing and the blankness on her face made him realize what a terrible error he'd made.

"I think you have everything under control here," she said quietly. "I'm going to go talk to Oliver and explain again that he's sleeping here, and then I'm hitting the road."

He sucked in a breath, his brow furrowing. "You're not staying?"

"I don't think so." She inhaled sharply through her nose, her lips pinched together. "Brian, Oliver doesn't come with a ready-made family. He's your son. You're going to spend time with him and have a hand in raising him. But us? Our job is to co-parent him and what we did last night makes that messy and we absolutely shouldn't have done it. And I'm going to go home so it doesn't happen again."

"A ready-made family?" He took a step toward her. "You're going home? What are you talking about?"

"We're not going to live here together as one happy little family. This is *your* time with him. I brought him here and spent the night to help him be comfortable. He did really good and I know you'll be fine so I'm going home. We'll come up with a time and place for you to hand him back off to me tomorrow."

The pain was so intense, he wasn't sure he'd be able to take a deep breath. He'd totally misread the situation and apparently for her, the sexual chemistry between them was only that. Chemistry. She didn't want him.

He was afraid to speak while his emotions were in turmoil because he didn't want to say anything that would make it worse. After the positive news from Kevin, a personal conflict between him and Siobhan would be a huge setback. "Sure. Okay."

Then he turned his back on her, returning to the sink, because it was anything *but* okay.

He listened as Siobhan went to Oliver, who was sitting on the floor, playing with his trucks with Stella curled up next to him.

"Did you like sleeping at Daddy's house?" he heard her ask, and he squeezed his eyes closed so they couldn't tear up. "Good. Remember Mommy told you that sometimes you'd sleep at Daddy's and it would be just you and Daddy?"

"And Stella?"

"And Stella. You're going to sleep at Daddy's tonight and then Mommy will get you tomorrow, okay?"

"Okay."

"I'm going to go upstairs and get my stuff and then I'll come kiss you goodbye and you can have fun with Daddy and Stella today."

He must have been okay with that because a moment later, Brian heard Siobhan's footsteps on the stairs. During the time she was up there, he did his best to reset himself—he'd been wrong about what was between them and because of that, she was going to distance herself.

And he had to let her. He couldn't make her feel something she didn't, and trying to would only complicate their tender new balance with Oliver. Their son was number one. Always.

Siobhan left twenty minutes later, after giving Oliver a huge hug and covering his face in kisses. Brian heard the tremor in her voice, despite her obvious effort to sound positive and upbeat for their son. He assumed it was because she was leaving her baby overnight, because when she turned to Brian, her face was blank again.

They agreed on a time and place to meet tomorrow and that was that. He listened until he couldn't hear her car on the road anymore, and then he emotionally dusted himself off and went into the living room.

"Who wants to go for a walk?"

Chapter Twenty-One

"Are you sure you don't want to go out?"

Siobhan let her head loll sideways against the back of the couch, so she was facing Robin. "I absolutely don't want to go out."

"I know it won't take your mind off things, but we could go to a sports bar and watch drunk men yell at the television screens."

"In the mood I'm in, I'd probably start cheering for the other team just to make them angrier." Plus, it would just make her think of being at Jasper's with Brian.

"Definitely no sports bars, then. I could grab a bottle of wine and we could throw on some reality dating show and yell at them, instead."

Siobhan chuckled. "That's tempting, but no wine for me. I want to be able to drive if…you know."

If Brian called because Oliver was inconsolable or if there was an emergency. Or if he realized he was in over his head and needed help. If their first solo overnight didn't go well, Siobhan wanted to be able to get to her son.

Robin sighed. "If you weren't ready to leave him, you should have stayed tonight, too. Brian wouldn't have minded."

"I'm sure he wouldn't, since we had sex last night."

She probably should have made sure her friend hadn't just taken a big drink of water before dropping that little tidbit, but luckily—with some coughing and spluttering—Robin managed not to do a spit take.

"I'm sorry, you *what*?"

After taking a deep breath, Siobhan filled her best friend in on not only the last twenty-four hours, but some of the holes she'd left in the story to date.

"Wait. Seriously. Don't move." Robin got up and practically sprinted out of the apartment and across the hall. She returned slightly out of breath, carrying a bottle of open wine and one glass. She poured herself a full glass before settling back on the couch. "What the hell, Siobhan?"

"I know."

"I'm going to forgive you for not having served up this delicious tea before now because I know your history with your family. Your mother and sister are good at manipulating emotions so you only like to express them when you're absolutely certain about what you're feeling. But this is…yeah. You need to talk this out with me."

"How do I know if he's really into me or if he just likes the idea of us being an instant family? There's no way to separate Oliver from the equation, so there's no way for me to judge how much he's a factor in Brian's feelings."

"I know you and I honestly don't think you would have ended up in bed with him if you weren't getting an authentic into-you vibe." She sighed and sipped more wine. "I don't think you doubt that he's into you. I think it was the jump from bed to cohabitation in the time it takes to eat scrambled eggs."

"I know that's how it sounds, but there's been something between us almost from the beginning." Siobhan groaned, closing her eyes for a second. "The second time, I mean. Not the time he was marrying my sister."

"I'm going to ask you a question that's probably going to make you mad, but as your best friend, I think I have to ask it anyway."

Siobhan sighed. "Okay. I'm ready."

"Janelle and Kelly are…" She paused, frowned, and then waved her hand. "They are who they are, so it's been just you and Oliver. And me, of course. But is there a chance that's why *you're* attracted to Brian? Because he comes with a big, ready-made family that sounds pretty awesome?"

Siobhan thought about the Kowalski family, and how much she'd loved spending time with them. They were loving and supportive and funny and very, very focused on being there for each other in all the right ways. She definitely loved his family and even though she knew she'd have to deal with feelings of not being enough for Oliver when he was older, she was so thankful her son got to be one of them.

"You're mad, aren't you?" Robin couldn't take the silence. "Like, so mad you're not talking to me right now?"

Siobhan chuckled, and then rolled her head against the couch to face Robin again. She really wished her apartment was big enough for conversational seating. "I'm not mad. It's a valid question and I'm just processing and trying to figure out just *how* valid it is."

"Oh, good. Our friendship would be one hundred percent more awkward if I had to do all the talking."

"The thing is, I already *have* the family. I'm Oliver's mom and they've welcomed me in. I could call Lisa to chat or for advice. I'll probably get invited for Thanksgiving. I don't have to be with Brian in that way to be a part of the family." She sighed. "But it was definitely a valid best friend question. You're very wise."

"I'm the oldest child. It's in my DNA."

Siobhan took the glass out of Robin's hand, downed a few swallows of wine, and then handed it back. "My problem is that I want Brian. He is everything I ever could have imagined wanting in a man. And more, really. Like there are things about him I didn't even know to put on my list, like I want a man who'll carry a rock around in his pocket because it was the first thing his son ever gave to him. When I'm with him, it just feels right."

"So when you're with him, it feels right, but when he asked you to be with him, you left."

"Yes."

"I'm going to need more to work with here, Siobhan."

"It feels so fast and it was all wrapped up with Oliver and yes, it *feels* right, but what if it's not? Right now, we can move on and be cordial and be great co-parents. If I quit my job and we move in with him and Oliver has his family, but it's not *actually* right, it'll be devastating for everybody."

"But what if it's right?"

Siobhan sighed. "There's too much at stake."

"That's exactly my point."

Being alone with an almost two-year old wasn't quite as terrifying as Brian had feared it would be.

He had a wealth of child-rearing knowledge at his fingertips. All he had to do was send an SOS text message and his phone would be flooded with advice. And if he needed hands-on help, his mom wasn't that far away. She'd drop everything and head over if they needed her.

It wasn't a surprise when Sean pulled up to the house

a little before noon. Brian had posted a photo of the damage he'd done taking out the gate at the top of the stairs, but in the original family group chat because it would hurt too much to see Siobhan's name coming up on his phone. There had been a lot of jokes, of course, but they also knew it would be tough for him to fix it while Oliver was there, and nobody wanted the little guy taking a tumble down the stairs.

Sean was there almost three hours, and Brian made small talk with him. But he didn't let on that maybe Siobhan hadn't left under the best of circumstances. It was too fresh and tender, and he couldn't take talking about it yet. And not only would Sean want to talk about it, but he'd tell Emma and then everybody in the family would want to talk about it.

Mostly, he tried to keep Oliver and Stella out in the yard as much as possible. Not only did the open sky and fresh air help Brian's state of mind, but his best strategy was to wear Oliver out so he'd be good and sleepy by bedtime.

Shortly after they finished supper—dinosaur chicken nuggets and fries from the oven because he wasn't going to fight food battles on day one—Brian's phone chimed with a text message from Siobhan.

How's Oliver doing?

Was the wording deliberate? She hadn't asked how *they* were doing or how he was handling things, but wanted to know specifically how Oliver was.

He's good. We finished eating and now he's telling Stella about all the kids at his school. He's told me several times that he's sleeping here tonight and will see you tomorrow, so he's reassuring himself.

Only a few seconds passed before the dots flashed to indicate she was typing, and then her response came through.

Okay. I'm not sure if hearing my voice would make it better or worse, so I'll leave it alone. But call me if he needs me.

I will.

And that was it. No more dots and no reply.

The next morning, he and Oliver were both a little out of sorts. Oliver had gone to bed alright, but Brian had tossed and turned, staring at the ceiling, and trying not to think about Siobhan being in this bed with him last night.

Maybe, if he'd kept his mouth shut, she'd be with him tonight. His mother used to tell him he was the most guarded of her boys because he was the opposite when he was little. He'd shared pretty much every thought and emotion in his head, but they were often used against him and he'd learned not to share.

Clearly, Siobhan had gotten through those defenses and here he was again.

Then, about two in the morning, Brian had awakened to Oliver calling for his mommy. He hadn't wanted daddy at all, but eventually he'd calmed down. Brian let Stella in the room to help Oliver feel better, and eventually he'd gone back to sleep.

There was oatmeal for breakfast and then a short visit from his grandparents. They'd managed to distract Oliver until it was almost time to leave, and Brian was grateful. He knew Oliver would adapt and get used to this new reality, but right now he felt guilty for changing up the boy's life. Even though he was handling it better than Brian expected, it was a tough age for a change in routine.

By the time they pulled into the parking lot of the store where they were meeting Siobhan, Brian was exhausted. He treasured the time he spent with his son, but his regret that he'd screwed things up so badly with Siobhan was turning him inside out. He'd thrown his own bags on the front passenger seat with Oliver's, and when they were done here, he and Stella were going to head straight north to the campground. He needed to be outside, doing hard work and sweating out the feelings he had no other outlet for.

"Mommy!"

Siobhan was leaning against the trunk of her car, and she offered up a huge smile and wave when she saw Brian's truck. Of course that was for Oliver, Brian told himself, but it still took his breath away.

He got Oliver's bags out of the truck while Siobhan freed her son from the car seat and covered his face in kisses. Oliver talked as fast as his little mouth could make words, telling her about the yard and Sean and the nuggets and he made it sound like he'd had the time of his life.

Since Siobhan had chosen a store parking lot and not a restaurant or a park, there was nothing to do but leave. He put Stella on the leash she hated and let her wander on the grass separating them from the next parking lot over, and then he brought her over to say goodbye to Oliver. The little boy hugged her, getting some kisses in return, and then Brian opened the door so she could get back in the truck.

Siobhan had Oliver buckled into the car, but she stepped back so Brian could lean in and give him a goodbye kiss. "I'll see you soon, little man."

"Bye, Daddy."

His heart squeezed in his chest, and he ruffled his son's hair before closing the door. Then, as he turned to face Siobhan, he reminded himself very sternly that he wasn't going to put his emotions on her again.

"He did good," he said in a remarkably steady voice. "He woke up in the night and was a little confused because you weren't there, but he calmed down and Stella helped. He went back to sleep pretty quickly, so I didn't see any reason to wake you up."

"It'll get easier." She gave him a shadow of a smile. "For everybody."

"Yeah. If I don't talk to you before then, I'll meet you at the courthouse, I guess."

"Brian, I'm sorry." She crossed her arms over her chest, tears shimmering in her eyes. "It's a lot and I'm scared and I handled it badly."

He wanted to pull her into his arms and hold her until that tremor in her voice went away. There was so much he wanted to say to her, but he couldn't pour out his feelings in this parking lot when she was about to get on the highway with their son. This was neither the time nor the place, and he couldn't do it.

"We're good," he said, knowing it wasn't enough.

She nodded slowly and when she realized he wasn't going to say more, she sighed. "I should get going. He gets bored in his car seat."

"Drive safe."

He turned away before he could change his mind—before he could back her up against the side of his truck and kiss her until she admitted that she felt the same way he did—and slid into the driver's seat. Stella whimpered, giving him an accusing look.

"You'll see him again soon," Brian promised as he buckled his seat belt. "Now, let's go split some firewood."

Chapter Twenty-Two

The past few weeks of co-parenting, since he'd blown it with Siobhan, had been hell on Brian's nerves. Not the actual parenting together, but the way it forced him to see and talk to Siobhan as she iced him out was tearing him apart.

Not icing him out, he thought. He'd seen her be cold and this wasn't that. She was hurting herself, too, and it didn't make sense to him. They could have been happy together.

They were actually doing okay with the co-parenting, so far. The second sleepover had gone very well, and he'd only had to call his mother three times. And *had to* was a stretch. He would have been fine without her advice, but getting it comforted him and giving it made her happy.

Siobhan hadn't brought Oliver to their meeting with the judge and there had been no ice cream after. She'd felt bad, though it was unavoidable due to her schedule, and he'd chosen not to let his disappointment dim the relief and joy at having the legalities done. He smiled and assured her he'd have ice cream with Oliver to celebrate next time he had him, but parting ways with Siobhan in front of the courthouse had hurt.

The next weekend, Brian had been at the campground. Though he wanted to spend as much time as possible with

Oliver, he knew that as a busy working mom, Siobhan treasured her weekends with him. He wouldn't take them all.

And last weekend, they'd met at the store halfway between their homes, transferring Oliver and what he needed for two days from her car to his truck. Oliver had been a little hesitant about this new arrangement, but Brian had brought Stella with him and she won over her favorite small human.

Could they continue on this way? Yes, they could. They both loved Oliver and put him first. The boy was happy and that was the real bottom line.

But did he *want* to? Absolutely not. He missed Siobhan so much it hurt. Even when they were standing ten feet from each other, he missed her. There was Oliver's mom Siobhan, and then there was *his* Siobhan—the funny, smart and captivating woman who laughed and kissed him under the fairy lights.

They'd be arriving at the campground anytime—Siobhan, Oliver, and Robin—to celebrate Oliver's second birthday with his family. Rob and Hannah had moved into the house, where they'd be spending the winter, so Siobhan could stay in the camper they'd been using before they winterized it. She'd assured Brian's mom Robin wouldn't mind sleeping on the folded-down dinette.

Most of the conversation about the party had taken place between his mom and Siobhan, without him. He wasn't sure if that was for practical reasons—why involve him when he didn't have any idea how to throw a toddler's birthday party?—or if it was Siobhan keeping him at arm's length.

Now he was in the store's supply closet, trying to find the box of paper goods his mother had shipped directly from the online store amid all the other delivery boxes that had shown up over the last week. When the bell over the door chimed, letting him know somebody had entered, he assumed it was his mother, out of patience with him and about to find the box herself.

"I can't move any faster," he called.

"That's strange because it looks like you're standing still."

It was his dad, and he backed out of the closet. "Sorry. I was expecting Mom."

"I'm sure she'll be along, but I thought you and I could use a few minutes to talk."

"Whatever it is, Bobby did it."

He chuckled. "Probably. But what's going on with *you*?"

"What do you mean? I'm getting stuff ready for the party."

"You were happy for a while, but something changed. With the legal business settled and Oliver getting to spend time with you, you should be *more* happy, not *less* happy."

"Siobhan and I, we…complicated things."

"Do you want us all to pretend we couldn't see that happening?"

"Yes." He snorted. "Anyway, the night she stayed over— Oliver's first sleepover—we…escalated the complications, so to speak. The next morning, she was talking about not being able to miss any more work or she'd lose her job and I said they should just move in with me and she just sort of shut down. We're co-parenting and that's all it's going to be."

"And you thought it was more?"

Brian's emotional walls crumbled under the force of his father's understanding, and he let the flood of sorrow and hurt in. "I *hoped* it was more."

When his dad reached out and grabbed his arm, Brian let himself be pulled into the embrace. It was a short hug, but it felt good and it helped. But when his dad pulled back and pointed at the leather chairs, he knew there was more coming.

Once he was seated, his dad went to the refrigerator case and grabbed two bottles of water. On his way to the chairs, he locked the back door so they wouldn't be interrupted— as if Lisa Kowalski wouldn't lay into that doorbell if she wanted her grandson's birthday napkins. Brian knew he should get up and write down the two bottles of water so they could be accounted for, but he didn't have the strength right now.

"Tell me what's going on, son," his dad said as he handed him one of the bottles and sat down across from him.

Brian told him everything. It came out a rambling mess because that's how it all felt in his head, but the gist of it was that he'd fallen for the mother of his child and managed to mess it all up in the process.

"And she accused me of wanting an instant family," he said when he'd gotten it all out. "Does she have a point? I don't know how to convince her that's not how I feel."

"You can't separate the woman from the mother. There are no boxes you uncheck or things you can cross off to see if you'd still feel this way about Siobhan if there was no Oliver and she'd just shown up here to be Steph's maid of honor. I mean, before the wedding I was led to believe you didn't even like her."

"I was wrong. We both were." He ran a hand through his hair. "All of our previous interactions had taken place with or about Kelly. When we had the chance to actually know each other it— it was…she's it for me, Dad. I love her."

"Let me ask you something," his dad said in response, which traditionally prefaced a hard question. "When you asked her to move in with you, did you list all the reasons it would be practical for the two of you and also better for Oliver?"

"I did."

"Okay. Did you also include your feelings for her on that list? Did you tell her you want her to live with you because you love her and you want to make a life together with her?" When he paused, Brian shook his head. "So basically you asked her to give up her job and move to a different state because it would be more convenient, cheaper and allow you to be with Oliver all the time with the benefit of his mom being there all the time to help take care of him?"

"No." Brian turned away, giving himself a moment to temper his tone before he looked back at his dad. "That's not what I said."

"But there's a good chance that's what she heard, son."

He groaned and scrubbed his hands over his face. "You know how I can be, Dad. It's all in my head and I blurt stuff out, but maybe not the right thing or in the right order."

"You should probably try again, but this time with added feelings. And a little honesty wouldn't hurt."

"I can't, Dad. She said we're co-parents from now on, full stop. We're still in the early days of figuring *that* out, and me ignoring her personal boundaries would make it so much harder. I don't want to make her mad."

"I think you need to relax. Enjoy the day, and let her enjoy the day. Everybody will be focused on Oliver and you need to act natural. Don't be pushy. Don't be withdrawn. Just *be*."

"That won't be as easy as you make it sound."

"Nope." His dad snorted, shaking his head. "Nothing about love is easy. But one thing I know for sure is that it's worth it."

* * *

They couldn't have asked for a more beautiful day to celebrate Oliver's second birthday. The sun was shining and it was warm without being hot and sticky, and the foliage was brilliant in its full autumn glory.

Siobhan pulled into the campground, her nerves ragged, and parked at the end of a line of cars belonging to the many Kowalskis she'd be spending the afternoon with. Including Brian.

She'd had no contact with him that wasn't about Oliver since the sleepover that had blown everything up. Other than giving Oliver to him on Fridays and taking him back on Sundays, the only time she'd seen Brian was in the judge's office when she'd approved the amending of the adoption papers and the custodial agreement they'd written up. There hadn't been celebratory ice cream after, despite their previous plan to do so. Oliver hadn't even been with them—he'd stayed at daycare because Siobhan had to get back to work in time for the meeting that was going to determine whether or not she got to keep her job. Luckily when she explained the entire situation, they'd been compassionate, but she was treading on very thin ice. And then there had been another weekend sleepover. She'd met Brian in a parking lot and handed her son over. Then she'd met him there and taken him back two days later.

"Where's the pool?" Oliver asked, pushing himself as high as he could in his car seat, trying to see.

"It's covered up because it's cold, but in the summer, it'll be there again."

"Daddy!" he yelled, and in the side mirror, Siobhan saw Brian walking toward the car.

"Here we go," Robin muttered, unbuckling her seat belt. "Wait. That sounded sinister, didn't it?"

"A little bit."

"I just meant, gee, this is going to be super fun and not at all awkward."

Siobhan laughed. "Surprisingly enough, awkwardness doesn't last long around this family."

The back door opened, and Brian leaned in to kiss Oliver's forehead before going to work on the car seat buckles. "There's my boy. Are you ready to have a fun party?"

"Happy birthday!" Oliver yelled.

When she saw the gift table, she stopped in her tracks, staring at the assortment of gift bags and wrapped boxes. "Are you serious, Brian?"

"It's not as bad as it looks—nothing extravagant, I promise. But there's a lot of us so there are a lot of gifts."

"I'd make a joke about needing a bigger car, but I'm afraid I might need a bigger apartment." Then she looked at him. "Oh, most of it will go to your house, I guess."

He shrugged, and she noticed it wasn't his easy shrug. His entire body looked tense. "Not necessarily. He lives with you and it wouldn't be very nice to make him leave without his birthday presents."

"Hi, I'm Robin." Her friend stepped in before things could get more awkward. "It's nice to finally meet you."

"It's good to meet you, too," Brian said, shaking her hand. "Oliver talks about Auntie Robin a lot, so it's great to have a face to go with the name."

"Nora!" Oliver shouted his friend's name and took off running toward her.

Cousin, Siobhan thought. Nora was his cousin. Regardless, the little girl met him like a long-lost friend, hugging him before leading him away to look at his birthday stuff.

It took almost half an hour to introduce Robin to everybody, and Siobhan wasn't surprised that her friend felt instantly at home. Robin was a social person and the Kowalski family was warm and welcoming by nature.

Siobhan hadn't been sure how much, if anything, Brian had told his family about the recent twists and turns in their relationship, but nobody was standoffish or reserved toward her.

Because Oliver was only two, the actual party segment of the day was kept short, leaving plenty of relaxed time for playing and visiting after. Knowing he wouldn't want to be pulled away from his new toys, she and Lisa had decided to do the cake first.

It was nice not to have to worry about taking pictures or missing anything, either. Rob was always circling, snapping shots she knew would be better than any her outdated phone would capture.

Ellie and Nora had decorated a child-sized folding camping chair—his gift from them—with ribbons and balloons and Oliver sat in it, clapping the entire time they sang "Happy Birthday" to him.

Mary had baked his birthday cake after confirming it wasn't something Siobhan wanted to do herself. It was a large sheet cake made to look like an open book, and on one page it said *Happy birthday, Oliver!* On the other page was a real blue pickup truck toy and two blue candles. It was so beautiful and so perfect for her son that Siobhan actually had to wipe a tear from her cheek. Brian caught her eye and gave her a wink, and she gave him a genuine smile, sliding back into the chemistry they shared.

"Beep beep!" Oliver yelled when he saw the cake, and when it was time to blow out the candles, Siobhan waved Brian in to help him.

"Let's each do one," he said, gesturing for her to join him.

They stood on either side of Oliver and after counting him down from three, they blew out the candles.

"Bobby, did you get that?" Lisa asked.

"Yes, Mom, I did," he said, and Siobhan heard the low-key annoyance at the childhood nickname that still slipped in at family gatherings. Or maybe it was due to the implication the photographer at the party would have missed the birthday boy blowing out the candles.

Beth and Keri had volunteered to slice the cake and add ice cream, with Johnny and Gage passing the plates out, leaving Siobhan free to eat with Oliver and Brian. Her son was thrilled to be the center of everybody's attention, and he kept grinning with a mouth covered in blue frosting that really brought out his eyes.

The gift-opening portion of the party was chaos and required a lot of chasing down bits of wrapping paper that got picked up by the wind. Siobhan was pleased to see that Brian had been right—there *were* a lot of gifts because it was a big family, but nothing extravagant. There were trucks and books and puzzles. She thought her favorite gift was from his uncles—a small blue sweatshirt that had the Birch Brook Campground logo on it, like the ones they wore.

But then Oliver opened his gift from his great-grandparents. It was a soft blue baby blanket, obviously knit by hand.

"I know he's a little old for a baby blanket," Mary said softly. "But all the kids have one."

When Oliver would have dropped it, because trucks were more exciting than blankets for a two-year-old, Siobhan took it and folded it carefully. "It's beautiful. And it's a perfect size for him to use when he curls up with his books. It will be very well loved."

Brian leaned in to see it, and Siobhan handed it to him. He ran his hand over the folded blanket and his eyes were soft and maybe even a little misty. While they didn't have anything like that in her family, she could see that these blankets from Mary were special, and his son getting one affected him deeply.

He had to clear his throat twice before he could speak. "It's beautiful. Thank you, Gram."

Once Oliver had opened his gifts, Robin got him to blow kisses to everybody and say thank you before helping liberate a few of his toys from the packaging. Siobhan was gathering the books and most of the other toys together, and Brian grabbed the empty boxes he'd saved from a delivery and stashed under a picnic table.

They ended up together, somehow, while everybody else was wandering around or talking or watching Oliver. The silence stretched between them as they figured out how to load the gifts into the boxes, until Siobhan couldn't take it anymore.

"Thank you for this party," she said quietly. "Robin and I threw a little party for his first, but there were really only the two of us."

He smiled at her and her heart flip-flopped in her chest. "But he was with you and I bet he loved it."

"He did. There was a lot of singing and clapping." She found the box Gram's blanket had come in and carefully repackaged it in the tissue paper. "Do you want to take this to your house?"

He stared at the box for a few seconds before shrugging one shoulder. "It should stay with him, probably. Maybe it can travel with him. Gram makes them from washable yarn because she likes them being used and loved rather than tucked away in cedar hope chests."

"Mommy, look at my truck," she heard Oliver call, and she turned to see him holding up a firetruck.

"Go ahead," Brian said. "I've got this."

Siobhan started to walk away, her hand going to her back pocket for her phone so she could take a picture of Oliver and his firetruck. It wasn't there and she realized she'd set it down next to one of the boxes.

She spun to grab it and, in that second, caught sight of Brian watching her. The raw, naked yearning grabbed her by the throat and she swallowed hard. In the blink of an eye, it was mostly gone and the relaxed, friendly Brian she'd seen all day was back. But a shadow of his emotions remained, echoing the same feelings she'd been trying to shove down for weeks.

How could she have doubted what this man felt for her, even for a second?

"Mommy!"

"I'm coming, sweetie."

She played with him for a few minutes before Nora remembered the horseshoe pits had sand in them, which was extra fun for playing trucks. Then she moved through the family, thanking people and making small talk, but a part of her focus never left Brian.

Though she told herself she could wait until the party was over and his family was gone, and Robin was with Oliver in the camper, everything she wanted to say to Brian was welling up inside of her. When the fear she might actually grab him and blurt out her feelings in front of everybody threatened to overwhelm her, she surrendered to the inevitable. At least the birthday party itself was finished, more or less, so she couldn't ruin that. If the rest of them were witness to coldness or tears for the rest of her visit, she couldn't help that.

"Could we go up to the store for a minute?" she asked Brian quietly, realizing she'd asked before coming up with a solid reason to go up there. Unfortunately, the Kowalski family was so good at this stuff, they'd forgotten nothing.

But he didn't ask. "Sure."

Siobhan looked over her shoulder to make sure Robin was still keeping an eye on Oliver. Her friend was watching her and Brian together, of course, and she gave her a quick thumbs-up before jerking her hand down in case anybody else was watching.

After he'd unlocked the door and stepped back to allow her in first, he locked it behind them. "What's up?"

"I know I should wait until everybody leaves, but I can't." Tears were welling up in her eyes already and she wasn't sure she would get through what she wanted to say. "I miss you."

She wasn't sure what she was expecting, but it wasn't his entire body relaxing as though he'd been holding himself rigid by force of will and finally let go. "I miss you, too."

"When you talked about us moving in with you and being a family, I wanted it so badly, but I was so afraid that we'd gotten caught up in being Oliver's parents and it was a way for you to have your family with you all the time." When he opened his mouth, undoubtedly to object, she held up her hand. "I know you would never do that on a deliberate level. We had been on this roller coaster for weeks and I needed to get off the ride and have my feet on solid ground."

"I went too fast," he said. "And I skipped some steps. Like the really *big* step of telling you I had fallen completely in love with you and the reason I wanted you to move in so quickly was that the sooner you lived with me, the fewer days I'd have to spend without you."

Tears ran unchecked down her cheeks. "I'm completely in love with you, too. And I think having time and space where we made co-parenting work and Oliver was happy made me see that neither of us needed to be in a relationship for his sake. That it was really about you and me."

"You and me?" He cupped her face in his hands, looking intently into her eyes. "What we have is unmatched, Siobhan."

"Like popcorn chicken and fries?"

"Yes. We belong together like popcorn chicken and fries."

She was still laughing when he kissed her, his hands sliding into her hair. Her arms slid around him, holding him close as joy coursed through her body.

"I love you," he whispered against her mouth before pulling back. "*You*, Siobhan. And I know if we'd met under any other circumstances, I still would have fallen in love with you."

"I love you, too."

Nothing made her happier than seeing the love she felt reflecting back at her from those pretty blue eyes. "Will you move in with me? I know the house isn't a lot, but there's the yard and land. I think we could be happy there. And here, sometimes, because I have to do my part at the campground."

She touched a finger to his lips to stop him. "Yes, I'll give my notice and Oliver and I will come live with you because the house is wonderful and he'll love the yard. And we'll be together. Maybe we won't be able to come up here with you all the time, but we'll be there waiting for you when you can get away."

He kissed her again before pulling her hard against his body and just hugging her. With his cheek resting on her hair and his heart beating under her palm, Siobhan was sure her life couldn't be any more perfect.

"Okay," she finally said, pulling away and scrubbing her hands over her face in what was probably a futile effort to hide that she'd been crying. "We should go out there and celebrate our son's birthday."

He grinned, holding out his hand. "Together?"

"Always."

They were halfway across the grass when somebody spotted them holding hands and everybody cheered. Even Robin and Oliver were clapping, even though the little guy probably didn't know why.

"I won," Keri yelled, running over to snatch some green bills out of Danny's hand.

"You bet on our relationship?" Siobhan asked as Keri fanned the money and shook her hips.

"The relationship?" Danny said. "No. You guys together was always a sure thing. Brian had some blue frosting smeared on the edge of his hand and we bet on which part of your body would have blue frosting on it when you came back."

When she immediately looked down at her chest, everybody laughed. But when she jerked her head around, trying to see the seat of her jeans, Brian chuckled and tugged at her hair.

"You've got a little frosting there," he said at the same time that Keri said, "I told you it would be in her hair."

He tucked the sticky strands behind her ear and then tracked his thumb down her jaw. "You sure you want to be part of this bunch?"

She'd never been so sure of anything in her life. "Always."

* * * * *

Harlequin® Reader Service

Enjoyed your book?

Try the perfect subscription for Romance readers and get more great books like this delivered right to your door.

See why over 10+ million readers have tried Harlequin Reader Service.

Start with a Free Welcome Collection with free books and a gift—valued over $20.

Choose any series in print or ebook. See website for details and order today:

TryReaderService.com/subscriptions

RSBPA2409